Echoes of the Past

Seeds of Autumn

By

H. B. Lyne

Acknowledgements

Chris, Agena, Arran, Phil and Andy, my friends and partners in creation.

The rich mythologies of this diverse and wonderful world.

My family, for their constant support and encouragement.

Nathalia Suellen for her wonderful cover art.

Prologue

The creature lumbered down the empty street. Tower blocks made of glass and steel loomed overhead, seeming to almost lean over and obscure the sky. He was vast, his body a mass of bricks, metal and glass. Tendrils of wire and cable flowed from him and rippled in his wake. It was difficult to tell his front from back, as elements of himself shifted around constantly, his body undulating and forever in flux. His innards were dirt, sand and soil, laced with small rivulets of water that directed the shifting plates of solid matter on his surface.

He was more than just the physical elements of the city though, he was its nature, its history. His existence connected every part of life together, every being that called Caerton home was represented by the King-of-Glass-and-Steel. He was as ancient as the city itself, and had been evolving in line with Caerton ever since the first wooden caer was built upon the hill, overlooking the wide estuary.

He felt the eyes of the goddess Artemis upon him and turned what passed for his face toward the cloudless, black sky, where the bright moon shone silver and clear. He was tired and he settled himself down right where he stood, just to rest a while in Her beautiful glow.

He didn't sense the figures moving silently in from all around him. He dozed peacefully, unaware of the deathly silent swirling mass of fear, chaos and evil sweeping gradually lower from the sky, a slight tinge of silver light weaving through it.

The figures had voices and they whispered a spell, the words chilling the air. As one they clapped their hands just once. And just like that, the King was gone.

Chapter One

14th September

Caerton City Hall was vast. The rooms used for competitions and events were among the grandest in the building, due to the council's intense desire to impress. This room had a high ceiling, was lined with marble pillars and carpeted in rich, red fabric. Golden, spindle-legged chairs lined the room in rows and were filled with spectators.

The nineteen year old defending Banshay champion prepared herself at the side of the impressive hall, holding her two ornate dha in their fine wooden scabbards. She stroked the varnished black wood, following the golden swirls as they licked their way up to each hilt. She ran her fingers through her short, dark hair, tussling the unruly mop.

As people gathered in the room, Ariana felt appraising stares and heard whispers of her name. The attention didn't phase her, she was used to it. But she did spot one striking-looking man watching her from across the room. He was very tall, dressed in loose black linen trousers and a black vest that displayed his athletic frame and impressive body art across his broad shoulders. Strange patterns twisted and knotted across lean muscle and tanned skin. His hair was dark and framed his rugged face and dark eyes. He leaned against the wall near the door, his arms crossed loosely over his chest, watching her quite unashamedly, with a small smile that took all severity out of his features.

'Ariana Yates,' one of the judges called. Ariana's focus snapped back to the competition, and she made her way to the mat. She briefly caught the eye of her mysterious admirer. She cocked her head at him in acknowledgement, and the room began to clap and cheer. She watched him uncross his arms to casually clap along, a smile tugging at the corner of his lips, and she felt butterflies in her stomach that had nothing to do with the forthcoming fight.

Ariana looked around to greet her first opponent, a young Banshay novice who looked petrified. Ariana smiled, but it wasn't a warm or reassuring one, it was the smile of a predator surveying her prey.

A bell rang out and the gathered crowd fell quiet.

Swords were not drawn, doing so was considered disrespectful to the Burmese tradition, so Ariana simply raised both swords in their scabbards. She paused for a long moment, watching the girl before her mimic the ceremonial movement, the girl's arms were shaking. Ariana grinned again and pounced forward with a cry, striking her opponent's raised sword with one of her own.

The competition didn't last long. Ariana took on the other entrants one by one, never losing a match. As her arm was raised the winner, her head pounded with exhilaration and her body ached with adrenaline. The room swirled around her, and her dha grew heavy in her hands as she walked slowly to the nearby bench where her belongings waited for her.

Sitting down, she reached into her bag for a bottle of water and drank deeply, hearing every gulp go down her throat and her pulse thumping in her ears.

'Congratulations,' a soft voice spoke nearby. Ariana's senses slowly returned to normal and she looked up into the piercing, dark brown eyes staring down at her. The intense-looking man lowered himself to crouch before her and he smiled again. 'I'm Rhys Blevins.'

Ariana smiled back at him, her heart pounded hard in her chest and not just because of her victory. Rhys looked down at the trophy hanging from her hand and gave it careful consideration.

'How many of those do you have?' he asked, his face serious.

'Well, this is my third consecutive win at this tournament, and I have two other tournaments under my belt. So, five.' She was exceptionally proud of her accomplishments and was more than happy to tell people about them.

Rhys nodded, looking impressed.

'You were pretty phenomenal. It's rare that I see someone with such an impressive spirit on the mat.' He had the trace of an accent that suggested he wasn't born and raised in Caerton.

'Thanks.'

Her eyes roamed over his tattoos and she felt an unmistakable heat inside herself. She cleared her throat and pointed at a swirl that darted out from under the neck of his black vest towards his ear.

'How many of those do you have?' she asked, deliberately echoing his question to her.

Rhys ran his eyes across his right shoulder and his smile broadened.

'Last count was sixteen. But only nine if you count the whole of this as one,' he answered, tapping the back of his neck where tongue-like shapes licked out on either side of his spine and disappeared under his vest. 'I got it done in stages, but it was always intended to be one complete work.'

Ariana nodded, looking over the tattoos with admiration.

'Are you competing?' Ariana asked him.

'No, I teach and some of my students were competing today.'

'Oh wow,' she replied. 'I teach too. At the Self-Defence Dojo in St. Mark's.'

'Good to know,' Rhys said with a smile and nod.

The room had almost emptied, and there was a slightly awkward pause.

'Okay. Well, it was really good to meet you,' Ariana said briskly, picking up her things.

'You too. Bye Ariana,' he said softly, then turned and walked casually from the room, his hands in his pockets.

Ariana watched him go, admiring the rear view. There was something so captivating about him, it made her uncomfortable and fascinated at the same time. The way he'd looked at her was both flattering and unnerving, and as Ariana left the hall she realised why. It was like she was a sumptuous meal and he hadn't eaten in a week. All the more unnerving was that she liked him looking at her that way.

After the victorious tournament Ariana left the venue alone, and stepped out into the baking September heat. It was just after 5pm on a Friday, so the streets were full of people leaving work or going away for the weekend. She crossed the plaza that connected the city hall, a museum and several large offices, past a large, ornate fountain in the centre where some young teenagers had stripped off most of their school uniforms and were splashing each other amid loud laughter and playful screams.

She took a turn down a bustling path between two tall buildings, and out into a major thoroughfare that was jammed with traffic and people. It was unbearably hot with the combined effect of the sun beating down on the concrete, all these people and the practically stationary cars chugging out hot smoke. As she walked, Ariana began to feel sick. Her stomach turned in knots and she grew hot and sweaty.

She walked slowly up the steep hill to the bus station and joined a queue for her bus out to St. Mark's; an area with a questionable reputation in the north of the city, the place she called home.

From her seat on the bus she stared up into the evening sky, which was still bright blue and hazy from the heat. It would be a clear night, but the people of Caerton would see few stars through the light-polluted haze, and the tiny slither of a crescent moon would be mostly obscured by that orange glow tonight. Ariana didn't usually know what phase the moon was in at any given moment, and as she thought about it she felt a wave of nausea roll over her suddenly. She clamped a hand over her mouth.

She was relieved to step off the bus and into the warm evening air. She took deep breaths as she walked slowly home, trying to tune out the sound of barking dogs and the clatter of bins in a dirty alley nearby.

She reached her home, a small flat on the middle floor of a converted three storey terraced house. She climbed the stairs wearily, unlocked her door and slipped inside. She kicked off her shoes, dropped her bag with her dha in it gently to the floor, and gave a satisfied sigh as she placed her new trophy carefully on the shelf in the living room with the others, then got ready for bed in an exhausted blur.

The world was wrong. It passed much too quickly and she was too close to the ground. Everything smelled strange, everything smelled. She shouldn't be able to smell the rubbish down the alley she was running past, or the fear in the young woman hiding there from the pack of wild animals running by.

Wait. The what? There were dogs either side of her, to her left ran a big dog with thick, long fur. To her right was

*a fox. Ariana shook her head and caught sight of her paws
pounding on the black tarmac.*

*Before the panic could completely drown her, there was
something else, she looked up and saw the moon in the sky
above, glinting down between quickly-moving clouds. It
was a tiny slip of a crescent moon, barely lighting the sky
and somehow she knew that it was waning, within a day or
two it would be a dark, new moon.*

*Her heart pounded in her chest and she skidded to a
halt. Why was she running? Whose dogs were these?*

Ariana sat bolt upright in bed, her head and heart were
hammering, and her light pyjamas clung to her sweating
skin. It was dark, the room glowing faintly orange from the
street light outside.

She tried to steady her breathing and focus on what was
real.

Her eyes drifted to the window and through a gap in the
curtains she caught sight of the moon above the building
opposite, just visible to keen eyes through the orange glow
in the sky. It looked exactly like it had in her dream and
she shivered. The moon normally made her feel warm and
loved, but she was unnerved by the dream. She forced it
out of her mind, and tried to get back to sleep. She tossed
and turned until the sky started to grow lighter. She finally
drifted into a deep and fitful sleep, but she remembered no
more alarming dreams.

The flu that threatened her didn't materialise, and the
next morning Ariana awoke feeling unsettled by the dream,
but not ill. Within a week the dream had drifted from her
memory, and life went on as normal through the balmy
September.

16th October

It was just another Tuesday in the middle of October. The Indian summer was over and the streets of Caerton were constantly wet. Ariana had woken up feeling sluggish, she was over worked. Her boss, Ron had wanted to roll out her popular classes to a full after-school programme and she agreed. She hoped she wasn't getting ill and managed to force the fatigue aside to get through the day.

St. Mark's Self Defence Dojo was a small studio above an abandoned electronics shop on the opposite side of St. Mark's to Ariana's flat. It had once been painted banana yellow, but the paint was faded and peeling now, revealing dull brown bricks beneath. The shop window was dusty, the sign over it was faded and worn and some of the large, plastic letters were cracked. Inside a few ancient items could be seen gathering dust on broken shelves, and paper notices pinned in the window were too faded to read. The first floor had windows all along one side overlooking the street. The dojo was accessible through a narrow door next to the shop window, with a slightly grubby swinging sign above it; the only indicator of the studio within.

Ariana went into her early evening Judo class feeling utterly exhausted, and didn't relish the prospect of teaching a group of rowdy teenagers how to throw each other to the floor.

Her students filed into the studio as she took great gulps from her water bottle. For once everyone assembled and got ready to start without her having to nag them, and she faced her class with a small glimmer of hope that it would be easier than she feared.

As Ariana warmed up with her students and began

issuing instructions her stomach seemed to settle a little, as if adrenaline itself were a soothing elixir.

The feeling didn't last, however, and once the class was over and her students filed back out of the studio, Ariana felt a wave of dizziness overpower her and she slumped to the floor.

She finally knew she would have to move when she heard Ron locking his office door, and reluctantly she stood up and gathered her things.

She slipped out quietly and walked home slowly through the light rain.

17th October

When Ariana awoke the next morning she felt so tired she didn't think she could move. She desperately wanted more sleep but the morning was bright and she couldn't hide from the day. She felt worse than she had the previous morning, and when she tried to stand up a wave of dizziness and nausea hit her so hard that she fell back onto the bed.

She lay there for a long time, just gearing herself up to trying to move again. When she did everything ached, but she managed to sit up and reach for her phone. She found the number for work and hit "call".

'Hi Ron. It's Ariana. I'm sorry about this but I'm really not feeling well at all. I think I have the flu coming on or something. Can you get my classes covered or cancelled today please?' She rubbed her head with her free hand and waited for his reply.

'That's fine Ariana, love. I'm sorry to hear you're not well. Not like you, is it?'

'No, it's not,' she sighed. 'I'll let you know how I'm doing tomorrow, hopefully it is just a 24 hour bug or something.'

'Of course. You take however long you need and keep me posted. Hopefully we'll see you back soon. Take care.' Ron spoke slowly, trying to lower his volume for her benefit, she assumed, and she couldn't help smiling weakly. She thanked him and hung up the phone, gingerly lying back down in bed. She slowly drifted back into an uneasy sleep.

When Ariana woke up again it was dark. With bleary eyes she grabbed her phone and checked the time. 11.15pm. She had slept all day and felt much more well rested, but hungry. Really hungry.

She moved carefully from the bed and stood still for a long moment. She swayed slightly, but once she found her balance she headed slowly for her little kitchenette and made herself a sandwich.

She sat down to eat it and her eyes drifted to the window. It was a cloudless night, and she thought of the moon; there was no moon tonight and it was deeply unsettling that she knew that. The sky outside was a dull orange from the light pollution of the city, but the moon would still be visible the fuller it got, and it did usually cut through some of the haze to cast its pure white light on Caerton. But not tonight.

As strange as Ariana found her awareness of the moon's phases, she felt at peace with herself. Thinking about the moon somehow filled her with a deep sense of warmth and contentment that she had never felt before.

When she finished her sandwich she had a shower and got dressed. She knew her body clock was all messed up but there wasn't much she could do about it, so she decided to catch up on some reading, with the intention of trying to get some sleep in a few hours.

As she sat on her sofa reading she realised how quiet the street outside was. Normally there would be sounds of people returning home from the nearby pub, or her neighbours opposite fighting, or cars going by. But there was nothing.

She moved to her window and looked out, there was no movement, no sound but for the more distant noises of traffic on the main road. Then something caught her eye up the street and she pressed her face to the cold glass to get a better look.

Two dogs were jogging across the road, both kind of wiry looking, with shaggy fur in need of a good brush down. They both looked tough, like they could take good care of themselves. She watched them mount the pavement on the opposite side of the street and continue in her direction. As they drew closer she saw that they weren't dogs at all, one was a fox and the other looked like a wolf.

Her breath caught in her throat and a half-remembered dream suddenly flashed into her mind.

A howl ripped through the air. As one, Ariana and the two canines in the street stopped suddenly and looked up over the houses opposite. Ariana often heard dogs howling around St. Mark's and didn't usually think anything of it, but there was something so urgent in this sound, cutting through the silence of the night.

The two odd canines sprinted past Ariana's house, darted up an alley and out of sight. Ariana's heart was pounding and a shiver went up her spine. It was almost like she could understand the cry for help in that howl, and she was drawn towards it, she wanted to run out into the street, to find the dog and help, somehow.

She paced in front of the window like a caged animal, looking out every so often, craning to see over the houses opposite, though there was no way she could from her first floor window. She felt frustrated and sick with worry.

Movement down in the street caught her eye, in the alley

she thought she saw one of the dogs, just hidden in shadow. It was looking up at her window, its yellow eyes right on her. She watched but the longer she stared at the spot the darker it seemed to be, and soon she began to doubt that she had seen anything.

Looking at her phone, Ariana saw that it was nearly 1am.

At that moment all of the street lights went out. Blackness fell like a cloak, and her pulse started racing. Something was very wrong.

Another howl rent the air. Ariana stifled a small, frightened cry by pressing her hand to her lips. This howl wasn't a plea for help, it was a battle cry.

She peered out of her window, straining her eyes in the darkness to see if she could make out anything.

There was a strange shape moving quickly down the middle of the street, an inky black against the dull grey. Ariana squinted to try and see it more clearly, but it was too dark. It seemed like the shape didn't want to be seen, though how she sensed that she didn't know.

Her eyes were drawn suddenly to quicker movement behind it, two dogs came running down the street and her eyes went back to the alley opposite, searching in the dark for those amber eyes.

A huge beast bounded out of the alley, running like a gorilla on its hind legs but with powerful forearms pounding the ground too. It was difficult to make out more detail in the dark, but she knew that it was not a gorilla, it was a monster, and the sounds that ensued as the beast and the wild dogs flanked the inky black shape were terrifying.

Ariana fought the urge to scream and struggled to breathe. Her eyes were fixed to the action in the street, no matter how much she wanted to tear them away. The dogs raced around the blackness and seemed to be ripping into it with their teeth. The beast tore at it with its huge claws.

She watched in horror as the two dogs changed shape before her eyes, their bodies stretching and twisting into two more huge beasts just like the first. The action was hard to make out under the cover of night, but the sounds were terrifying. Shrieks issued from the black shadow, ripping and tearing sounds that sent chills right through her as Ariana stood, transfixed. Two of the savage beasts broke away and drove the blackness down the street, disappearing into the dark night.

One figure remained outside her window, the beast shrank and stood on four paws in the middle of the road, just in time for the street lights to flicker back to life.

The fox's piercing amber eyes turned upwards to look directly at her and Ariana leaped back from the window, clamping her hand hard over her mouth to swallow the terrified cry.

18th October

The next morning Ariana woke up confused. Her memories seemed unclear and she couldn't figure out what she had dreamed and what had been real, so she made a conscious effort to force the stranger memories firmly into the "dream" category.

She still felt ill and took a second day off work. She slept more and slowly her appetite returned to normal. By the evening she felt more like herself and decided to return to work the next day.

As the sun set over the city Ariana felt uneasy. Every time she looked towards the window she felt fear creeping up her spine, though as time passed, it became harder to understand why.

Chapter Two

22nd October

'Why do you want me to go?' Ariana asked, hating that she was whining.

'Because I am up to my ears in paper work and have no time for a field trip.' Ron slammed one pile of papers down on top of another and Ariana flinched. 'You know how it is with Central, they regularly gut the place and flog their old kit, but it isn't old! It's only a couple of years since the last refurbishment. I can't let a bargain slip through my fingers.'

Ariana gave a resigned sigh and set off towards the bus stop. She wasn't waiting long before a bus heading for the city centre arrived, and she boarded quickly with several other passengers.

Ariana cursed herself once again for not owning an umbrella as she sat on the bus looking out at the pouring rain. The route took her south through St. Mark's, along the edge of China Town and then into Burnside, the financial district of the city. She reluctantly stepped off the bus and ran from the bus station to the Central School of Martial Arts. She darted in and out of office doorways, past huge buildings and across the central plaza, right into the heart of the city where the prestigious martial arts school stood.

She ran in through the big, glass doors of the school, into the pristine foyer, and shook out her hair and extremities, sending splashes of dirty rain water showering down onto the polished wooden floor.

She ran a hand through her unruly hair and looked around. There were several people in the waiting area and one very well-dressed woman behind the reception desk, all staring at her and the dirty puddle she had created with her entrance.

'Sorry,' she said meekly, her cheeks reddening.

Ariana approached the sour-looking receptionist. She tried her best to smile and pull through the bad first impression she had made. 'Hi, I'm Ariana Yates, I'm from St. Mark's Self-Defence Dojo. I've come to look at the equipment for sale.'

The receptionist gave her a fake smile and picked up the phone. She spoke to someone in clipped tones, relaying Ariana's introduction, and when she hung up the phone she turned to Ariana with that hideous fake smile again.

'Someone will be with you shortly.'

Ariana nodded in thanks and moved away from the desk.

She waited for a few minutes, staring out at the wet street and the people scurrying by under their umbrellas. Her vision started to blur as her attention drifted away from what was in front of her and odd memories started to prickle at her mind.

A moment later, the sound of light footsteps jogging down the stairs next to the reception caught her attention.

A ripple of surprise and recognition ran through her when she saw Rhys approaching and a small guttural noise stuck in her throat, which she promptly cleared and tried to smile casually.

His dark eyes went straight to her as he stepped into the reception area and he approached her without so much as a glance at the receptionist, who, Ariana noticed, was looking incredulous about not being needed.

'Ariana,' Rhys greeted her with a smile. He held out his hand to shake hers and she willingly accepted. A little jolt went through her as they grasped hands and she found herself a little short of breath. She felt goosebumps break out all up her arm as their hands parted.

She suddenly felt far more self conscious about her bedraggled appearance but tried to force confidence to the fore, hoping that it would mask her wet clothes and hair just a little.

'Hi. Good to see you again,' she replied after a moment. 'I had no idea you worked here.'

'I teach taekwondo here,' he said. 'I'm just helping the manager out with a few things as we're so busy at the moment. So, I'll show you the kit that your boss is interested in. Is that okay?'

Rhys showed her around the impressive training centre, it was so clean and shiny, compared to her run down little workplace. Everything smelled new but still carried an authentic feel to it.

Rhys didn't pass one comment about her drowned-rat look, for which she was grateful.

He took Ariana into a large studio at the back of the building, all along one wall were pieces of gym equipment and crash mats in nearly new condition. She looked closely at the stock and he let her try a few things to make sure they were in working order.

She pulled out a mat into the middle of the floor and slipped out of her wet shoes to walk on it. It was a little faded in the middle, but still had just the right amount of spring in it.

She looked up to see Rhys watching her carefully, his eyes roaming slowly up her body from her bare feet. It sent shivers right through her to see him watching her like that.

Suddenly he took a step towards her.

'Want to test it out?' he asked.

Flustered for only a moment she gave him an uncertain nod before taking a defensive stance. She knew absolutely no taekwondo, but she did teach jieishudan, which was a self-defence style that was effective against pretty much anything.

Rhys tried to hide a smile, but she saw it playing at the corner of his mouth. She couldn't tell if he found her funny or if he was being cocky. Either way, she wasn't going to stand for it, and she steeled herself against whatever he had to throw at her.

When he initiated the attack she was ready and easily blocked.

They sparred, neither one of them landing a serious blow, but there was a glint in his eye that told Ariana he was waiting for his moment and she recognised it the instant he thought it had come, the moment he was going to stop holding back.

In a flash she spun him around, grappled his arm and threw him to the ground, landing squarely over his chest with one of his arms still tightly held, and her free hand slammed firmly onto the mat beside his head.

Their noses were mere centimetres apart. Ariana felt the exhilaration of victory begin to fade and be replaced with a strong heat in her gut that spread quickly downwards, leaving her tingling.

His eyes were feasting on hers, his breath hot on her face and he smiled, it was a look that told her she was exactly where he intended her to end up. He had let her pin him to the floor.

Quickly pulling herself together she leaped up and went straight to her shoes, clearing her throat and wiping her clammy hands on her jeans.

'It all looks great. I'll give Ron an inventory and he'll let you guys know which pieces he wants. I guess he'll arrange a van to collect them too.'

'Fine,' he said, casually standing and walking over to her.

He stopped right in front of her, his eyes held hers for a

long moment then he stepped back, a satisfied smile on his lips and held out a mobile phone. 'I think this must be yours, it fell out of your pocket on the mat.' He passed it to her and as she took it she saw that a number had been tapped into the phone and was dialling.

'I take it this is your number?' She raised an eyebrow, impressed with his quick wit and ingenuity. She let it connect to his voicemail and felt her insides flip about.

'You will call me,' he said, turning and walking towards the door. He looked back, flashing a wicked grin and she stared at him, open mouthed as he left the studio. She didn't know what to make of his attitude.

He was arrogant, intimidating and manipulative. But he was also painfully attractive, charming, in his own way, and very sharp. As she quietly left the Central School of Martial Arts she couldn't get him out of her mind.

23rd October

```
Hi. I've been thinking about you. You
didn't call :( - Rhys xx
```

Ariana laughed a little, she liked his directness and, if she was honest with herself, she liked being pursued.

```
Hi. I was going to give it a couple of
days ;) You're not used to being kept
waiting, are you?
```

She waited, watching her phone.

```
No. I'll see you tomorrow... I'm coming
to St. Mark's with the van.
```

Ariana's pulse quickened at the thought of seeing him again so soon, which was definitely a good sign.

```
Well, I don't know if I'll be there, my
hours are erratic. What time are you coming
up?
```

She was lying, she already knew what time Ron had arranged for the delivery of the new equipment, but she didn't want to appear too eager. He was doing enough of that for the both of them and she could tell he liked the chase.

```
We'll be there at 11. I hope you can be
there xx
```

24th October

The following morning Ariana arrived at the dojo just after eleven, she didn't really need to be there, but she did want to see Rhys, while not appearing too keen.

The van was parked at the end of the building and someone had rigged up a winch system to lift the gym equipment up the side of the building and in through the fire door on the first floor.

Ariana stood and watched in awe as two men hauled a treadmill up the side of the building on a pulley and she caught sight of Rhys climbing the fire escape, helping to guide the machine smoothly. Smiling to herself she went inside and ran up the stairs and into the studio.

Ron was in there, leaning out of a window and shouting directions.

Moments later Rhys backed in through the open fire door with another man, pulling the treadmill in with them.

'Where shall we put it?' Rhys asked, turning to Ron. He

caught sight of Ariana and she thought she saw a flicker of excitement pass across his face.

Ron directed them and together they positioned the machine.

Rhys made his way over to Ariana and flashed her a wonderful smile.

'Hi,' she said, trying to be nonchalant. She didn't know if it worked.

'Hi. Good to see you,' he replied.

They were enlisted to help with the rest of the equipment and hardly had chance to speak again before the van driver was ready to leave.

As Rhys jumped up into the cab, hitching a lift back to Central, he called Ariana over. 'I'm going to take you out. I'll give you a call to set it up. Okay?'

She laughed as the door was slammed shut and she nodded helplessly. It seemed she didn't have much choice in the matter, but she found that she didn't mind.

Over the next few days a few messages flew back and forth. Ariana's friend was throwing an elaborate Halloween party and she suggested Rhys go with her as her "plus one".

It's fancy dress. Spooky sexy. She told him.

No problem. He replied. Ariana gave a wry smile. She had trouble picturing Rhys in a costume and wondered what he would come up with, what any male attending would for that matter.

31st October

Ariana adjusted her costume. It was not going to be a comfortable evening, she could tell she would be tugging bits of it out from crevices constantly, but her friend Ben's invitation had been very clear: "Sexy costumes only", so here she was, dressed as some sort of evil fairy in a black and green corset, black hot pants covered in sequins, stockings and suspenders and tattered black wings strapped to her back. She retained a hint of her own personality by wearing untied combat boots to finish off the outfit.

She leaned close to the mirror to finish applying her mascara and just as she was applying the last stroke her door bell rang, sending a sudden flutter of anticipation right through her.

Grinning, Ariana grabbed her little black clutch and left her flat, jogging down the stairs to open the door. She flung it wide to find Rhys stood waiting for her.

'You're not in a costume.' Ariana frowned at him, looking him up and down. He was dressed more or less as he had been every time she had seen him, in black combats and a vest. To be fair to him, he had dressed up the look this evening with a smart jacket, but it was decidedly not a costume.

'The scariest things in this world are the ones that look completely normal most of the time,' he shrugged.

'That is such a cop out,' she huffed. She locked her door and he led her to his car. 'Well, on your head be it if you're refused entry to the party.'

Rhys chuckled and opened the passenger door for her. She slid inside and tried to get comfortable with the wings on her back.

'You look amazing,' he said softly, sliding into the driver's seat and starting the car.

'Thank you.' Ariana smiled to herself as they set off towards the city centre.

Rhys parked in a small car park close to the venue, which was at the heart of Caerton's night life. The streets throbbed with music from the clubs and bars and people swarmed outside, queuing to gain entry to some of the most exclusive venues. Halloween costumes were everywhere, some bright and humorous, others alarmingly realistic.

Rhys put his arm around Ariana's shoulders as they negotiated the bustling pavement, steering her away from the slightest hint of aggression or over exuberance.

On the corner stood an impressive cocktail bar, its large windows looking out onto the brightly lit and lively streets. A red rope was strung across the door and two big bouncers in suits flanked it. A cluster of young women in varying degrees of skimpy clothing stood begging for entry.

'I'm sorry, this is strictly a private party,' one of the bouncers said, firmly but politely.

Ariana pulled her invitation out of her clutch as they approached the bar and smoothed out the crease from where it had been folded in two. They squeezed past the persistent girls and she showed the invitation to the polite bouncer. He gave them a brief nod before admitting them. Rhys's lack of costume didn't raise so much as an eyebrow, perhaps because he was as big as either of the bouncers. Or perhaps Ariana's costume got them both past the rope.

Music blasted out as the bouncer opened the door and Ariana led the way into the bar. She rolled her eyes in apology back at Rhys when she recognised the cheesy music.

'Ben is, well, he's not afraid of clichés,' she called over the thumping bass. Rhys grinned at her and bent low to speak into her ear.

'I don't mind a bit.'

Inside was hot and dark, red and orange paper lanterns were strung across the ceiling and ornately carved pumpkins were displayed on almost every available surface. Not the typical toothy grinning faces of Ariana's childhood, but expertly carved spiders, headless-horsemen and witches glowed in the darkness.

Low sofas and tables filled the two large windows and all seats were filled by people in outrageous costumes. A woman walked past wearing only a leather thong and a small cross of black tape over each nipple, Ariana couldn't help but stare.

Rhys nudged her towards the bar at the back of the building, his eyes firmly on Ariana.

The couple moved through the bustling bar. There was a small stage off to the right of the bar area, with a small dance floor in front of it. A DJ stood behind decks at the back of the stage, while caged dancers flaunted their bodies to the pounding music and a man in a devil costume juggled fire at the front.

Ariana spotted Ben sat on a tall stool at the bar, surrounded by a small cluster of people but he shooed them away with a flick of a hand when his eyes locked onto Ariana. Ben was dressed in a sharp suit with a vibrant red shirt undone almost half way down his chest, reminiscent of a young John Travolta.

'Well hello gorgeous!' Ben called, hopping down from his stool, his arms open to embrace Ariana. She grinned and moved in to give him a hug but at the last second he swerved to avoid her, his eyes fixed firmly on Rhys. 'Not you, darling. Him.'

Ariana laughed. Ben passed for straight easily when sober, but after a few drinks his inner queen came out to play.

'Ben, this is Rhys,' she introduced them and smirked as Ben made no attempt to disguise his admiration. 'He is straight,' she added pointedly and glanced at Rhys for confirmation.

He gave a slight nod just for her and placed his hand on

the small of her back under her fairy wings as he shook Ben's hand. A tingle ran up her spine.

'Fine,' Ben grumbled. 'I'm spoken for anyway.'

'How does your costume fit the brief of sexy scary?' Ariana asked, raising one eyebrow.

'The 70's scare the hell out of me!' Ben cried and his laugh rang out above the din of the music.

'What do you do, Ben?' asked Rhys as a round of drinks appeared on the bar before them.

'Ugh, I work at the city council's Environment and Planning office. Boring,' Ben replied, looking around a little anxiously.

'Oh, I assumed you owned this place or something.' Rhys gestured to their surroundings.

'No, no. Ben's boyfriend, Marcus, is in PR. He throws the best parties,' Ariana supplied, grinning at her friend.

'Where has he got to any way?' Ben was still distractedly looking around. 'Excuse me. Here,' he thrust a stack of tickets at Ariana. 'Drinks tokens. Have fun, I'll catch up with you later.'

Ariana watched him dash off to hunt down his beloved then gave Rhys an apologetic smile.

'He's,' she searched for the right word.

'Very impulsive?' Rhys suggested and they both laughed.

The evening passed quickly in a blur of cocktails and loud music. Ariana saw old friends and enjoyed introducing Rhys around. He joined in with enthusiasm and didn't seem to mind being interrogated by her nearest and dearest as they endeavoured to confirm that he was good enough for her.

It was past midnight before Ariana caught sight of Ben again, he had found Marcus, who was clad in red hot pants, matching feather boa and devil's horns. The two of them were dancing at the heart of the dance floor, surrounded by friends and admirers. She joined them, leaving Rhys at the mercy of some friends and danced until she could hardly breathe.

Red-faced and thirsty, Ariana returned to Rhys and he quickly supplied her with water.

'Hmm, looks like I should be getting you home,' he sighed as she slumped sideways into him, a tired smile filling her face.

Ariana said her goodbyes to everyone and the couple left the heat and noise of the bar, stepping out into the cold October night. Ariana shivered and clutched her arms, cursing herself for not bringing a coat. Rhys cast a nervous glance up and down the busy street, which was filled with people abandoning their revelries, or moving them on elsewhere. He removed his jacket and took Ariana's wings off her back. He wrapped his jacket over her shoulders, carried her wings and took her hand in his.

Ariana smiled up at him, thankful for the gesture and caught sight of the bright moon low in the sky over his shoulder.

'Oh look. It's a full moon, on Halloween. How spooky,' she giggled.

Rhys turned to glance at it and gave a little shrug.

'It's actually full tomorrow.'

Ariana frowned at him, it looked full to her, but a prickle at her senses told her he was right. Something cut through her slightly intoxicated haze, a memory, a perception that had lain dormant for a while. She tried to shrug it off, but it tugged hard at her mind and as they walked in silence towards his car she felt eyes on them.

Rhys seemed to sense it too and gently urged her to walk faster. By the time they reached the car the feeling had passed and Ariana quickly forgot it.

They drove in easy silence back to St. Mark's. Rhys helped her from the car and walked her to her door.

At her front doorstep she paused, hoping that he was going to kiss her. While she hesitated, he reached out and gently swept her hair back off her face, tucking it neatly behind her ear. She felt her face flush with the heat of his touch and she cast her eyes down.

He stepped closer and caressed her cheek with his thumb, his fingers still entwined in her hair. He was so warm and so close, she could feel his breath on her face. She looked into his dark eyes and surrendered to what she knew was coming.

Their lips met and brushed together gently. Ariana's heart was racing and she could feel his thumping madly in his chest too. The heat building inside flared uncontrollably and she deepened the kiss. He reciprocated and their kiss became frenzied and passionate; their bodies pressed together and his hands held her firmly against him.

Finally he released her, softening the kiss again before pulling back. She took a deep, shuddering breath and let out a small, nervous laugh.

'Wow,' she whispered to herself and he chuckled in response. 'Would you like to come in?' she asked, her heart pounding.

Rhys pulled back a bit and groaned with frustration.

'I would really, really love to, but I have to be at work at 7am. I'm sorry.' He gently tipped her chin up and looked deep into her eyes. 'Next time though.'

He leaned in for another smouldering kiss and Ariana tried not to let the disappointment interfere with the goodbye kiss, which was almost as intense and passionate as the first one. Ariana felt heat in all the right places and it was with deep regret that she let him end the kiss and step away from her door.

'Next time,' she whispered. Ariana handed him his jacket and he went, reluctantly, back to his car. She waved as he set off and went up to her flat feeling both elated and frustrated.

Chapter Three

1st November

The moon hung low in the sky, full and bright. Ariana was perched on a rooftop, watching clouds skidding across the beautiful moon that bathed her in soothing light. The night was almost silent and she felt at peace. An itch tickled at her ear and she raised a paw, licked it and rubbed it over her head, ear and whiskers, just like a cat.

Ariana woke with a start and looked urgently at her hands. Hands, they were hands. With a frustrated sigh she dropped them back onto the bed. She was too awake to go straight back to sleep and with resignation she got out of bed to fetch a drink. As she stood at the kitchen sink she noticed a man standing in the street outside. He was leaning against the wall opposite, his hands wedged into the deep pockets of a baggy old army jacket. The hood was up, hiding his face from sight. She looked at the digital display on her microwave, it was just after 4am. Looking again at the shadowy figure outside, a chill went through her.

Ariana moved cautiously back to her bedroom and went to the window there, she looked down and watched him for a few minutes. He hardly moved a muscle, just stood there letting the rain pour down over his coat. Fatigue dragged her back to her bed and she slept restlessly until the dull light of dawn crept in through the bare curtains and a familiar tone from her phone roused her. Ariana picked up her phone and opened the new message.

Are we still meeting for coffee? Ben xx

Ariana smiled, glad to be reminded of her plans for the day. The memory of her strange dream and the haunting figure in the street came upon her and she looked out of her window. He was still there. Unnerved, she distracted herself with responding to her friend.

```
How are you up so early?! I'll see you
later xx
```

Ariana showered off the glitter and remnants of make up from the party, her mind running over the fun she had had and lingering longingly on the kiss she shared with Rhys.

She dressed and ate breakfast, trying to focus on happy thoughts, rather than the creepy stranger still standing outside her house. Each time she passed a window she took note of him. Sometimes he was looking up and down the street, at others his gaze was fixed on the entrance to her building. Just after 9am Ariana saw him push away from the wall on which he had been leaning for so long and walk casually away up the street.

'Creepy guy,' she muttered under her breath.

When it was time, she picked up her coat and set off to meet Ben in the city centre, again regretting her lack of umbrella. She jogged to the nearby bus stop and took shelter there with a handful of people. No one spoke. St. Mark's was not some leafy suburb where strangers made cheerful small talk, it was a risk to make eye contact with anyone here and as everyone pressed forward to greet the arriving bus, Ariana wondered, not for the first time since moving to Caerton, if any of the people around her were armed.

As she took a seat on the busy bus, the hooded figure from outside her flat walked past her to take a seat near the back. A sudden breath caught in her throat and she tried to hide it, her whole body tensed up. She liked to think she had good instincts and a knack for noticing things, but his presence on the same bus had blind sided her completely.

Her heart hammered in her chest and a lump sat uncomfortably in her throat. Caerton city centre could not approach quickly enough and Ariana rang the bell and moved up to the front of the bus just before her stop. When she demounted and set off walking again she glanced back and sure enough, her new best friend followed her off the bus and walked behind her through the city centre. The bustle of the city was not enough to shake him, and as she approached her destination she was close to turning and confronting her stalker. The presence of innocent passers by who could easily get hurt in a physical altercation was just enough to make her quicken her step instead.

Ben was sat in the café window and waved as she approached. She tried to grin back at him, but faltered. She squeezed her way through the crowded café to Ben's table.

Ariana took off her coat and slung it on the back of her chair. Sitting down, she looked anxiously out of the window and saw that her hooded follower had sat down on the steps of the shopping centre across the broad road, traffic sloshing by between them. People rushed past him, eager to get out of the rain and cast him incredulous looks as they passed.

'I ordered your usual,' Ben said quietly, drawing her attention. 'Is everything okay?'

Ariana shrugged. A waitress brought their coffees over and Ben thanked her.

'You look rough,' they both spoke at once and then cracked up laughing.

'It was a great party,' Ariana said. 'Marcus pulled it off once again.'

'He does that,' Ben said, grinning.

'How's work?' she asked, sipping her cappuccino.

'Busy,' Ben groaned. 'Maybe I've taken too much on. There's this big new project, but same old story, I can't actually tell you about it. Sorry,' he said, sipping his coffee. 'But between you and me, it is about bloody time, it is ridiculous that Caerton doesn't already have one,' he teased, but Ariana was too distracted to bite.

Her eyes moved back to the hooded figure on the steps opposite and she chewed her lip.

'Everything okay? You keep looking at that guy,' Ben asked, a frown etched deep into his forehead.

'Yeah, fine,' Ariana waved her hand in the air dismissively. He looked at her disbelievingly. 'It's nothing,' she insisted but he raised his eyebrows at her. 'Look, don't overreact, but he's been following me.'

'What?' he hissed, glaring over at the guy and half getting to his feet. Ariana pressed her hand on his arm and looked around, checking that they weren't drawing anyone's attention.

'Sit down. If I thought there was anything to it, I'd take care of it myself. Like you could do better than me in a physical confrontation,' Ariana snorted with laughter and Ben joined in.

'No I suppose not. Weird though, creepy hooded stalker, Ariana hon. Be careful.'

Ariana shrugged off his worries and tried desperately to keep her eyes away from the stranger.

'What did you think of Rhys?' She promptly changed the subject.

'Oh my, your boyfriend is just delicious.'

'Boyfriend might be a stretch at this stage, we only just started seeing each other.' Ariana's blood rushed to her face as she remembered the passionate kiss on her doorstep.

'What? What happened?' Ben gasped, seeing her face go red.

Ariana hid a big grin behind her hand and shook her head.

'Nope, I'm not kissing and telling.' She laughed and Ben's mouth dropped open.

'Oh I bet he is a fantastic kisser.'

Ariana gave a non-committal jerk of her head. Rhys had made her dizzy when he kissed her, but she wasn't going to give away the juicy details, even to her best friend. She wasn't usually the kind of person to go into such details about her love life.

They drank their coffees and chatted aimlessly for the rest of Ben's lunch break. Ariana tried to forget about the hooded figure across the street, but she felt his eyes on her and it made her extremely uncomfortable.

Ariana left for work, parting from Ben with a brief hug. As she walked away, she glanced back to see her new friend crossing the road and falling into step behind her.

Somewhere between the city centre and the dojo in St. Mark's, the stranger stopped tailing her, but it was little comfort. Throughout her classes that afternoon and into the evening she felt uneasy and as she left work late in the evening she cast furtive glances into the black sky, knowing that the full moon shone somewhere behind the clouds.

5th November

Ariana huddled with Ben on the edge of Redfield Park. A thick coat and gloves providing inadequate protection against the bitter November night but at least it wasn't raining.

A huge bonfire raged in the centre of the park and

overhead brightly coloured flashes filled the sky, accompanied by booming explosions. Children ran past with sparklers and little stalls lined the field selling toffee apples and candy floss.

Ben "oohed" and "ahhed" appreciatively beside Ariana, a big grin lighting his face, but Ariana was finding it difficult to get into the spirit of the occasion. She could feel eyes upon her, more than one pair. She hadn't seen the hooded figure for days and was just beginning to feel comfortable in her skin again, but now she sensed him nearby. She knew it was him, though she couldn't see him in the dark and crowded park.

Somehow she knew he had friends with him and she tried to convince herself that it was a coincidence, he was here enjoying the festivities, just like all of her neighbours in St. Mark's and Redfield. But try as she might, she couldn't make herself believe it.

The firework display came to a glittering end and gradually the crowd began to disperse. Ariana stuck close to Ben, her heart was racing as they moved towards the trees that lined the park.

'That was so much fun.' Ben beamed at her, linking his arm through hers.

'Yeah.' She tried to smile back and shake off the feeling that someone was walking close behind them. There were hundreds of people moving away from the park. You're being paranoid. She told herself.

Ariana glanced over her shoulder towards the bonfire, still burning brightly with stragglers gathered around it. The faces of people walking behind them were all hidden in shadow, the blazing fire at their backs.

Ariana and Ben walked briskly away from the park and headed south towards St. Mark's. The streets became quieter as the crowds dispersed and went their separate ways.

Somewhere to the south another public firework display was still in full swing and the loud explosions echoed across the city. Each one made Ariana's heart leap into her throat but she fought her fears and tried to respond to Ben's cheerful babble by her side. Other smaller, private fireworks displays popped and crackled behind fences and walls that they passed and the air was thick with smoke and the smell of gunpowder.

Each step they took brought them closer to Ben's flat and Ariana looked around cautiously all the way. She saw no signs of being followed and by the time they reached his home she felt almost at ease.

'Will you be okay walking home on your own?' Ben asked at his door, his face full of concern.

'I'll be fine,' she said, trying to convince herself as much as him. 'I think I can take care of myself.' She smiled and gave his arm a playful punch.

He drew her into a warm hug, Ariana hugged him back, a little reluctant to let go and go on her way. Ben was the one to release her and she stepped away from him with a heavy sigh.

'See you next weekend, I expect,' Ben smiled. 'Cocktails at the new bar by the river.'

'Of course.' Ariana made a gallant effort to give him a broad smile and they said their goodbyes.

She set off walking quickly, she lived on the opposite side of St. Mark's. She knew the route like the back of her hand and although she was eager to get home as quickly as possible, she decided against taking the little short cuts through alleys that she knew so well, instead sticking to the bigger, well-lit roads.

A low snarl behind her made her pick up the pace, afraid

to glance over her shoulder. Her heart hammered in her chest and she started running. There were more unfamiliar noises behind her and she let out a frightened cry and picked up the pace. At the next corner she grabbed hold of the iron fence and used it to pivot around the corner with extra speed and agility. She chanced a glance back and saw two huge dogs sprinting down the pavement towards her.

Ariana leaped up onto the wall next to her, still clinging to the iron fence that topped it and watched in stunned silence as a rangy fox leaped out of the shadows on the opposite side of the road, followed by a long haired dog that looked suspiciously like a wolf. The two new arrivals intercepted the vicious dogs heading for her.

Snarls and sharp barks filled the air and teeth snapped in warning. It was a stand off. Ariana watched, open-mouthed. The two dogs that had been chasing her were definitely wolves, as was the other canine that had come to her rescue, she was sure of it. The pursuing wolves slowly backed down, they turned and jogged back the way they had come. Her wolf saviour followed them, his nose to the ground, apparently escorting them off his territory.

The fox turned to look at her, his eyes were amber and glistening under the street light. She stared into the familiar eyes, a nagging sensation of a lost memory tugged at her and she slowly stepped down from the wall and took a few cautious steps towards the fox.

He stared at her, breathing heavily and sending out little puffs of hot breath into the cold air. She stopped and watched him, trying to read him, there was something about those eyes.

Suddenly the fox snapped his jaws and jerked towards her. Too much, too long. She understood him instantly and she stepped back, acutely aware of her surroundings once more, the spell was broken. She turned and walked briskly away, desperate to get home.

She didn't look back, but she knew he was following her, seeing her safely home.

10th November

Ariana hadn't told anyone about the encounter with the wolves and fox in the street. It was all too strange and she instinctively knew it must be kept private. Not just because it made her sound crazy, but she felt the inexplicable need to protect these strange animals by keeping their existence secret.

She went to work each day, aware of the hooded stranger's eyes on her. He never left her now. She felt safe, protected. She decided he was her guardian angel, not her stalker. Even when she had gone with Ben and Marcus to the new bar as promised, her guardian was there, hooded and hidden from view. He blended into the background somehow, but she knew he was there.

As she left work that Saturday night it was raining, the rain seemed relentless now that November had taken hold, she pulled her coat around herself and set off at a brisk walk. She looked around, waiting for him to appear from the shadows and follow her home.

After a block there was still no sign of him and she started to feel anxious. Her eyes darted around, searching the darkest corners, the deepest alleyways as she walked quickly through the wet streets.

A passing car shone its lights into the mouth of one such alley and she was startled to see two yellow eyes fixed on her. The lights quickly passed and the eyes were gone, but Ariana knew the fox was still there, hidden in the dark. She took a cautious step into the alley, her hands open at her sides, hoping that the fox would accept the gesture.

'Where is he?' she asked. She laughed a little at herself, surprised by the question, surprised at saying anything to the fox that she couldn't even see. For a moment she wondered if she ought to be embarrassed at herself, but decided quickly that it felt right to talk to this fox with the amber eyes. 'I'm worried about him. He's been there every time I've been out on the street for days now. Is he okay?'

She felt movement in the alley ahead of her and she took another cautious step, engulfing herself in the shadows, away from the orange glow of the street lights. Her eyes began to adjust to the darkness and she latched onto a shape nearby that seemed about right to be the fox. She knelt down, bringing her eyes level with his and slowly his form became more clear.

He stood looking at her, his eyes not quite making contact with hers, there was no other light to catch his eyes, so they were dark too. He let out a small noise in his throat, so dog-like and normal that Ariana was startled; she had almost expected him to speak. She stood abruptly and shook her head. What was she doing?

Without another word, Ariana turned and walked quickly back onto the street. She wasn't far from home and she finished the journey shaking her head and scolding herself.

Chapter Four

She was being chased by a dog that she couldn't see, but the world was wrong: twisted and frightening. She was running on four paws again, but she was in a panic, terrified of something she couldn't identify with her conscious mind. Maybe she was only scared of herself. She was sprinting along the street on all fours but she was wrong. Her run was more of a gait, glancing at a shop window as she sped past she caught sight of a twisted creature; part fox, part human, part bear. It was some awful combination of creatures and she howled in terror.

The dog chased her down, she couldn't outrun it, she found herself backed up a dark alley. She turned to face it as it prowled slowly towards her. It wasn't a dog, it was a sleek fox, shrouded in darkness, but for those yellow eyes. Suddenly she was not afraid. His eyes were soft, familiar and so comforting. Then just as she relaxed enough to feel her horrific form shifting into something more human, the fox shuddered and twisted before her and disappeared. In his place was a huge cobra. It launched itself at her and bit her arm.

Searing pain woke her and she leapt out of bed and went straight to the window, searching for her guardian, but he was nowhere to be seen. Staring out of the window at the empty street her arm gave a twinge. She looked down at it, eerie in the orange street light and saw wet blood glistening on her skin. With a small cry she dashed to the bathroom and ran cold water over her arm. The blood ran off down the drain and she watched as strange marks were revealed.

Scared, she went back to bed, wrapping a cloth around her arm and wincing with pain. She told herself that she had grabbed her arm while she was sleeping and that her finger nails had left those marks. But she didn't really believe it and she lay awake, afraid to close her eyes.

11th November

Ariana woke with a start. She had fallen asleep despite herself but still felt shaken. It was just beginning to get light outside, and the dull light was enough to see by. She looked carefully at her arm. Clear as day were fresh puncture marks on her skin, not deep, it had only been a nip by the looks of it and they were healing cleanly and remarkably quickly. She tossed the bloody cloth that she had wrapped her arm in into the laundry and paced her room. She searched her memory for something, some tangible explanation. She couldn't remember leaving her flat in the night, the fox definitely hadn't bitten her in the alley and the marks on her arm were clearly not the bite marks of any kind of dog. They were two neat puncture marks from a snake. She had to make sense of it all. The nightmare still felt as vivid as it had when she was in it and when she looked at her hands they were shaking.

Ariana dashed to her flat door, tried it and found that it was still locked, there was no way anyone or an animal like a fox could have followed her into her home and bitten her in her bed. But a snake could have found its way in without having to use the door. Ariana looked around her precious little flat cautiously, peering into corners and under her bed. There was no sign of a snake anywhere, but she knew it could be hiding. She collapsed, her back against the bedroom door and closed her eyes. Tears began to leak out of the corners of her eyes, she made one small effort to stop them but quickly gave into it, sobbing loudly into her hands.

She felt so confused and afraid. Vicious wolves were chasing her in the street, bold as brass, a strange man was following her almost everywhere she went, and now she was turning into some monstrous creature in her nightmares and had woken with a real snake bite on her arm. How could this be happening? Was she going insane?

Anger fired up inside her, frustration both at herself for being so self-pitying and with the lack of available answers. She was the sort of person who always needed an explanation and who was self-sufficient. She felt anger towards her so called guardian, what use had he been in her sleep?

She strode to her bedroom window and looked out. He stood there, in his usual spot, looking right at her, his clear grey eyes sharp and bright. At his heel was the fox, his yellow eyes fixed on her too.

Ariana's anger faltered as she looked down into their eyes. All in one moment, she finally consciously acknowledged the possibility that the man and the fox were one and the same; then dismissed the idea, now she had proof that they weren't. The fox looked sad and concerned for her and so deeply apologetic.

A sudden urge to go to them took hold of her, she turned from the window and dashed for the door, grabbing a rain coat on the way and shoving her feet into her running shoes. She charged down the stairs two at a time and burst out of the building into the rain. They were gone. Her eyes flew up and down the empty street, she ran across the road and into the alley opposite. A metal bin lid was spinning its final circle before landing flat with a clatter at the far end of the alley, but they were already gone; over the tall, wooden gate.

She was about to turn and go back to her house when her fierce determination asserted itself once again and she sprinted for the end of the alley. She leaped up and vaulted the gate, landing squarely in her neighbour's overgrown back yard. With just a moment's pause she followed her gut and charged for the opposite fence, climbing it quickly, if a little clumsily, and dropped down into the next street. She ran blindly for a few seconds, the street was empty, but for a passing car. It was barely daylight, people were still in their dry houses eating breakfast before greeting the wet, November morning.

With a frustrated snarl, Ariana turned and trudged back home, sticking to the streets and keeping out of her neighbours' gardens.

Why had they run from her? If they were there to protect her and were sorry about the bite then why couldn't they talk to her?

Some dark and deeply buried memory began to stir as she reached her front door. She stopped and looked at the alley and then up the street. She remembered a blackout and strange animals fighting. She reached into her memory, clawing at it, searching for the rest, but it was like a wispy thread, just too thin and too swift to grasp.

12th November

```
I'm taking you out tomorrow night. Wear
something warm and comfortable and
practical shoes! R xx
```

Ariana found a smile as she read the message over a few times. Something stopped her from replying, some sense of wrongness with the world that made her want to hide away from it. She looked out of her window at the empty street. Had they abandoned her? They hadn't returned.

All the way to work that afternoon she looked around for

a sign of either the man or the fox, but found none. Throughout her classes she was distracted and foggy, half remembered images of an inky blackness troubled the back of her mind.

Her last class of the day was a private lesson in Banshay and she went to fetch her precious swords from her locker in the staff room. The other instructor had finished and cleared out, but she could hear her manager, Ron, talking on the phone in his office. As she slid the dha out of their case, Ariana felt the steel humming within their scabbards. Ariana took the swords through to the small studio and unsheathed one of them. Running her fingers gently along the blade, she felt at peace.

Closing her eyes, Ariana lifted the sword and slowly passed it across her body, under her arm and back again. She repeated the move a little quicker and gradually picked up the pace, moving around in a circle as she twisted and spun the blade ever closer to her body. It became a dance, one she knew well.

Ariana felt energised and cleansed. She sheathed her dha again, ready for her student and pulled out her phone, quickly she punched in a reply.

```
Sounds intriguing. Looking forward to
it :) xx
```

13th November

Boots on and coat zipped up, Ariana was ready at 7.30pm exactly when her doorbell rang. She ran down the stairs and flung open the door to greet Rhys. They grinned at each other for a moment before he drew her into a warm embrace, kissing her cheek.

'Hi,' she breathed in his ear, butterflies soaring through her stomach and up into her throat.

Rhys stepped back and gave her a quizzical look before gesturing to his sleek, black car behind him. Ariana locked her front door and allowed him to open the passenger door for her. He looked at her curiously again as he closed the door and Ariana felt a tug at her gut. She shrugged off the strange feeling and smiled at him as he slid into the driver's seat next to her. He smiled back and started the engine.

'I have something to show you.'

'Okay,' she replied slowly. She noted his heavy combat trousers tucked into big boots and his thick, hooded sweatshirt. This was no ordinary date.

He drove quickly across St. Marks, through a particularly rough neighbourhood a few blocks from her flat. Ariana tensed up in her seat and watched Rhys carefully, intrigued and a little nervous. The deserted, industrial streets gave way to wide, leafy avenues as they entered Crossway, one of the wealthier parts of the city. The houses here were large, terraced town houses, boasting elevated positions back from the road and cars much like Rhys's sat outside each house. Tall trees lined the road, their roots beginning to burst up out of the grey concrete.

On they went, out into the beautiful suburb of Fenwick. Once a separate village, Fenwick had retained its unique identity as the city of Caerton had sprawled east to meet it. It was a very green part of the city, with several large parks and wide streets lined with old trees. It was a very affluent area, with large detached houses behind electric gates and high walls. It was right on the eastern edge of the city and backed onto large woodlands. There was only one major road through Fenwick which passed right through it and out of the city, all other roads ended before the woods, which gave it the feeling of being nestled and protected by the ancient trees.

Fenwick sat higher than most of Caerton and Rhys drove them to the topmost hill and parked up by the side of the road. The forest lay ahead of them, there were no houses in sight and it was with a growing sense of apprehension that Ariana got out of the car.

It was a clear night and very cold, but Ariana was thankful for a break in the near constant rain and she looked up at the crystal clear stars above. Rhys appeared by her side and switched on a torch, which he shone at his own face and grinned.

'Have you ever been up here before?'

Ariana shook her head in reply and Rhys's face lit up with glee.

'You are going to love this.' He took her hand so tenderly and gave it a firm squeeze before dragging her at a brisk walk towards the trees and then bearing north through the forest.

They walked in silence for a minute, Ariana was watching the ground where Rhys shone the light and picked her way carefully along the roughly trodden path. She kept pace with Rhys but it was clear that his enthusiasm was getting the better of him, as he was almost breaking into a jog, navigating the rough terrain with expertise.

Suddenly they came to the edge of the forest and Ariana stopped abruptly, her breath catching in her throat. They stood at the top of a high cliff, Caerton spread beneath them as far as the eye could see. It shone brightly in the night, lit up by a million multi-coloured lights. Ariana gasped.

'It's incredible,' she whispered. 'Obviously, I knew the

city was big, but to see it like this,' she tailed off, lost for words.

'I know. The first time I came up here I couldn't believe my eyes. Below us there is Burnside and the city centre,' Rhys stood behind Ariana and wrapped one arm around her, pointing down into the city with the other. 'We're facing west. In summer the sunsets from here are just breathtaking. There's your neighbourhood, St. Mark's and there's Redfield.'

'Oh look,' Ariana interrupted, 'the Telecoms tower, there!' She pointed out the tall tower with its red light blinking at the top, it lay in the heart of St. Mark's, not far from where Ben lived. Beyond the familiar St. Mark's was the river, winding right across the city. It flowed from some place inland, through the city centre and out to the docks in the north. Finally spilling into the estuary with all of the detritus that it had picked up on its course. 'I can see the river too.' She grinned back at Rhys and he returned her smile.

Ariana nudged her nose up to his and felt him draw in for a kiss. Their lips met and she twisted in his arms to face him. The kiss was deep and dizzying and when Rhys pulled back Ariana took a clumsy step forward. He caught her easily and set her on her feet. Ariana felt her cheeks redden and didn't want to look straight up at him, but there was something unsettling that dragged her eyes up. She felt physically sick, the dizziness wasn't just from the kiss, her head was pounding and she saw spots before her eyes.

'Are you okay?' Rhys put a gentle hand on her arm and she leaned into him for support.

'Sorry, I'm not feeling well all of a sudden.' She turned and looked up at the sky. The stars blinked and the slip of a waning crescent moon wasn't enough to shine any light on her tonight. Her stomach lurched and she clamped a hand over her mouth, but nothing happened, the wave of nausea began to subside.

Rhys held her by the arm and rubbed her back gently.

'I'll take you home,' he whispered.

Rhys guided her carefully back to the car. They sat in silence on the drive back, Ariana rested her head against the cold glass of the window and kept her eyes closed to keep the dizziness and nausea at bay.

When they arrived at her home, Ariana could hardly move her legs, they felt so dull and heavy. Without a word, Rhys lifted her from the car and carried her easily to the door. She fumbled for the keys in the pocket of her jeans. As she passed them to him her arm ached and she began to feel sick again. She clung tightly to him as he carried her inside and up the stairs to her flat. Her vision was blurred and she closed her eyes again, when she opened them he was lying her on her bed. He took her boots off her feet and sat down on the floor next to her, holding her hand. She tried to squeeze his hand, but wasn't sure whether she had managed it or not.

Her eyes slowly closed. She saw the fox with amber eyes watching her, until a slick, black nothing slid over him and engulfed her too.

14th November

The fog was lifting, Ariana's mouth felt dry and her throat ached, her head was heavy and when she tried to lift her hand to her face that felt heavy too. Her eyes opened slowly. It was daylight, but only just, and her eyelids flickered closed against the light. A quick movement next to her gave her cause to try again to open her eyes, with a little more success.

'You're awake.' The voice was barely above a whisper, mercifully.

'Meh,' she managed to whimper and she rolled onto her side. Her eyes focused on Ben by her side and confusion set in.

'Rhys called me this morning, I've been here for about an hour. He had to work.' Ben settled down on the bed next to her and put a reassuring hand on her shoulder. 'How are you feeling?'

'Like death,' she croaked.

Ben held out a sports bottle and she shuffled nearer to take a sip. The water was cold and soothing. Gradually, Ariana felt able to sit up and Ben passed over her phone.

'You got a message about ten minutes ago.'

Ariana took the phone and opened her messages.

```
Hi. How are you feeling? I hope Ben is
taking care of you. I'm sorry I couldn't
stay. Keep in touch and I hope to see you
when you're feeling better xx
```

Ariana put her phone aside, she would reply later, when she had some progress to report.

'Why didn't you have to be at work?' she asked Ben.

'I'm half there,' he smiled and pointed through her open bedroom door to his laptop on the table in the living room.

Over the course of the day Ben helped her to eat and drink and even take a shower. As he helped her get undressed he saw the bandage on her arm and gave her an enquiring look.

'Oh it's nothing,' she lied. 'I burned myself on a pan making chilli.' He seemed to believe her and when she gingerly unwrapped the bandage alone in the bathroom she found that the fang marks were almost healed, silvery scars remained and a little redness, but nothing too noticeable.

The shower helped clear her head and by the evening she felt almost normal, but with that lingering fatigue of a bad flu.

'You should head home. You've been great today, nursing me back to health, but I think I'll be okay,' she insisted.

'Are you sure? It really is no problem for me to stay.'

'Really. I can always call you if I change my mind,'

He nodded sympathetically and took his time leaving, somewhat reluctantly.

Ariana went to her window and watched him go. There was no sign of her guardian angel or the fox and she felt a deep longing for one or both of them. She couldn't explain the feeling, but she knew she needed them nearby, she wanted to talk to them, certain that they could explain to her why she kept falling ill and recovering again so frequently. She had no one that she could talk to about all of the strange things she had seen and experienced, even Ben wouldn't understand it if she told him that her stalker had turned out to be her body guard or that she had been saved from a pack of wild wolves by the odd couple of the wolf and fox. She hardly believed it herself.

Ariana looked at her phone and thought carefully about how to reply to Rhys. She felt deeply embarrassed about being taken so ill on their date. She wished she could give him some concrete explanation, but as she had none herself there was nothing she could offer him.

Hi. I'm feeling a bit better, thanks. Thank you for bringing me home and getting Ben to come over, I really appreciate it. Assuming I'm at full strength at the weekend, maybe we could try that date again then? Xx

She hit the send button and tossed her phone down on the bedside table. She lay down and drifted quickly into a restless sleep.

He came to her out of the shadows, he circled her, his amber eyes fixed on her, unblinking. She looked up at the black sky and could see clouds rushing overhead. As they parted the full moon shone brightly over her and illuminated the trees around her. The trees shifted into tall buildings and span around her in a confusing blur. They twisted and became crooked old things with broken windows and crumbling walls. The city turned to ruins all around her and then she was among the trees again. She looked up and the moon was changing rapidly before her eyes, waning from full to half, quickly shrinking to a crescent and then it disappeared. The new moon was black and she could no longer see the trees. Her body began to shake violently and when she held out her arms they were monstrous, with huge claws jutting out from thick fur. She screamed, but the noise that came out was a hideous howl.

Ariana woke with a start, sweating and shaking. She looked at her hands, but they were fine; totally normal and human. Tears were streaking down her face and she couldn't stop trembling. She knew these were not just nightmares. They were connected to the strange animals, that nagging memory that she couldn't quite place and the mysterious bite on her arm. It was all too real and she finally acknowledged to herself that she was deeply afraid of what she was changing into.

Chapter Five

15th November

It was with some fierce determination and sense of obligation that Ariana dragged herself from her bed and got ready for work. She felt awful; still full of this "new-moon-flu", as she had decided to call it, still shaken by her nightmares and her head spinning with questions. A lifetime of martial arts training wasn't for nothing, however; she could be disciplined and diligent when she set her mind to it, and that afternoon she had classes to teach. She shoved the thoughts and feelings that were so unwelcome deep into the darkest recesses of her mind where they could not trouble her.

She walked through St. Mark's in the rain, again. One of these days she would stop off at a shop and buy an umbrella. It was early in the afternoon and cars sloshed by, sending torrents of water across the pavement. Ariana trudged on, knowing that dry clothes and shoes were secured in her locker at work.

She arrived and got changed, made idle chat with her colleagues when she saw them, greeted students as warmly as she could muster and warmed up her body for her first class of the day. Regular deep, cleansing breaths helped to keep unwanted thoughts and feelings at bay throughout the afternoon, but as the sun set outside and the windows of her studio grew black, the aching set in.

Throughout her last class, Ariana felt her body growing more and more tired. She shouted instructions to her students and leaned against the wall to take the weight off her aching feet. Her eyes felt tired and she closed them briefly to rest them. Her head pounded. All of her senses seemed to be on overload, crowding her head up. She could smell the sweat of her students so strongly it almost made her retch. The studio lights were too bright and she cursed Ron out loud for not installing dimmer switches. The teenagers in her class were so loud and boisterous that she felt like her ears might begin to bleed.

As her class drew to a close she hurriedly threw her kit into her bag and bolted out of the door ahead of some stragglers. She ran out into the street, hoping that the air would quieten the noise in her head. She breathed deeply and looked up into the sky. There was no rain, the downpour had stopped and she stared at the clouds overhead as they drifted across the sky and parted. It was so black and Ariana knew without needing to look that it was a true new moon.

As that thought took root something shifted in her gut and she thought she was going to be sick. She ran to the kerb and retched, but nothing came up. She felt her bones groan and muscles stretch. She stumbled backwards and slammed into the window of the old electronics shop as a strange sound rose in her throat, part growl and part howl, it was a sound so alien to her that she started running, trying to flee from herself.

Her eyes darted around for her guardian, but he was nowhere to be found so she just kept running. She knew she needed to get to him, wherever he was. She didn't know how she would find him, just that she had to.

Her heart pounded, she was terrified and her body felt so alien, it was as if she were no longer inside it, but rather watching from somewhere just above her head. Sometimes she was sprinting on all fours, at others she was leaping along in huge bounds, her hands grazing the pavement at the same time. When she looked down she saw wolf paws pounding the pavement one second and the huge claws of a lion the next. Her arms and hands were no longer her own, they were covered in thick fur. Her throat felt strange, the noises coming from it were wrong. She was aware of her tail, swishing behind her as she ran, and of the strength of her legs as they propelled her along at an alarming speed. She felt she could launch herself twenty feet into the air if she tried.

The street around her kept changing too, flickering like an old TV with bad reception. It was normal one second, but another it was twisted and wrong, the cracks in the pavement became gaping maws to be traversed, which she found she could do easily with those powerful legs of hers. The buildings alongside her loomed overhead, bigger and darker and looking down on her as if they were alive. In the road to her right, a sleek, black shadow glided along beside her, turning out each street light as it passed, keeping her in darkness.

Her head was filled with panic, she had no idea how far she'd travelled, fear and pain were ravaging her mind and body.

Suddenly the street went black, all the lights went out, there were no cars, no people, nothing and she collapsed in a shop doorway, shivering. Her clothes were torn, hanging off her in shreds and she began to scream, her body convulsed and tears streaked down her face. She looked at her human hands, they were covered in scratches and scrapes.

It's just another nightmare, she thought, just another nightmare. I'm going to wake up any second now. Any second now.

Her vision began to clear and she saw them running towards her, her guardian and the fox. She could hardly see them in the blackness of the night, but she knew it was them. Her guardian dropped to his knees by her side and unzipped a large duffel bag, pulling out clothes and trying to cover her with them. She resisted at first, her mind a fog of uncertainty, she twisted and writhed and scratched out at him. He stayed utterly calm and silent, but persisted in his efforts to cover her and calm her body down. He caught hold of her wrists and pulled her into his strong embrace.

Ariana sobbed against his chest and gave in to him, a feeling of warmth and safety gradually overtaking the terror. The fox sat silently beside them, his amber eyes connected to her own and as she stared into them she felt his thoughts inside her mind.

We are family.

She felt the heartbeat of her guardian against her ear and gradually his thoughts entered her mind too.

Shhhh. I have you. You're going to be just fine.

Further away she felt others. She could almost see their faces.

My pack? She asked in thought. The fox glanced at the man, who pulled away from her in order to look at her.

'Yes,' he said aloud. 'Our pack.'

Ariana felt a wave of calm wash over her, followed by complete and utter exhaustion, and before she could say or do anything about it, she slipped into blackness.

Chapter Six

When Ariana woke she was in a bed in a dimly lit room. She felt the residue of sweat all over her body and her skin was covered in goosebumps, though she lay under a warm blanket and had been dressed in loose sweats. Her eyes adjusted to the low light emanating from a lamp in the corner. She could hear traffic and the occasional yells of passing people from the busy street outside. Ariana sat up slowly, her arms shook under her weight as she pushed herself up.

There was a tall glass of water on the bedside table and she took it, and holding it with both hands she sipped slowly. Her eyes scanned the room, the walls were faded and peeling. As her eyes passed the dark corner next to the door her heart leapt into her throat and she let out a cry, sloshing water over herself at the sight of someone sitting silently in the shadows. He leaned forward, his arms resting on his knees, his face slowly entering the reach of the lamp light.

Ariana drew her knees up to her chest and put the glass down slowly, not taking her eyes off him. She felt suddenly very confused as the memory of what had happened in the street came rushing back to her. Her breathing quickened and her eyes left her watcher to dart around the room. Her gaze went to the bare window, but all she could make out was that she was in an upstairs room, orange street lamps cast their eerie glow.

'Be easy,' the dark figure finally spoke and Ariana's eyes snapped back to him. He was staring intently at her, his dark skin glistening in the odd light, the whites of his eyes standing out in stark contrast. 'You are perfectly safe here and you will soon understand everything that has happened to you.'

Ariana was shivering slightly but she stopped at the sound of his voice. She had expected to hear a Indian tang to it, but there was none. She looked at him carefully and saw something familiar in his eyes, there was a spark there that she had seen before and as she stared into them she saw the amber eyes of the fox.

'It's you. This is your human face.' A trace of confusion prickled at her senses as they worked hard to wrap themselves around this reality, but she had faced the worst of it already; her own change. As she remembered the panic, the disorientation, the random shifting of form, her heart began to pound furiously and her senses again started to feel too big for her body. She shook violently and felt her body start to change. 'No!' she screamed. 'Not now!'

The man stood and moved swiftly to her side. He was whispering words she could barely register through the pounding in her ears and the overwhelming feeling of her senses being amplified. Something about the sound of his voice soothed her and she felt the panic begin to dissipate. Every now and then she recognised a sound he was making as he drew closer to her and gently stroked her clammy arms.

'Quiet... safe... help you.' The familiar words penetrated her foggy mind.

She fell into an uneasy sleep again, with this stranger at her side, stroking her hair and speaking those soothing words.

She didn't sleep for long, however, and when she woke again it was still dark. She opened her eyes and looked towards the chair in the corner. He was sitting there watching her intently, a small smile on his lips. 'Are you ready now?' he asked softly, and she sat up slowly and nodded. She knew he had answers for the thousand questions she was ready to ask now that the shock was wearing off a little.

'What's happening to me?' she asked, her throat felt hoarse and dry and she reached for the water by the bed. He watched silently as she sipped the water and took a deep breath before speaking.

'You are changing. You have always felt different from those around you, your passions have always bubbled close to the surface and you've been in trouble for your short temper before.' Ariana blinked at him, surprised at his insight. 'Your body is now catching up to your feelings, you are...' He paused, considering her for a moment.

'Please,' she whispered, 'please don't be afraid to tell me the truth.' He nodded slowly and moved forward in the chair.

'In terms you will understand, Ariana, you are a shape shifter. As am I. You have always been one, but you have never shifted fully before tonight.'

'I don't understand,' she said slowly, rubbing her temples. 'How can I be a shape shifter? How is this possible?'

'I know it's a lot to take in. Your entire perception of the world is changing. It will take time for you to accept it. Ariana, tell me, have you always felt connected to the moon? Have you ever dreamed of being an animal and woken up needing to check in a mirror to reassure you that it was just a dream?'

Ariana remembered her recent nightmares and the occasional dream throughout her life that had had that effect. He was right. She nodded slowly as images flashed through her mind, memories of the monsters in her dreams.

'It wasn't a dream, running through those twisted streets, the fox...' She faltered and looked into his eyes again. 'That was you.' He nodded and looked at the floor.

'I am Shadow's Step. The one who was following you for the last few weeks is Fortune, he is the leader of our pack. This awakening of your abilities is not a sudden one, it builds gradually and over recent months you have been slowly changing, sometimes even crossing into our own realm, Hepethia. I found you there, tracked you and tasted your blood so that we could easily find you when you changed in this realm. I am sorry that it had to be that way.' He looked sad, his eyes fixed resolutely to the floor. She watched him closely, looking for any sign of deception. She could see none.

'You were the snake too?' She spoke slowly, her mind racing to catch up to everything.

'Yes, though not all of us can take multiple forms.' Shadow said, a small smile playing on his lips. 'We all have an animal form, which is determined by which moon we change under. You, like me, changed under the new moon, the fox's moon.' He smiled and she couldn't help smiling back.

She was going to be able to change into a fox and run through the city at night. That thought ignited her enthusiasm.

'Hepethia?' she asked, her curiosity was intense and hopped from one subject to another.

He smiled and looked up.

'We are not human, we can live like humans most of the time, but we are not of this realm. Our magic comes from another place, Hepethia. It's a sort of alternate reality. It's a place we can go to recharge our spirits, get away from the white noise of the human world and shift freely away from prying eyes. There is a veil that separates this realm from Hepethia, a sort of cloak that hides Hepethia from human eyes.'

Ariana listened, fascinated by his words and this entirely new reality unfolding before her.

'You asked if I had always felt connected to the moon. I've been getting sick at the new moon recently. I changed under a new moon. So does the moon control us?'

'We are creatures of Artemis, the goddess of the moon, the hunt and wild animals. Luna's form is ever shifting, just like us. Artemis created us and gives us our abilities, but no, she doesn't control us, nor does the moon itself. She casts her beautiful light down on those who walk the night, guiding and ever watchful.' Shadow's Step spoke with a serene smile. Ariana shifted her weight uncomfortably at these words, this was the first thing he had said that she didn't quite understand, it didn't seem to relate to her and she twitched her mouth, wanting to speak up but unsure which words to choose.

He paused and looked at her for a long moment, then he moved over to sit at the end of the bed. 'We are different, we were born under the new moon, you and I. Our path is not lit with silver moonlight,' Shadow's Step said softly, locking eyes with her. 'Ours is to walk in the dark places, to see when others are stifled by the black oppressive sky. The others of our kind bathe in her light, we do not, but she cares for us too. We are the chosen few who must keep humanity close to our hearts, for if we fail to do so we fall into despair. Sometimes you will need those who loved you before to remind you of all that you are. It is lonely in the blackness and most shifters will never understand, that is why it is me here with you now and not Fortune, with whose human face you are more familiar. He changed under a full moon, so he is our opposite in some ways.'

She nodded, though she didn't really comprehend everything that he said. It was so much to take in. His last words hung in the air for a long moment as she considered them. A wry smile tugged at Shadow's lips and Ariana caught his eyes with hers.

'What does he change into?' she asked, though she suspected she knew the answer.

'A wolf.' Shadow smiled.

Ariana laughed, she couldn't help herself. A hysterical sound bubbled out of her. As the shock of his words subsided she thought of the wolf who came to her rescue with Shadow that night that the feral wolves chased her. That was Fortune, her guardian angel, or guard dog.

'Who were those other wolves who chased me on bonfire night?'

'They were from a rival pack,' Shadow said with a sigh. 'We share a border along Redfield Park. They must have caught your scent and were attempting to claim you for their pack. Fortune saw them off our territory. They won't bother you again now that you've changed and become one of us.'

Ariana swallowed the hard lump that had formed in her throat. She shuddered at the thought of being bitten and claimed by those wolves, like she was property.

'We have a pack? I think I could feel them, after I changed.' Her heart started pounding again as images of her terrifying change ran through her mind, but she steadied herself.

'We do. We call ourselves The Blue Moon. You met Fortune, there are two other experienced packmates and three youngsters, like you. You'll meet the rest tomorrow. You'll also begin training. I'll teach you to fight.'

'We'll see,' she laughed. She doubted there was much he could teach her but she stopped laughing as his lips curved into a slight snarl. A submissive sensation spilled over her, which unnerved her, it was unlike anything she had felt before.

'You will need to forget almost everything you know about combat, young Ariana. You have a whole new body now, it won't move the way it used to.' She nodded meekly. 'I mustn't burden you with too much at once,' Shadow said, standing slowly. 'Try to rest and I will see you in the morning.'

'Shadow?' Ariana reached out a hand, grabbing his and he looked down at her, his eyes soft and caring. 'Will I change in my sleep? I don't feel completely in control.'

He placed a warm hand on her shoulder.

'I do not believe so, you have adjusted from the initial change. But we are all nearby and we will sense it if you become afraid enough to change again. Fear, I'm sorry to say, remains a powerful trigger for change however long we live. But you will grow more accustomed to it and learn to dominate it most of the time.' He smiled reassuringly and left the room quietly without another word.

Ariana sat for a long time looking out of the window by the bed. She recognised the road, she was still in St. Mark's. As she watched the night go by she understood that this was her territory, the beast in her claimed this place and somehow that helped her feel safe. Eventually she drifted off to sleep once again.

Shadow's Step's words drifted through her fractured sleep, along with images of changing, but the fear didn't overtake her.

16th November

She woke again late in the morning. On the chair in the corner was a small stack of her own clothes, the wet ones that had been in her bag. Now they were cleaned and dried. She tentatively got up and dressed and cautiously opened the door. There were noises coming from below as Ariana stepped into the narrow corridor. The wallpaper was peeling and there were two other doors on the passage. Ariana moved quietly to the corner and looked down the stairs, she could hear the noises more clearly here, raised voices and the sound of a dozen televisions blaring sports' commentaries.

She jumped as a door opened and closed behind her. Her head snapped to face the sound and she saw Shadow's Step smiling calmly.

'I'm glad you're up. We have much to do.' Ariana was relieved, for a second she had felt like a naughty school girl caught out of bed and about to be scolded. He moved down the corridor, passed her on the corner and set off down the stairs. Ariana followed, eager to see what he had to show her. At the foot of the stairs a passage led back to what looked like a kitchen and in front of her was an open door to where the noise was coming from. It was a smoky room, full of people all jostling and shouting. Light spilled through the doorway and Ariana took a step towards it, drawn to the energy, but a gentle hand on her shoulder stopped her. She looked at Shadow and he gave a single shake of his head. He turned and moved towards the kitchen, after one glance back towards the source of the noise, Ariana followed him.

Just before the kitchen door he slipped through a small door under the stairs, moving silently down a narrow stair case. Hesitantly, Ariana looked down into the dark and slowly followed, chewing her lip nervously. Her better judgement knew that it was foolish to follow a stranger into an unknown basement and yet she trusted this man utterly. Something inside her told her that he was her brother.

She trotted down the stairs after him and blinked as a light flared up to her right. A single bulb swinging on a cord lit the dry and surprisingly clean basement. A punch bag hung from the ceiling to one side and free weights stood on a rack to the other and she smiled broadly.

'I will teach you to use your body. You will be strong and fast and deathly silent.' Shadow spoke softly, his voice deep and enticing. Ariana nodded and moved into the room.

'You know I can already fight, right? You've been watching me for weeks, you and Fortune.' Shadow nodded and lifted his shirt over his head, tossing it to one side. His dark brown skin glistened under the light and she noticed his extremely sculpted physique. All over his torso were scars that shimmered slightly in the light. There were a few old wounds, but most of the scarring looked deliberate and she stepped closer to look more carefully. A delicate string of tiny runes wound its way around his body, they were branded onto his dark skin.

Suddenly he turned to face her, catching her off guard.

'You haven't begun to know what your body is capable of. What skill you possessed in your human life will certainly help you now, but it doesn't even compare.'

Ariana frowned and wrinkled her nose, she felt put out at this dismissive attitude toward her skills. She had always taken great pride in her abilities with her fists and blades and as she stood there feeling indignant she was taken aback to see Shadow suddenly transforming before her. His limbs changed shape and he dropped to all fours, thick hair sprouted all over his body, his jaw jutted out into a muzzle and ears sprouted up on the top of his head. He stood before her, a beautiful fox, but he was big, too big and looked dangerous. His trousers had completely vanished, they had merged with his body and been replaced by fur.

Ariana stepped back reflexively, but when he didn't move she swallowed hard, recovered herself and looked him over. Ariana felt energy surge through her body as she realised that she too could take this form and she longed to try it.

'How do I...?' she asked eagerly, stepping under the light bulb in the centre of the room. Shadow's Step moved around her, circling her, his breathing becoming more like a growl as he moved. She turned her head to follow him and waited to see what he would do. She sensed it coming, the strike, saw that his teeth were bared as he lunged for her arm. She whipped it out of his path and spun away from him. She wasn't afraid, she was fuelled by a roar in her gut and as she spun she dropped to her knees and felt her bones changing length, her muscles shifted and her face cracked and strained. Moments later she stood eye to eye with him, her skin also covered with thick red hair and her body that of a wiry city fox. With a start of surprise at seeing her altered form, Ariana let out a low growl. Her clothes had been shredded and she scowled.

'My clothes,' she tried to say. She wasn't sure what she expected to come out of her mouth, but no words came, just a strange snarl. A surge of panic coursed through her and she stumbled around, clumsy on four feet. She slid back across the concrete floor and crashed into the weight rack, which rattled behind her.

Shadow's Step moved over to her and nudged her shoulder with his nose. She looked into his familiar yellow eyes, and she could feel him inside her thoughts. He wanted her to fight with him, to show him what she could do in this body. Although she also somehow understood that this was not the shape she should use when she needed to fight, this was where she was quickest and the most stealthy, but not the most powerful.

There was something else, something he didn't want to frighten her with but he couldn't hide it from her and she

67

grasped out with her mind, trying to latch on to the elusive thought. She caught images of herself running from the dojo, her body rapidly fluctuating between different animals, messy, clumsy and terrifying. She could be a lion, a bear, a gorilla. Any number of beasts that could easily kill a person with their claws, teeth or strong fists. But more than this even, was a terrifying monster not known to humanity. Something else that was far more deadly.

As she stood taking in this new realisation, Shadow began to change in front of her. His body shrank initially, the fur receded and made way for scales. His form lengthened and his small head rose up to be eye level with her. He was a snake, a huge cobra with powerful muscles to crush with and venomous teeth to bite with. For the first time she was truly alarmed.

She stumbled away from him, whimpering and lowering her nose to the floor. Shadow shifted gracefully into his human form, sitting cross legged in front of her. His thoughts became more fuzzy, harder to comprehend but she understood that he was offering her some relief, some privacy and she understood at once that it went both ways, he could feel her thoughts too but it was much less pronounced in their human shape.

She thought about her first change, sprinting along the street shifting like that. What if someone had seen? She looked sharply at Shadow and with great focus she forced her body to change. Everything groaned and cracked and when she ran her eyes over herself she was frustrated to find that instead of her human self, she had managed to shift into a sleek, grey cat. She focused again and concentrated on shifting back into her human form. She found herself crouching on the floor, shaking violently. Her clothes a tattered mess hanging over her shoulders and scattered on the floor around the basement.

'Damn,' she muttered, looking around and trying to cover her body.

Shadow moved quickly and passed her some more sweats from the corner cupboard.

'What was that?' Shadow asked as he helped her cover herself.

Ariana stopped and looked at him. His question caught her off guard. She had wanted to ask him the same question, she expected answers from him, not questions.

'What do you mean?'

'You took the form of a cat. You shouldn't be able to do that. It takes a great deal of practice and some ritual magic to be able to take forms other than the one Artemis, or another of the gods blesses us with. Aside from the Agrius, the bestial form you find so frightening. I'm sorry, we all struggle with that one at first. Only those born under the gibbous moon can turn into cats right away.'

Ariana felt confused and vulnerable. She shrugged her shoulders and tried to make sense of his words.

'I thought it was normal. When I changed last night I shifted through lots of animal forms. Didn't you see that?'

'No, we only caught up with you when you were changing back into your human self at the end.'

'So I should only be able to take the form of a fox and that, that other thing?' she asked, shuddering at the thought of the beast within.

'Yes,' Shadow said softly, a deep frown etched onto his face.

'Why can I change into other animals?' Worry filled her.

'I don't know. Best we keep this between us for now. I'll ask some discrete questions and see if any of my associates have heard of this before.'

Ariana nodded in agreement. She didn't want to draw any attention to herself. It was a big enough shock to discover that she was a shape shifter, never mind finding out that she was an unusual one.

'I'll give you a moment.' Shadow said softly. 'I think that's enough for now. I will be upstairs in the kitchen when you are ready, we will eat and I think it would be a good time for you to meet the others.' He moved silently up the stairs and out of sight.

Ariana quickly put the clothes on, they were a woman's but were too long for her. She rolled up the trouser legs and paced the basement in her bare feet. She was afraid of the monster within her, the beast that she could be if she lost control. The news that she was somehow odd for a shifter was unsettling too. How was it possible for her to change into other animals? What was she?

Sitting down on the bottom step of the stairs, Ariana rubbed her face and covered her eyes with her hands. Hot tears stung the corners of her eyes as the reality of what she had become finally took hold of her. She wept, her shoulders shook. Her life would never be the same, everything had changed, not just her body but the whole world. Things she never knew existed before were real now and she was one of them. She could be a mindless killing machine rampaging through the city of Caerton, and although she knew that she could also be a graceful fox, or cat, silent as the shadows, the knowledge of the other side of her new nature was overwhelming.

Eventually the tears slowed and stopped and Ariana sat for a few minutes feeling the cool air dry her face. Giving herself a shake all over she stood and walked slowly up the stairs. The front of the building was still noisy and again she felt drawn towards the hubbub. Pausing in the hall, she could hear voices and smell bacon frying in the kitchen behind her. Suddenly a fierce hunger fired to life in her stomach and she moved quickly towards the sound of the frying pan spitting fat and the voices talking over one another.

Ariana approached the kitchen and she could feel the presence of her pack before she saw them. She also knew that they had sensed her approaching, although their voices did not change. This new heightened awareness was going to take some getting used to, but so far she quite liked it. She had never had a close family, but now she had brothers and sisters clamouring for attention inside her head.

'Ariana,' a warm voice carried towards her, the others dimming around it and she entered the large kitchen to be greeted by smiling and welcoming faces. She couldn't help but return the smiles with one of her own. She felt as though she were coming home to dear family. Her familiar stranger, her guardian for so many weeks was standing with his arms open toward her and she moved straight into his embrace.

Fortune was tall and covered with dark brown hair, it fell to his shoulders and his jaw hadn't seen a razor in some time. Thick hair covered his muscular arms and was visible at the neck of his t-shirt. He was painfully attractive and appeared to be in his mid forties, but she sensed a great wisdom and depth of experience from him and it occurred to her that his apparent age might be deceptive. She could feel his power emanating from him, she felt automatically submissive to him and knew without any hesitation that he was her alpha male, her leader. But she felt safe and warm in his arms too and could tell how protective of her he felt.

He released her and gestured to the other people in the room. 'Shadow's Step you already know, of course.' Shadow was sat at the big, pine kitchen table. He nodded once and Ariana smiled to him. 'This is Flames-First-Guardian.' Fortune indicated the man sat opposite Shadow. He was big, she couldn't tell how tall, but he was heavy set, it was largely muscle but he carried some extra bulk, and he carried it well. His hair was fairly short, but it was thick and wild and his face was hard with a prominent jaw and cheekbones. He was wearing several layers of clothing and had a dozen or more necklaces on display, each adorned with small trinkets, some of which looked like bones. He nodded and tapped the table with his thick fingers.

'If you would like to meet me later I will place a blessing on you, so that your clothes change when you do.' He looked her up and down, taking in the too-big clothes she had on and her bare feet. She felt a flush of embarrassment.

'Yes, thank you, that would be much appreciated,' she said softly, in a voice quite unlike her own.

'Don't mind Flames,' a bold, female voice darted from by the cooker. Ariana looked over to see a very tall woman with long auburn hair stood over the bacon frying in the pan. She was watching them and smirking. 'He has a way of making people feel like kids again, but he's mostly harmless. Mostly.'

Ariana gave a hesitant smile. The woman crossed the room and extended a hand, which Ariana took and shook briefly. 'I'm Speaks-with-Stone. You can just call me Stone.'

'Are these yours?' Ariana asked, looking down over her clothes. Stone nodded and smiled.

'Yeah, don't worry, keep them as long as you need them.' She smiled and went back to the bacon.

Fortune gave Ariana's arm a friendly squeeze and flashed a reassuring smile.

'You'll meet the others later, they're sleeping now. You're the fourth new pack member in recent weeks. We've never had such a large pack before and it is challenging for us to see that you are all well educated and well looked after.' He gestured around the room. 'The Blue

72

Moon has been the four of us for a long time, seeing our numbers double so quickly tells us that something big is on the horizon and we must make sure we take care of you all.' He released her arm and moved over to the cooker to help with lunch.

Ariana took a seat at the table next to Shadow and the conversation began to pick up again. She sat and listened to them chatting, some of it she understood, other parts passed her by. They were talking about names and places she didn't recognise, and some of what they said just didn't make any sense to her at all. She thought of the other newly changed pack members and she sat thinking about what it might mean to be the youngest of such a group. She felt a little insecure and somewhat less special.

Stone passed her a bacon sandwich with at least four rashers stuffed into thick bread and Ariana took it gratefully, polishing it off quickly with very little thought of table manners. The others each took a similar sandwich and all ate in much the same fashion. Stone sat next to her and leaned close while the men talked loudly around them. The air almost stilled around this strange woman, like a calm aura touching those closest to her.

'How are you?' she asked, her voice very soft. Ariana finished a mouthful of her sandwich and smiled weakly.

'Oh well, it's a lot to take in. But I think I'm okay. It all makes sense.' She glanced at Fortune who was reeling off names from a list and pointing at a small hand-drawn map on the table. 'Well, not everything, but just the existence of shifters and me being one. I don't know, it doesn't feel wrong. Am I making sense?'

Stone chuckled.

'Yes, completely. We were each born to this. We don't just change over night, or even over several months. We are born shifters, and it will affect us our entire lives, long before we first take an animal form. Some of our kind are raised by their shifter kin, and will know much about our world before they ever shift. Others, like you, will have no contact with our kind and have a lot of adjusting to do. But that's what the pack is here for, we're a family.' She smiled warmly and Ariana felt a bubble of gratitude well up inside. This was her sister, she felt it with all of her being.

Chapter Seven

That afternoon Ariana went with Shadow's Step to her flat to collect some clothes and other things that she could keep at the pack's headquarters.

'There are many of our kind in Caerton, not just our pack, but many others,' Shadow explained in a quiet voice as they walked briskly through St. Mark's. 'Each area of the city is claimed by a different pack, except for the very heart of the city.'

'Why?' she asked, frowning.

'None of us are entitled to it. There are certain traditions, certain bloodlines.' Shadow's voice tailed off as a man rushed past them.

'Do you mean royalty?' Ariana asked him.

'Yes.'

'Is there an heir somewhere, then?'

'Yes. And Artemis help us if he ever makes a serious move to claim his throne.'

Something in Shadow's tone told Ariana not to pursue the matter further and a few minutes later they arrived at her door.

Shadow waited outside while Ariana quickly packed a bag and checked that all was in order. She planned to stay with the pack for a day or two to get acquainted with them and learn as much as she could about her change. She changed into some black boarders and a white vest top, adding her favourite, most comfortable trainers and a smart black jacket.

As she stood in front of her mirror checking her outfit she focused on her eyes; they looked more sharp, more alive than ever before and the blue of them was far more striking than it had been before she changed. Her skin looked pale but had a healthy glow to it and her short hair felt thicker and a bit more difficult to tame. It was like she had grown into her own features, she looked the same but healthier and more vibrant.

She stared at herself for a long time, examining every curve of her face carefully. She found herself wondering if anyone would notice and she quickly banished the thought, afraid of what it might mean having to face up to; whether or not she could keep close ties to her friends, her work and her human life. With a quick shake of her head she grabbed her overnight bag and the bag with her precious dha in and ran for the door.

She locked up and ran down into the street to meet Shadow and they set off back to the headquarters. Shadow walked half a step behind Ariana, his eyes ever watchful and she couldn't help but feel on edge the whole way back.

The Blue Moon Betting Shop was on a fairly wide and busy street, with terraced houses on both sides and a few shops in a row on the opposite side. The betting shop stood between two normal houses that both looked suspiciously empty. Shadow led her in through the shop and he held the door open for her.

Ariana cast her eyes around the space. The front of shop had a large window with dark blue printed on it to conceal the inside of the shop from passers by. Mounted on the walls around the room were several televisions each blaring out a different sporting event, several dedicated to horse racing. The walls were painted dark blue, the floor was faded blue linoleum and discarded betting slips littered it. At the back of the shop was a partition with four cashier windows, two of which were open and Ariana saw Stone behind one and a new face behind the other. Filling the space were at least a dozen men, nearly all were smoking heavily. There were shouts of frustration and enthusiasm at the events on the screens, and the whole shop was filled with smoke and noise.

It was overwhelming for Ariana and she put her head down and quickly followed Shadow to a small door at the back of the shop. Shadow punched a code into a keypad and opened the door. He held his hand out, indicating for her to head on through into the back area and she made her way ahead of him. Stone gave her a warm smile as she stepped through the little door and the young woman next to her gave a friendly wave, Ariana regarded her carefully and sensed that she was human.

The back area was well sound proofed, the noise of the televisions was little more than a faint buzzing. Ariana's eyes went to the safe under the counter between the two middle windows, out of sight of any punters. Shadow greeted Stone and nodded at the other assistant.

'How are the takings looking today, ladies?' Shadow asked, leafing through a few papers in front of Stone.

'About the same as usual,' Stone replied with a shrug. 'Ariana, this is Lily, my little sister.'

'Oh,' Ariana gasped. 'Pleased to meet you.' She stepped closer and shook hands with the girl.

'Hi,' Lily replied. 'Nice to see another new face around here.' She grinned and bounced slightly on her stool.

Ariana regarded Lily carefully, she was young, probably a year or two younger than herself. She had long red hair, like Stone's, and a fresh face. She was dressed in skinny jeans and a t-shirt that fell off one shoulder, revealing a hot pink strap.

'See you both later,' Shadow said cheerfully, before leading Ariana out into the back of the building.

She sat down at the kitchen table. Shadow moved around the kitchen, tidying, moving meat from the freezer to the fridge and other little chores.

'Stone has a little sister?' Ariana asked quietly, unable to conceal the disbelief.

'She does,' Shadow said, chuckling. 'Lily hasn't changed yet, she may never change, but we have raised her and she knows all about us. That's the way it often happens.'

'I was adopted,' Ariana said quietly. She had tried not to give too much thought to who her birth parents were. They had abandoned her for some reason and she had bounced around the care system during her early years. She was adopted when she was four. Her adoptive family were nice enough, but she always felt different from them. Now she knew why.

'Do you know who your biological parents are?' Shadow asked cautiously.

'No, I have no idea.'

'Would you like to find out?'

'Not really,' she said dismissively.

'One of them at least will have been a shifter,' he said, a leading tone to his voice.

She raised a curious eyebrow. It was all too much to take in, everything had changed and this was one thing too many. She shook her head and pushed the idea of finding her birth parents right to the back of her mind.

'No. I can't deal with that right now. Maybe later.'

'Okay,' he said simply and went back to tidying.

'Shadow?' she asked tentatively. 'You were so cautious on the walk over here, I wondered if you could see something that I couldn't.'

He shook his head.

'No. I was just keeping a cautious eye on you and making sure nothing untoward happened. There are other things that might try to take advantage of your recent change.'

'Those wolves on bonfire night?'

'Maybe,' he replied solemnly. 'But perhaps other forces.'

Ariana wanted to ask him to explain but his demeanour suddenly changed, a bright smile appearing on his face. 'Tonight I will take you patrolling. You need to take a tour of our territory so that you know where the borders are.'

Ariana nodded in agreement. Her thoughts turned to running through the night as a fox, she was longing to get out and do that. She remembered seeing the animals from her flat window and the terrified howl she had heard. Her grin faltered and she looked down at her hands, remembering the eyes in the alley. A half forgotten memory jerked into her mind, an inky blackness, canines shifting into beasts and fighting in the street. Her hand darted to her mouth as the memory became clear again at last.

'Oh!' she exclaimed and Shadow looked thoughtfully at her. 'I remember now. I saw a fight. I saw you change and fight that blackness. That has been bothering me so much. What was that? Why did I forget?'

'Blackness?' Shadow asked, a frown creasing his brow. 'Oh, I remember. It was about a month ago. There are all sorts of things in this world that you are close to discovering, Ariana, so many things. Not all of them are good. We try to protect people from discovering the truth and that sometimes involves hunting down rogue demons and other creatures and clearing up the mess they make.'

'Demons?' she blurted out. Shock and fear sent a shudder through her entire body.

'Demons,' he repeated calmly. He looked her in the eye and gave a sad smile. 'I'm sorry, it's a lot to take in.'

'It is,' she whispered in reply. Her eyes dropped to the table and her thoughts tumbled around in a chaotic jumble. She thought of his words about clearing up messes and cringed as her thoughts turned to her first shift. The memories were overpowering. She realised that it was possible that someone saw her changing, just as she had seen Shadow and the others. 'What happens, if we change in public? People must see sometimes.'

Shadow regarded her carefully.

'Yes, sometimes they do. They usually forget the details of what they have seen, as you did. Later they rationalise it. They believe they saw a vicious dog or some other reasonable explanation. We don't normally take the Agrius form in front of humans if we can possibly help it.'

Ariana was shocked that they had this power over people's memories. Shadow looked deep into her eyes. 'It's our defence, Ariana, it's for the best. Humans must not know about us, this protects them from realising the truth and protects us from humanity. What do you think would happen if people found out about us?'

'I suppose,' Ariana spoke slowly, gathering her troubled thoughts, 'they would hunt us.'

He was right, of course, and she supposed that in time she would grow used to the idea. She looked to the floor and gripped her own arms across her chest. She felt Shadow's warm hand on her shoulder and looked up into his striking yellow eyes.

'I don't believe anyone saw you change, Ariana. It happened very quickly, it was late at night. Half of your rampage took place in Hepethia, away from human eyes, and we tried to hide you in darkness once we knew that you were changing. That same darkness elemental that you saw last month has been brought back into check and is working with us again. It caused the lights to go out as you ran, hiding you in shadow.'

'My students were leaving their class, there must have been some still getting into their cars or leaving the dojo behind me. There must have been.' Her voice shook.

'When we caught your scent and followed you there was no one else on the street. You had run a fair distance from the dojo in your frenzy. Please try not to worry. If there are any repercussions from your change then we will handle that too,' he paused only for a moment. 'Now, we need to see Flames.'

He stood and walked briskly to the top of the stairs to the basement. 'Flames,' he called out in a clear but calm voice. Ariana moved across the kitchen, her sword bag clutched tightly in her hand. She heard muffled noises below and then footsteps on the stairs. Flames-First-Guardian emerged from the stairwell and behind him came a man a little older than Ariana, in his early twenties. He was well built, tall and with a confident air, almost a swagger. He gave Ariana a quick once over and nodded in greeting.

'Ariana, this is Wind Talker, he joined the Blue Moon a few weeks ago.' Flames spoke authoritatively, but barely looked at her as he passed her and headed towards the shop at the front of the building. Wind Talker paused by Ariana and smiled, which looked a little odd on his severe face and she smiled nervously back.

'Hi, nice to meet you,' she managed to mumble. He barked with laughter and followed Flames. Shadow took her hand gently and gave an apologetic look. He led her after them into the back of the shop. As they reached the doorway she watched open mouthed as Flames and Wind Talker shimmered out of existence right in front of her. 'What the...'

'We're crossing the veil into Hepethia now,' Shadow whispered at her ear. 'I will lead you this time, but I want you to feel everything so that you can try it yourself next time.'

The back area of the shop was empty but for Lily at one

of the windows and beyond the partition a few people shouted profanities at the televisions, but they were out of sight of the doorway. Ariana concentrated and stepped through the doorway with Shadow. She felt something wrench at her navel and the world spun around her. As her foot hit the floor she stumbled awkwardly but Shadow still had hold of her and she corrected herself quickly. She was shaking slightly as she looked around.

They emerged in a space that looked like the betting shop, but there were no people, no partition and everything looked a little different. The room was taller than in the human world, and much darker. The corners seemed to stretch away into blackness and the walls were hung with strips of paper money. The safe, tucked away out of sight in the human world was dominant on this side of the veil, it was tall and well secured with a large and elaborate locking mechanism. On the walls around them were mounted televisions but they were broadcasting only static, commentaries babbled over one another through the fizz in chaotic and eerie voices.

Flames and Wind Talker stood watching her carefully and she felt they were waiting for her to react. She was unnerved but she felt safe with Shadow at her side. Casually, Ariana dropped Shadow's hand and took a step away from him, looking around with wide eyes.

'Okay. I wasn't expecting this. I don't know what I was expecting, but not this.' Her voice echoed slightly and there was a flutter of movement on the other side of the glass shop front. Her eyes darted to the source but she didn't see anything. The others didn't react so she concluded that it was nothing to worry about and she didn't want to appear to be too jumpy.

'Shifters can create safe places in Hepethia with our thoughts and actions,' Shadow explained. 'This is ours. I wanted a field with a protective dome over it, but the others wanted it to be like the betting shop.' He sighed and Ariana stifled a laugh. He smiled and winked at her.

'Flames?' Ariana spoke up tentatively. He looked at her expectantly. 'Is it possible to do something to these as well? So that they change with me?' She unzipped the bag and slipped the dha out of it.

He came over to her for a closer look and a knowing smile crossed his lips.

'Burmese, yes?' he asked, looking carefully at the ornate wooden scabbards.

'Yes.' She was surprised and pleased to find that he recognised them.

'I will make them blend to you, so that they change with you and become invisible until drawn, we can't walk around the streets of Caerton with weapons on display.'

'Of course,' Ariana grinned.

'Do you mind me marking them? I will need to engrave the hilts and scabbards with special runes.'

Ariana clutched them close for a moment, unsure that she wanted them marked. But she knew that she wanted to be able to use them so she nodded in agreement.

'At a later date I can imbue them with special properties, make them more fun to use.' Flames flashed an excited grin, Ariana could tell he enjoyed this.

Flames cleared his throat and began issuing instructions to Wind Talker in setting things up for their ritual. In the centre of the room sat a small fire pit, which had clearly seen a lot of use. It was nothing fancy, just a blackened metal dish the size of a wok, it may have once been an actual wok. In it Wind Talker placed some herbs and what Ariana thought may have been incense. The fire was lit and the air filled with the smells of smoke and the ritual herbs. Ariana watched as Flames began casting a circle. He walked around them chanting words she didn't fully understand.

The money on the walls fluttered gently and the sound of the televisions hushed in response, the air all around them grew still and Ariana realised by its absence that she had felt eyes on her before but now felt sure she was alone with her pack mates. Whoever was watching them had been banished from the space and the circle protected them.

Shadow stood very still next to her and he leaned close to whisper in her ear.

'You should stay in this form now until Flames invites you to change. Your clothes will then change with you. Don't worry, you'll be fine.' He gave her hand a gentle squeeze and she turned her head to smile at him. She did feel nervous, she was going to have to control her shift in front of the others and she didn't know if she could. She tried to follow what they were saying.

'We give thanks to Luna, may her light protect and bless us always.' Flames spoke with a clear and authoritative voice. He produced a long, beautiful knife with a bone handle and swiftly swiped it across his palm. Blood ran down the blade and dripped onto the floor. Ariana looked down and saw dozens of little blood drop stains all over the linoleum, undoubtedly from previous rituals. 'We offer life to Grins-Too-Widely, thanking him for his patronage and many gifts to The Blue Moon.'

Wind Talker took some more incense and lit it, he tossed it into the fire and flames rose up in a sudden burst, sparks showered out onto the floor.

'We offer this incense, made of our shadows and our blood to the fae of secrecy and adaptability.' Wind Talker spoke with confidence, though Ariana sensed a touch of apprehension behind his eyes, she could tell this was the first time he had actively participated in this ritual.

Flames approached her and held out a large ritual goblet carved from wood. He held it out and spoke to her.

'I will offer your blood in sacrifice now, please do not be afraid.' His voice had a soothing lilt to it and for the first time Ariana felt trust for him well up inside her and she felt the bond between them. She held out her arm and looked into his eyes as he pushed the sleeve of her jacket up her arm, then brought the knife down on her forearm in a swift movement. She felt the sting of the cut, but not as keenly as she would have before the change, she looked down in surprise to see her blood seeping out from the deep cut along her skin and she flexed her fingers to keep them from going numb. Quickly Flames took hold of her arm and twisted it gently over the goblet, spilling blood into it. Ariana was fascinated and watched carefully. Flames chanted as he dipped his finger into the blood and drew swirling circles and what looked like runes onto her skin and clothes, moving around her as he did so. Wind Talker was watching carefully, clearly taking mental notes and Ariana gave him an encouraging smile, which he returned and she felt a kinship with him swell within her.

Flames gently positioned her arms out in front of her, then placed her two swords across her palms. He took the blood-stained knife and very carefully began to scratch runes into the wood.

'I invoke the fae of secrecy, hidden things and those of ownership. Make these blades bound to this blood.' When he finished carving, he carefully placed both swords across her back by their straps and Ariana adjusted them so that they hung comfortably on her.

Flames took a step back and stood before her, his arms raised above his head. He nodded once and she understood that he meant for her to shift now. With a steadying breath she willed her body to change and it came surprisingly easily this time as she shifted into her fox form. She looked down her legs and back over her shoulder and along her orange-brown back to see that her clothes and dha had melded into her body. She shifted back, her clothes and dha restored perfectly and she beamed at Flames in thanks.

She felt Shadow lightly touch her arm and she looked at him, he was pointing toward the shop door, following his finger with her eyes Ariana was startled to see a fox slinking silently in through the now open door. His orange fur was in stark contrast the purple-blue of the shop front and it gleamed in the daylight flooding in through the unpainted top half of the front window. His face was contorted into a huge grin. It should have looked like a snarl but didn't, though there was something deeply unsettling about it. But she couldn't find the fox frightening, she could feel his being within her, just like she could feel her pack and she leaned close to Shadow, unable to take her eyes from the fox.

'What is that?' she whispered, though her voice carried on the silent air and the others followed her gaze. The fox sat down on the edge of the ritual circle, his head tilted to one side and looking at Ariana, grinning.

Flames lowered his arms and held one hand out to the fox in welcome.

'This is Grins-Too-Widely, guide and ally to the Blue Moon. He is a very old, wise and powerful shifter who has slipped into Hepethia and lost his humanity. Think of him as an elder, like in tribal societies that venerate the eldest and wisest members.' Flames explained. 'Please greet the newest member of our pack and welcome her as your own.' His voice was full of command but Ariana sensed that he was not in control of this fox, it seemed to be more the other way around. Grins-Too-Widely blinked at her a few times, then nodded and she instantly felt her connection to him deepen. He had accepted her. She didn't fully understand what that meant but she felt the weight of it. She felt Shadow reach out to her with his thoughts,

You'll get used to all the more... unusual things. She giggled and immediately felt all eyes on her. She muttered an apology and nodded respectfully to Grins-Too-Widely. The fox locked eyes with her and spoke; somehow his voice penetrated his grin without his huge teeth parting or his lips moving, that grin was relentless.

'I will take you on the hunt tonight and help lead you to your true name.'

'You will?' Ariana wasn't sure what to make of that. Shadow stirred beside her.

'Grins-Too-Widely rarely makes his presence known during the day, but you will feel him with us tonight when I take you out. He may show you something that will have a lasting impact on you. It's good of him to forewarn you.' Shadow smiled and bowed to the fox. As silently as he had approached, Grins-Too-Widely slipped away.

'The Blue Moon gives thanks to Grins-Too-widely, Luna and all of the fae who bestow their gifts of change, adaptability and secrecy to our packmate.' Flames drew the ritual to a close by walking around the circle with his knife held out towards the floor, blood dripping from it every few steps. He stood next to Ariana and gave her a slightly awkward pat on the shoulder. 'You did well.'

Ariana smiled in gratitude and followed the others back to the doorway and this time, holding no one's hand, she stepped across the veil on her own.

Chapter Eight

The evening meal was a lively affair in the kitchen of the Blue Moon betting shop. Ariana sat sandwiched between Wind Talker and Shadow, Flames sat opposite them with piles of notes that he didn't lift his eyes from and yet still managed to join in with the general banter in the room. Fortune flash fried steaks and tossed them, still so rare they were bloody, onto a large platter in the middle of the table at regular intervals for people to tuck in to, making loud jokes and laughing heartily. Ariana liked Fortune very much, he was friendly and confident, he had warmth and just the right amount of rough edge, she couldn't help but grin in his presence.

Stone entered having shut up shop, with two new faces in tow, a man and a woman who couldn't look more different from one another. The man was lean with a smart haircut and expensive-looking suit. He was handsome and in his early thirties, clean shaven and with a confident grace. The woman had long blonde hair just past her shoulders and mousey facial features, she wore glasses but her eyes pierced right through them. She wore loose clothing and lots of layers, with half a dozen necklaces hanging from her long, slender neck.

Fortune gave the man a warm and masculine hug, patting him hard on the back and on releasing him stood with one arm slung over the man's shoulders. Ariana saw the pride in Fortune's eyes, this must be his new protégée.

'Ariana, I'd like you to meet Fights-Eyes-Open.' The newcomer smiled graciously and Ariana returned the gesture. 'And this is Teri Melrose.' Fortune gestured towards the young woman, who seated herself next to Flames at the table and gave Ariana a friendly smile.

'I wish I'd seen you sooner.' Teri spoke softly and with such poise that Ariana's focus went immediately to her.

'I'm sorry. What do you mean?' she asked, leaning across the table.

'Teri is our resident prophetess. She has visions.' Stone leaned across the table to help herself to some meat and Ariana glanced at her serious face before returning her gaze to Teri.

'Wow. Cool.' Nothing that she was learning really surprised her, but Ariana found that each new layer of this world that she peeled back was infinitely more fascinating.

'Sometimes.' Teri looked down at her hands, her fingers spread open on the table. Ariana noticed ink stains on her fingers from a well-used pen. 'I saw you changing, but only moments before it really happened. Though Fortune and the others sensed your blood strengthening long before. I'm still very new to this life myself, I don't fully understand my talent yet.'

The conversation in the room had picked up around them, but Ariana only wanted to hear Teri talking, she was thirsty for more and found Teri's voice very appealing. It was as though she was born to plant images in other people's minds with her words.

'So are you the most recently changed here? Apart from me?' Ariana asked, leaning right across the table.

'Yes. I haven't found my true name yet, I only changed ten days ago. But Eyes only changed a few nights before me.' She grinned over her shoulder towards the man in the suit, who was deep in conversation with Fortune.

'What is the deal with the names, anyway?' Ariana asked.

'Artemis sends us our true name some time after we change. They are the names that truly reflect our souls, as opposed to the human names we are given at the whim of our parents.' Teri gave Ariana a playful wink.

Beside Ariana, Wind Talker shifted in his seat and cleared his throat. The two women looked at him expectantly.

'I changed two months ago, but I only arrived in Caerton a few weeks ago.' His voice was deep and authoritative. 'I was brought up in a shifter community and was sent here once I changed, a sort of cultural exchange. I don't think anyone saw the Blue Moon growing so rapidly, otherwise I might have ended up in another pack.'

'Can a pack be too large then?' Ariana asked, looking at him quizzically.

'Maybe,' he shrugged. Ariana looked back at Teri, who rolled her eyes and shook her head.

'It is a gift from Luna,' Flames muttered, still poring over his notes. 'We have been sent new blood to strengthen us and renew what was becoming stale.' They all looked at him and Shadow chuckled.

'That's one interpretation,' Shadow said, barely hiding his smile.

'Luna?' Ariana raised an eyebrow and glanced between faces.

'The embodiment of the moon,' Teri explained. 'Artemis is the Greek goddess who gives us our abilities and Luna is literally the moon, according to the Romans anyway. As I understand it, different pantheons are all real.'

Ariana nodded, masking her lack of full understanding.

Shadow didn't give her chance to dwell on it though, he finished his steak and stood up, clearing his throat and gesturing for her to follow him. Ariana stood to follow and Teri looked at her with wide eyes.

'Shadow, do you mind if I come with you?' Teri asked, full of eagerness.

'Of course not, that would be fine.'

Teri jumped up out of her chair, falling into step with Ariana as they followed him. He took them out through a door at the back of the kitchen and out into the back yard. There was a fire escape snaking up the back of the building. Its black railings and ladders were difficult to see against the pollution-blackened brickwork of the building, and it was almost dark. Ariana watched carefully as Shadow leapt up onto the first tier of the fire escape, then silently and smoothly climbed and twisted up the metal frame, ignoring the ladders, and disappeared onto the roof.

She looked at Teri, her mouth open in awe and Teri gave her a flash of a grin before following him, almost as quickly and quietly.

Muttering to herself in disbelief and doubt at her own ability to be so graceful and stealthy, Ariana stepped up and grabbed hold of the first railing. A little awkwardly she climbed up the ladders of the fire escape. At the top she clambered up onto the tiled roof. Shadow was looking out across St. Mark's and Teri had her eyes firmly on the stars above, though they were barely visible through the haze from the orange street lighting.

'We can and do patrol our territory at ground level, but the rooftops afford us a good view of everything,' Shadow whispered, but Ariana easily heard every word. She looked out across the area. It wasn't the pretty view she had seen from the cliff top with Rhys; stretching out were rows and rows of brick terraces. In the distant north, just inside Redfield, the telecoms tower jutted up toward the sky, a red light blinked at its peak. Over to the north-west the terraces gave way to the factories of Northgate, and beyond them the river snaked through the city. In the dusk light all Ariana could really make out of the factories were the chimneys and the continuous smoke that issued from them.

That part of the city never shut down. In the north-east Ariana knew her dojo was hidden among the rows of familiar streets and beyond it was Fenwick.

'Almost everything that you can see is ours,' Shadow spoke softly. 'From the river, across Northgate and Redfield, here in St. Mark's, of course and over to Crossway in the east.' He swept his arm across the landscape, pointing to each area. 'It is a big territory, we will need all of you to take your turn in helping to patrol its borders and keep a careful eye out for unwanted visitors from across the veil. Tonight we will run the border. Teri, you've done this with Stone. Ariana, I'd like you to use your sense of smell to familiarise yourself with the scents around you. You should be able to smell each of us three, Fortune patrolled recently and his scent may linger, but no other shifters should be present.'

Ariana felt the adrenaline beginning to race through her system and the moment Shadow set off she was right behind him. She felt Teri half a step behind and with a huge grin she ran nimbly across the rooftops.

At the end of the terrace Shadow led them quickly down onto the street using a garage and a wall to find the ground safely. It was a dark side street and he shifted into his fox form, giving the two women a short bark. They both glanced at each other and with excited looks changed themselves.

Teri shifted into a beautiful black cat. Ariana took the shape of a fox, like Shadow. She felt free in this form, her senses were at their peak and the night wrapped around her. In an instant Shadow was gone and the two females set off after him, jogging briskly along the pavement, keeping close to the shadows and ducking into alleys away from the glaring headlights of passing cars. They would make for an odd grouping, two foxes and a cat.

After a block or two Ariana felt the presence of Grins-Too-Widely, though she couldn't see him, she knew he was there, running with them. Night had fallen completely now but the city streets still buzzed with activity, so they had to be careful. Ariana could feel the influence of Grins-Too-Widely on their journey, guiding them safely down the quietest streets and steering them into the deepest shadows. She kept her senses sharp, sniffing the air for traces of anything out of place.

They ran quickly through Northgate, where the factories tirelessly worked and nothing of interest caught their attention. They circled east into Redfield, another industrial and commercial area. They ran north of the looming telecoms tower and up to the northern edge of Redfield Park, where Redfield met Runmead, a very rough area of Caerton.

Ariana immediately smelled something odd, she knew it was a shifter but she didn't recognise the scent and she slowed down to track it. Shadow hung back and let her lead them. She remembered that they were at a boundary and her senses reinforced it very vividly. The scents changed abruptly, as though someone had deliberately marked this area. She knew to hang back and not cross over into Runmead. She looked into Shadow's eyes and picked up his loose and primal thoughts. This was the edge of their territory and beyond lay that claimed by a rival pack. She saw alarming flashes of some very violent clashes, but Shadow's deep eyes calmed her.

Shadow took the lead again and set off south, back towards St. Mark's and Crossway, the nicer area that bordered Fenwick. Ariana could sense his caution as they entered Crossway. The streets were wider here, with avenues of trees standing tall in front of larger residential properties. There were no convenient alleyways for them to hide in here.

Ariana caught a familiar scent, but very faint and not familiar enough to place, and a few blocks on it was gone. She pushed the thought into Shadow's mind and at once he replied with a mental image of their packmate, Fights-Eyes-Open. He lived in this neighbourhood with his family.

They went on but Ariana began to feel uneasy. Teri was jogging along at the rear, but Ariana was totally focused on identifying the unsettling tugging sensation. Something felt very wrong and she slowed down, letting Teri overtake. She let out a small whimper and Shadow stopped, trotted back to her and caught her eyes with his. As she tried to form her thoughts for him a powerful and foreign scent assaulted her senses. Shadow caught it too and his head whipped around to identify the source. Both foxes became hyper-alert, something wasn't right. Where was Teri? Ariana looked for her pack mate and caught sight of her a little way ahead, she immediately set off after her, Shadow racing along at her side, but they were too far behind to prevent it. Ariana saw the intruding wolf dart out from the shadows and bite into Teri's flank.

As fast as lightning it was gone again and Teri was left meowing in pain in the street, as she writhed her form shifted and she lay human and clutching her bleeding thigh. Shadow was in his human form by the time he reached Teri and he stooped to examine her as Ariana caught up.

'She's fine, she will heal quickly but we should help her home.' He spoke calmly but his eyes didn't rest for a second, he was scanning the area. Ariana shuddered and her heart pounded an erratic rhythm. She sniffed the air, she could make out the intruder's scent clearly but could tell it was beginning to fade. She sensed that they were very close to the edge of the pack's territory but couldn't smell anything beyond their border, unlike in Redfield where the other pack's scent was all over the place, clearly marking the boundary.

She took a few steps after Teri's attacker, who had retraced their own steps through a large garden, returning from the exact direction they had come. They had been tracking Ariana, Teri and Shadow, she was sure of it, they had been followed at a distance. This attack was probably pre-meditated, but she had no idea why. She looked back at Shadow, who was lifting Teri up into his arms and standing to leave. Ariana felt an overpowering instinct to track the attacker, she wanted to follow the trail and see where it led and she tried to push these thoughts to the front of her mind so that whatever small ability Shadow had in his human form to read her thoughts he would see. He looked right at her and sighed.

'No, it's too dangerous for you to go alone. Come with me back to the shop.'

Ariana growled in frustration. She knew that the trail would go cold; if someone was going to follow it, it had to be now.

'I know who did this and where they are, roughly. Please just come with me and help make sure she's all right.'

Ariana regarded him carefully, then bowed her head and set off with him.

'Don't worry,' Teri moaned. 'I'm all right.'

Ariana whimpered in sympathy, feeling the pain coursing through her friend's body.

Shadow led them directly across St. Mark's, close to Ariana's dojo and through the streets of houses. All the way back to the shop Ariana was on edge, she could tell

Shadow was too. He was difficult to read in his human form, but one word came through loud and clear: *Witches*.

Chapter Nine

When they arrived back at the betting shop Fortune and Fights-Eyes-Open were waiting for them, their faces full of concern. They had felt Teri's attack through the bond they shared and were ready for them. Eyes held the back door open as Shadow carried Teri through, and Ariana quickly shifted as she entered the kitchen.

'What happened?' Fortune asked as Shadow sat Teri down at the table.

'We were tracked as we entered Crossway,' Shadow said, as he cleaned Teri's wounded leg with a damp cloth. 'I'm sure it was just one of them, but she crossed our border and took Teri by surprise. Ariana got a better sense then me.' He glanced at her and Ariana's cheeks burned as Fortune's eyes fell upon her.

'Yes, it was just one shifter, a wolf. It happened so quickly though and I didn't smell them until it was too late.' She felt terrible, like she should have sensed it sooner or kept Teri closer. Fortune put his arm around her and gave her a warm hug.

'Don't worry. She's fine and there was really nothing you could have done.'

'I could have tracked it. I had the trail.' Her voice tailed off, she didn't want to sound as though she were ungrateful to Shadow or angry at him for preventing her from following the trail. She understood his concerns and in her right mind she knew how stupid it would have been to follow someone onto their territory alone, when she was so freshly changed and had so much to learn.

'There was no need to track her, Ariana,' Shadow spoke softly, nearly finished with Teri's wound.

'How do you know it was female?' she asked, suddenly curious.

'The smell for one thing, we can distinguish male from female with a little practice. But we know who borders our territory there and they are all female,' Fortune said, releasing Ariana and slumping down into a chair. He looked frustrated but his voice was level.

'Witches?' Ariana asked, recalling Shadow's thought. Fortune looked at her sharply.

'Yes,' he spat. 'They are the enemy. They're not like us, they're dangerous and evil.' His voice was so full of hatred that it took Ariana by surprise. There was a finality to his words and she didn't dare push the issue.

'Fortune,' Shadow's voice was soft but insistent. 'You know what this means. That Witch tasted Teri's blood, she can track her easily now.'

'I know.' Fortune hung his head. Teri sat up straight and scanned the room, her eyes full of worry.

'Am I endangering the pack by being here?' Ariana smiled sadly, it was so sweet of Teri to think of the pack's safety before her own. Ariana was just worried for her new friend. Fortune turned to her and placed a hand gently on her shoulder.

'No, not at all. You'll be healed within an hour and the pack has dealt with this kind of intrusion before.'

Ariana watched Shadow's face carefully, he was almost as stoic as ever, but there was a flicker of something there in his expression for an instant, and she knew she was the only one to notice it.

'I'll take Eyes over to Crossway now and we'll guard the border tonight. Make sure everyone else gets some rest.' Fortune said, his hand on Shadow's shoulder.

Fortune and Eyes set off through the back door. Shadow helped Teri up and the three of them trudged up the narrow staircase. They got Teri settled in a bed in one of the small rooms, then left her to rest.

Shadow headed to one of the other rooms. Ariana followed him closely, she had no intention of letting this lie, no matter what Fortune said. She slipped into the room behind Shadow and closed the door. He looked around, clearly not surprised to see that she had followed him.

'So,' he said quietly. 'You want to know what that was all about.' It wasn't a question. Ariana didn't respond, she just sat in a chair and waited for him to continue. 'I bit you before you changed, deliberately. We do that. It is easier for us to track someone whose blood we have tasted as it grants us a sort of empathy. I have no doubt that is exactly what happened tonight. A Witch bit Teri in order to be able to track her, presumably to track her here, to find out where our headquarters is. Yes, her being here does put the pack in danger but we wouldn't have it any other way. We won't hide her somewhere, she would be vulnerable on her own or with minimal protection. Some shifters learn the hard way that it is far more dangerous to be on ones own. The pack is what makes us strong, so we stick together, no matter what.'

'There's conflict with the pack to our northern border too. But it isn't like this thing with the Witches,' Ariana whispered, almost to herself.

'The Wrecking Crew are rivals, we compete for territory and have an uneasy truce at the moment. But we're all basically on the same side. The Witches are, well, there is a very long war waged between us, we're enemies. There are no shades of grey. We're just enemies, always have been and always will be.' He shrugged and sat down on the bed in the corner of the small room. 'There are some shifters who have different ideas about the way we should live and the Witches are among them. They have close ties to the feral shifters outside the city, the rural ones who don't have a clue about city life or what it takes to keep control. The Phoenix Guard and The Rutherford Estate are two elite packs who live just outside the city. They would love to be in a position to take Caerton and rule it. The Alpha of the Rutherford Estate is believed to be the heir to the throne of the city.'

Ariana nodded solemnly.

'You mentioned a royal bloodline to me earlier.'

'The Witches have likely noticed our pack double in size recently and assume that we are preparing for an offensive attack on them. Which we are not,' he added quickly. 'That's not it at all, we can't help it when three new shifters change on our territory. Perhaps Wind Talker could have found another pack, but he was here first and is one of us now. But I can see that the Witches might be paranoid.' He sighed and rubbed his face. 'This attack by the Witches is probably them reacting to our pack growing, but it could be part of something bigger.'

Ariana felt deeply troubled to learn of this war, she hadn't asked for this and to be dragged into it was a lot to take in. She wondered how likely it was that a battle might be approaching rapidly and began to feel scared that she was so unprepared.

'We have to get on with training.' She broke the silence, a slight tremble to her voice. 'Shadow, I have to be ready.'

He smiled, but it was tinged with sadness.

'Oh Ariana, we are never ready. This life brings us a new challenge every day and we are never ready for any of it. But,' he stood up suddenly, 'we can be as prepared as possible with what time and resources we have.' He strode to the door and held it open for her. Eagerly she dashed out into the hall, they moved quickly down to the basement to continue with her physical training.

'You've never seen me use these, have you?' Ariana asked him, removing her dha from her back. 'You've followed me to and from the dojo, but never seen me teaching. Right?'

Shadow took a seat and nodded.

'You want to show me what you can do, which I understand. But you realise that I am not skilled with blades, I can't offer much expert opinion or tips for improvement.'

'I know, but I'm already one of the best in the country. I'm not looking for a teacher.' Ariana puffed up her chest and fixed Shadow with a firm stare. He let a small smirk form on his lips and cocked his head to one side.

'Okay then.' He stood up and approached her slowly.

Ariana kept her dha sheathed, but readied herself for an attack. The pair of them circled each other slowly. She wasn't accustomed to using her swords against an unarmed opponent and felt a little lost, she realised just how artificial the world of competition was, with its rules and traditions. It all meant nothing in a real fight.

Ariana was ready when Shadow made his move and she easily blocked his arm with the back of one of her blades, following it with a body strike with the other. Shadow blocked her and twisted free of the wood-sheathed weapons. Ariana moved gracefully, in her element. Each strike and parry was carefully placed and she landed a few hard hits.

Shadow was very quick, however. He slipped under her thrust and as he moved under her she drove the butt of her sword down on his shoulder. He flinched but his arms found their way around her torso and he grappled her to the ground.

He let her up immediately and she didn't waste a second, springing an aggressive attack on him as he shook out his arms. One of her dha struck his back and she heard the distinct sound of a rib cracking. She stopped at once as he winced, and dashed to his side.

'Oh my gosh, I am so sorry,' she cried, trying to look for an impact mark, wanting to see if the rib was properly broken. But Shadow grabbed her arm and twisted it behind her back, forcing her sword to go clattering to the floor.

Ariana felt a spasm shoot through her from her arm and swiftly swung the other sword back over her shoulder and struck Shadow hard on the top of his head. He cried out and reeled backwards, breaking his grapple. She spun to face him as he stumbled backwards clutching his head. She took a swift step towards him and pressed her dha threateningly to his throat, a roar on the tip of her tongue but just held in check.

'I yield,' he groaned. Ariana stepped back and let her arm drop to her side. She was panting, yet not from physical exertion, her stamina had barely been tested, but the adrenaline was real enough and she had felt the beast flare in anger for a moment. She struggled to subdue it.

'I had to get creative there. My old teacher and peers would be appalled.' She reached out a hand to help Shadow up, which he slowly took, still rubbing his head.

'Thank you,' he said, graciously. 'Now put them aside and show me what you can do without them.'

She did as she was told and laid her precious dha down on the bench before returning to face Shadow.

He was tough on her, he didn't hold back and at the end of the session she had real injuries, though they healed almost instantly. She barely landed a scratch on him, he was so fast and strong that she was truly outclassed for the first time in a very long time. It might have frustrated her in her former life, but she accepted that this was all new to her and it motivated her to practice and improve.

After several hours of hard training, Shadow showed her back to the room she had first woken up in and she nursed what felt like a cracked tibia, just below her left knee. The sky outside was tinged with pink, dawn was approaching.

'You can sleep here if you like, but there's a lounge upstairs in the attic and mostly we all sleep up there together.' Shadow moved towards the door. Ariana rubbed her eyes, her shin was already completely healed and she almost laughed with satisfaction. She knew that Teri must be fine too and wondered where she would be sleeping.

'I'll meet you upstairs in a minute. I just need a little processing time.'

Shadow nodded courteously and left her alone. Ariana found her bag under the bed and searched for her phone. She had two text messages from Rhys and she felt a stab of guilt for forgetting about him so completely.

```
15/11. 11.17pm: Hi. I hope you're OK.
16/11. 4.54 pm: Please can you let me
know you're OK?
```

Ariana bit her lower lip and thought hard about how to respond. She hadn't contacted him in nearly two days and the last he knew, she was in bed with a horrific flu. Had it really only been two nights since she changed? So much had happened, so much had changed that she couldn't tell him. Eventually she settled on a reply.

```
Sorry, just got your messages. Phone
died. I'm fine thanks. You?
```

It was 7am, he should be up and getting ready for work so she waited for a reply, though her eyes were growing heavy. Worry gnawed at her over whether she would be able to remain as close to Rhys, or any of her friends, as she had been. A few minutes later her phone buzzed in her hand.

```
I'm OK thanks. Let me know if you want to
meet up soon.
```

She smiled wearily, she didn't feel she could reply to that right now. Though she would need to see him soon to see if he could sense the change in her or not. It seemed obvious to her already that shifters wouldn't find it easy to have friends who were human, they were too different, and there was an oddness to everyone she had met so far. She didn't think they would blend in too well among normal people.

She turned off her phone, plugged it in to charge and left the room in search of the others. A narrow staircase at the end of the hall led up into a wide open space. It had a thick carpet and two skylights at opposite ends of the room, there was a large sofa and a small space heater plugged into the wall. In front of the heater were several thick rugs and piles of cushions. Curled up on them was the oddest assembly of animals she had ever seen. She identified Shadow immediately, he was the only fox and his yellow eyes were fixed on her. The others she could vaguely identify by sense, Fortune was there, the only wolf among them, Wind Talker had the form of a badger, which seemed oddly fitting, and Stone perched on the back of the sofa, a beautiful tawny owl. Flames must be taking a shift on watch, Teri seemed to have stayed in bed and Eyes was missing.

She shifted into her fox form, and went and laid down next to Shadow. He put his muzzle down on his paws and gave her a warm rumble of a noise from his chest, almost a cat's purr. She smiled inside and rested her head on the soft rug, drifting easily into an exhausted sleep.

Chapter Ten

17th November

Ariana had woken too soon, she hadn't managed to fully catch up on her sleep. But the pack was moving around her and she couldn't sleep through it. She followed them to the kitchen, where another meal was served and Ariana tucked in heartily. It was already lunchtime and the betting shop hummed with activity. Lily was holding down the fort and Ariana took her a chicken sandwich.

'Thanks,' Lily said, beaming at her. 'How are you getting on?'

Ariana glanced through the window, all of the customers were noisily riveted to the action on the screens and were paying the two young women no attention.

'Okay, thanks. Do you know what happened last night?'

'Yes, my sister told me this morning. Is Teri all right?'

'She seems okay. I haven't spoken to her properly yet today.' Ariana glanced back towards the kitchen.

'Go on, you'll be missed soon. Fortune will want to dote on you for a while yet before he moves on to the next shiny thing.' Lily winked and turned her attention back to a trashy magazine on the counter in front of her.

Ariana felt a mixture of amusement and caution as she made her way back down the hall. Lily was bold and friendly, undoubtedly very capable with the patrons, despite her youth. She was painfully honest too. Ariana knew that Lily had not meant anything negative in what she said about Fortune, but the idea was planted in Ariana's mind that Fortune was fickle in his attention and she realised that each new recruit had had their moment to bask in his fatherly warmth, but it soon passed. Perhaps not so for Eyes, there seemed to be a deeper connection there.

'Flames, I need you here, out front as much as possible. Teri, you will help him. Stone, you and I will take Eyes and Wind Talker out to secure the border.' Fortune barked his orders and everyone gave curt nods of acknowledgement.

'Can I come?' Ariana spoke up. Shadow smiled slightly as he sipped his coffee.

'No. You must continue working with Shadow. I need you up to speed as soon as possible,' Fortune snapped, his genial tone missing. 'Another time,' he said a little more softly with a sympathetic look her way.

Ariana tried to shrug off the disappointment as the pack went its separate ways. She and Teri just managed to catch each other's eye briefly and exchange the mental promise to catch up properly later. She followed Shadow down to the basement.

'Sit down.' Shadow pointed to a bench along one wall as Ariana reached the bottom of the stairs. She went immediately to it and sat down, looking at him expectantly. She felt like a schoolgirl again. 'I am going to teach you how to read your opponent and glean something honest about them.'

Ariana raised a sceptical eyebrow.

'Really? That's such a variable thing though, isn't it? Every individual has different tells.'

'I'm not talking about tells. I'm talking about reaching into their soul with your mind and sensing their deepest fear, or greatest love, their current mood, sometimes even a very specific thought.'

Shadow was fetching items from the cabinet. Ariana watched him carefully. She wasn't sure what to make of his words. She had never believed in souls or mind reading, but a few days ago she hadn't believed in shape shifters either. She had already taken part in a ritual that resulted in her clothes moulding to her body as it shifted between human, fox and monster. She definitely had some sort of telepathy with her pack. Was this really so far fetched?

Shadow moved into the middle of the room and sat down on the floor. He laid out a small dish and a selection of herbs, which he set light to with a match. Thick smoke immediately spiralled up from the dish and the air filled with a strong smell. Ariana wrinkled her nose against the unusual fragrance.

'The incense will help to focus your mind. First you must learn to look inside yourself and draw the power from within. Look into the smoke.' His voice was faintly hypnotic and Ariana felt compelled to do as he said. Her eyes drifted out of focus as she stared at the smoke and the vague thought occurred to her that the incense was fogging up her mind rather than making anything more clear, before everything became a blur.

She blinked a few times and the room came back into focus. Shadow was still sitting in front of her, on the other side of the smoking incense. She felt calm, but her thoughts seemed sharper. Her mind latched onto each fleeting thought and seemed to take an instant to absorb every nuance.

'This feels strange.' Even as she said it the words punctured her mind, sharp and deliberate, each leaving its mark within her.

'Everything is clear now, isn't it? You know your own thoughts with a clarity you have never felt before.'

'Yes.' She wasn't really seeing the room, she was seeing her own thoughts. She pictured herself, as she was days ago, normal, and as she was now. She saw herself as the ginger fox, a beautiful lion and a soaring eagle, then as the monster; tall, powerful, dangerous. 'I know myself.'

She saw herself at the Caerton Martial Arts tournament in the summer, winning another trophy, her face smug, she saw herself with Rhys. She was boasting about her victories. There was something in his face that she hadn't seen at the time, just a hint of reservation towards her as she casually glanced at the trophy in her hand.

Her thoughts returned to the present and she focused on Shadow, sitting before her, watching her carefully.

'You saw something about yourself that you didn't like.' It wasn't a question.

'I can be, well, kind of smug and annoying.' She grimaced.

'I have observed this too.' There was a trace of a smile on his face and Ariana had to laugh.

'Okay, so what now? I have seen my own soul, but I can't go into a trance like that in the middle of a fight.'

'You won't need to do that again. You have tapped into the ability within yourself and will be able to recall it at will now.' He pressed his fist into the smoking dish and snuffed out the burning embers of the herbs without flinching. He stood and tidied up briskly. 'On your feet,' he barked as he put away the ritual tools and Ariana did as she was told. Her head felt clear, the bizarre sharpness had left her and her normal senses returned, still sharper than they had been before she changed, but manageable.

She moved into the middle of the room, still thinking about what she had seen, yet she saw the attack before Shadow struck and she blocked his fist easily. He spun around her and ducked below her arm as she tried to land a blow. They danced their dance, neither of them taking a hit. Ariana evaded him easily, jumping over a sweeping leg, rolling across his back and ducking under an attempted strike. But he evaded her just as smoothly and she began to feel frustrated. As she twisted under him and blocked a strike, she allowed her body to change, she needed an advantage and so she took the biggest one she could muster. Thick hair sprouted instantly all over her body, she shifted form and became enlarged and empowered as the monster inside took shape on the surface.

Ariana leaped up and out of their tight dance, changing the rules in an instant and went for his shoulder with her massive jaws. As her teeth sank in, he shifted to match her and her mouth met with fur and sinewy tissue. Shadow snarled and recoiled away from her bite, then leaped in low for his own attack. Their dance resumed, but this time it was vicious and feral and both of them tore flesh with claws and teeth. Shadow had the advantage as the larger and far more experienced beast, and he sank his teeth hard into her shoulder and pinned her firmly to the ground. As one, they shifted back into their human forms, Ariana was panting hard and her body shook with pain. Shadow drew a deep, steadying breath as he continued to hold her firmly to the floor, and Ariana watched in amazement as the open wounds on his shoulder and chest healed before her very eyes.

Her hand shot out to touch his near-black skin where seconds before had been a gaping wound from her teeth.

'So fast,' she murmured and he glanced at the spot where her fingers rested. He cleared his throat and jumped up, releasing her.

'Yes. You too.' He gestured toward her and as she sat up she looked herself over, her flesh and skin were sealing themselves up. The blood stained her skin and a little had got onto her clothes where she had continued to bleed for a moment after she shifted back into her human form and exposed her clothes to the blood. 'I wasn't expecting you to shift. Did you forget the lesson?'

Ariana stood up and met his eyes.

'I must have.'

'Well, remember it later. You may need it. Perhaps it was too much of me to expect you to use it in combat right away.' Shadow turned away and reached for a large bottle of water in the cabinet.

Ariana watched his back and focused her thoughts, she reached into him, not just his mind, but into the very essence of her mentor. She saw him watching her, she felt his thoughts and feelings as he had fought her and knew that he had been working very hard to keep up with her. Like a knife, the truth penetrated her mind: that he hated how hard it had been to beat her. He should surpass her easily at this stage and his jealousy was almost tangible.

'Huh,' the sound escaped her lips before she could stop it and Shadow's attention turned back to her as he held out a bottle of water.

'What?'

'I had better not let that go to my big head.' She smirked and took the water from him, turning and leaving him to ponder her words.

She returned to the kitchen, where Teri sat with a pile of books and notes, reading and scribbling while idly playing with one of her necklaces with her free hand. Ariana sat down opposite her new friend. She noticed the necklace Teri was toying with was a silver-coloured Celtic knot with a gibbous moon at the centre. Ariana smiled and glanced over the books on the table, all science texts and totally lost on her.

'That's pretty,' she said, pointing at the necklace.

'Thanks,' Teri smiled at her and dropped the charm. 'Fortune gave it to me. It's not real silver, obviously.'

'It's not obvious to me,' Ariana said, stifling the sting of her own ignorance.

'Silver hurts us, just like in the myths about werewolves. It burns the skin. I think this is nickel.'

Shadow placed a careful hand on Ariana's shoulder and gave it a light squeeze. She startled, having not heard him follow her.

'I will see you later.' He was gone through the back door before Ariana could react to his warning tone. She shrugged it off and returned her attention to Teri.

'What's all this?' Ariana asked, gesturing the books and papers.

'Before I changed I was in the middle of a PhD.' Teri explained. 'I want to finish it.'

'I can understand that,' Ariana replied. She too felt that she had unfinished business with her old life. With a sudden stab of guilt she decided that the following morning she must call Ron at work and excuse herself, take some annual leave to come to terms with all of this, it was too late in the evening to call him now.

'Seeing as Fortune won't let me leave the betting shop right now, I am trying to get something productive done. I was supposed to meet with some other new friends tonight, but he won't let me go. It's so stupid, it's in the city centre. The Witches are hardly going to get right through the city to get to me.'

'Why do they want you, anyway?' Ariana was suddenly struck with the question and as she asked it, a dozen more flooded into her thoughts.

'I don't think it's me in particular. Is it? Fortune thinks they just want to be able to track the pack to here, to find out where we live.' Teri looked at Ariana with confusion in her eyes.

'Then why did you say that? About them tracking you into the city centre?'

'I don't know.' Teri's brow furrowed. 'It just popped out. I guess on some level I am afraid that they might be after me. I grew up in Fenwick. Even though I've lived here for over a year maybe they still see me as theirs.'

'I think it is really important to listen to our gut instincts about this stuff. Especially now. I mean, that's what this is all about isn't it? Our gut, animal instincts. We are closer to beasts than humans, after all.' As Ariana spoke she felt the truth of her words acutely, realising it consciously for the first time. Teri and Ariana looked at each other in silence for a long minute.

As night fell, the pack reassembled and Fortune gave out assignments for the night over a dinner of yet more meat, which Ariana felt obliged to eat with some salad, for the sake of variety. She felt thankful that she had never been inclined towards vegetarianism.

Flames and Wind Talker were planning to continue Wind Talker's training in rituals, while the rest of the pack were to patrol the border in pairs.

'I'll take Eyes East, to the Fenwick border. We are the most physically capable, if we encounter the Witches.' Fortune gave Eyes a pat on the back and Ariana cocked a sceptical eyebrow at the be-suited Eyes. Sure, he looked lean, but she had yet to see him fight and couldn't remotely imagine this straight guy being up to much in a serious fight. 'Stone, you take Teri north.'

Teri sat up straight in her chair, her eyes bulging.

'I can leave the shop? Really? Can't I go to...'

'No, I need you on pack duty.' Fortune pressed firmly. Teri's face sank a little, but Ariana gave her a reassuring smile. At least she was getting out to patrol and be of use to the pack. She knew Teri would be pleased about that at least.

'We'll take south then,' offered Shadow's Step. Fortune nodded in agreement.

'What about west?' Ariana asked.

'Our territory borders the river, we have no pressing concerns on that side, but we will check it tomorrow. I need Flames and Wind Talker here tonight.' Fortune finished as the pack began to move out.

Shadow took Ariana south from the betting shop, they walked briskly as their human selves and Shadow was on edge, his gaze darting around, his fists clenched at his sides. They approached a small independent petrol station on the main road south into the city centre. Shadow led her across the forecourt and into the little shop. A buzzer sounded their arrival and a spotty young man at the counter behind the glass looked up from his magazine expectantly. He took one look at Shadow and gave a wary nod of recognition. Shadow swept through the shop with an air of familiarity, scooping up a packet of nuts and bottle of water before stopping at the counter. The young man behind it gave them half a smile, but he looked as though he were fighting the urge to back away from them. Ariana frowned slightly, bemused by this reaction to them and she wondered if this was going to be typical.

'Thank you. Are you working until midnight?' Shadow asked, his voice sounded odd and Ariana stifled a laugh when she realised that he was trying to be friendly.

Ariana backed off and wandered around the shop for a minute while Shadow engaged the poor boy in conversation. She felt a prickle over her senses and looked out onto the forecourt. She could feel power reaching out to her. She stood staring out of the window, breathing deeply and feeling everything. Her senses were deeply diminished in this form and it frustrated her slightly. She wanted to bask in the sensation but it was like feeling sunlight through a tinted window. With a sigh she went back to Shadow just as he was turning to leave. Together they left the shop and Shadow spoke softly as they crossed the forecourt, between the pumps.

'Can you feel it?'

'Yes. What is it?' she whispered back. Shadow glanced at her and then disappeared, it was as if he had stepped around a corner. With a cautious glance around at the deserted street and petrol station she followed him across the veil. To the boy in the shop, it would look like they had stepped behind one of the tall pumps.

When she steadied her feet and looked around she gasped. The pump next to her was a twisted pillar of metal with cables flowing from it like tentacles and petrol pooled around the base. The smell was overpowering. Ariana looked around at the rest of the station. Right in front of her in the centre of the forecourt was a spiralling column of fire. Ariana screamed and leaped backwards, bumping into the pump behind her. The column of fire seemed to move towards her and she scrambled around the pump. Shadow stepped between her and the fire and Ariana watched open mouthed as the fire diminished and in its place was a roughly human sized fiery shape.

Shadow took her by the elbow and helped her to her feet, his other hand held up towards the fire creature, commanding it to keep back. Ariana stood and stared open mouthed at the flaming thing as it twisted and flickered before her.

'How goes the night?' Shadow asked loudly. The flames flared and died again and a soft whooshing sound escaped it.

'Quiet,' it seemed to say.

'Good,' Shadow replied as he politely bowed his head. 'Ariana, this is a fae, a fire elemental, to be precise. It guards this property for us,' Shadow said authoritatively.

'But it's fire!' Ariana exclaimed. 'Isn't that really dangerous?' A fire elemental at a petrol station seemed like utter stupidity to her. Shadow chuckled.

'Yes. Yes it is, but this being feeds off the potential for fire, not the flames themselves. It's more of a danger sprite really. We allow it to feed on that danger in exchange for keeping an eye on this part of our territory for us.' As Shadow spoke, the fae lost interest in them and drifted away, sinking into the ground nearby, leaving a small puff of smoke. Ariana raised a sceptical eyebrow.

'Okay,' she whispered. 'I thought we were patrolling the border?'

'We are,' he replied. 'We need to do regular sweeps on both sides of the veil. This side of our territory doesn't share a border with any other shifters. From here to the other side of the city centre is unclaimed. We have little to guard against in the human world. But Hepethia needs our attention.'

'Couldn't the Witches circle south then, and come in over our southern border with no interference?'

Shadow chuckled, an odd sound from him, and he shook his head.

'No, they would have to get through the Glass Wolves. They hold Burnside.'

Ariana took a deep breath as her thoughts leaped back to her old life. Burnside was the financial district of Caerton, but it was also where the main bus station was and she had had cause to pass through the area more times than she could count. It was so strange now to think of all of the times she might have passed shape shifters in the street. The Blue Moon had sensed the change coming in her, they had smelled her shifter blood in passing, as would almost any other shifter she had encountered. How many times over the last few months had a shifter caught her scent and tracked her back to St. Mark's? Would they have been relieved that she was not their problem? Or disappointed that she would be embraced by a rival pack? Knowing now that the city was full of these hidden creatures caused her to re-frame everything she thought she knew.

Shadow gave her a considered look, but asked no questions, nor gave any gesture, he simply waited for her moment of realisation to pass. There would be weeks ahead of her, if not months or years, when these moments would capture her briefly. He knew it too and wasn't going to baby her, he would simply let her deal with the memories in her own way.

After a minute, Shadow led Ariana off the petrol station forecourt and onto the street. The buildings around them were darker, taller and more oppressive than in the human world. They were twisted and the corners seemed to stretch into deep recesses with shadows as black as pitch. Ariana felt a shudder run through her and she looked about cautiously. She felt the eyes of unfamiliar beings all around them, darkness and fear demons peered at them from their shadows, urban constructs of brick and glass twitched in the windows of the buildings.

Shadow walked cautiously ahead of her. He moved down the middle of the street, keeping to the pools of light cast by the orange street lamps, and seemed to cast his gaze everywhere at once. Ariana kept close behind him and her eyes darted in the direction of every little noise.

'Shadow?' she whispered. 'If Hepethia is our world, why is it full of these things? I can feel them everywhere.'

'The fae are as much a part of our world as the trees are a part of the human world. Try to think of it like that, they are part of the wildlife. Usually harmless to us, sometimes totally unaware of us. Every once in a while something sentient manifests and can cause us a problem, or a demon will find its way here from one of the demon realms, but we are perfectly able to handle it.'

'Have you told Fortune about my strange ability yet?' she asked, keeping her voice very low.

'No, I haven't. I honestly don't know what to make of it and I would rather take him something concrete. This attack on Teri has taken over the attention of all of us. I apologise for that. You need our attention, our time and our experience and that has been taken from you.' He gave her such an apologetic look that Ariana was almost moved to tears.

'It's absolutely fine. It's no one's fault. We just have to get through this and then there will be time to consider my stuff.' Ariana waved a dismissive hand in front of her face.

She meant what she said and was surprised at her own humility. There was the strangest look on Shadow's face, though, just for a moment and she wanted to ask him what he was thinking when just ahead of them a silent figure slipped out of the shadows into the street. Grins-Too-Widely sat down and waited for them to reach him. Ariana felt a little calm settle over her at the presence of the strange ally. The fox cocked his head to one side, regarding her in that same, careful way. Without a sound, Grins-Too-Widely stood up and trotted away down the middle of the street. Shadow shifted into his fox form and broke into a jog and Ariana followed suit to keep up.

The three of them ran swiftly and silently through the twisted streets of Hepethia. The buildings resembled the red brick terraces of St. Mark's, but they were a twisted maze that Ariana couldn't dream of traversing alone.

Her sense of smell was of little help to her here, she

sniffed the ground but it was almost devoid of any scent she could identify. Not that it didn't smell of anything, just nothing she was familiar with. There were no people, no animals, no shifters, no rot, just the strange mixture of nameless scents that had to be unknown fae.

They jogged down the middle of the street, under the orange glow of the street lights, which on this side of the veil gave the streets an even more eerie quality. The orange was bright and the shadows much darker, contrasts seemed exaggerated here, angles more severe and as Ariana turned her eyes to the sky she was shocked to see thick, purple storm clouds rolling over one another in no discernible direction. They weren't driven by wind, the clouds were alive and tumultuous, Ariana could feel their power even from so far below them. Somewhere in the distance lightning flashed behind the clouds and a moment later the rumble of thunder reached them. Ariana watched as the clouds shuddered, the ripple of sound was visible in the reaction of the clouds as they fought with each other. As the wave passed by, the clouds settled again into their hypnotic war dance.

As she gazed upwards, Ariana had slowed to a walk, and as a heavy rain drop landed on her face she stopped and shook her head. Another drop followed, then another. She looked up again and the clouds had darkened, they were heavy with rain and were about to unleash it on the city. She looked ahead for Shadow and Grins-Too-Widely, they had just turned a corner and she dashed after them, cutting the corner and darting into the shadows.

The moment her paws touched the black pavement something snatched at her from the darkness and a tightness wrapped itself around her leg. She let out a yelp as she struggled to free herself from the thick, formless shadow.

119

A moment later Shadow was by her side, his teeth bared and a threatening snarl trembled from his chest. Ariana felt the grip on her leg tighten for an instant and then it slipped away. She leaped backwards into the safe pool of light and felt her heart rate start to settle.

Shadow looked up at the sky and then his amber eyes met hers. Run, he urged and set off at a gallop, Ariana followed, sprinting along behind him. Grins-Too-Widely seemed to glide along silently just ahead of them. The rain drops felt heavy on her fur and caused large splashes on the street. Puddles formed far too quickly and soon Ariana was leaping over and skirting around them as they reached out to her from the sides of the road. She suspected that a wrong paw could mean being dragged down and drowned if the rain elementals were in a wrathful mood.

Before she could get her bearings, they were skidding to a halt outside the betting shop. Shadow launched himself at the door, and it opened of its own accord to admit them.

Grins-Too-Widely slipped silently in through the front door and Ariana followed. The shop was silent and Ariana felt unease seeping through her body. Grins-Too-Widely stood still next to the door into the back of the building and Shadow shifted form smoothly. He bowed to the fox, Ariana shifted form too and also gave the fox a respectful nod. Grins-Too-Widely cocked his head and nodded back, but that eerie voice of his that came from him without his teeth so much as snapping caught Ariana off guard.

'Cross over now, you are needed.' His voice was almost lazy and he slipped back out through the door without another word or backwards glance. Shadow and Ariana exchanged worried glances and the two shifters crossed the veil into the human world.

Ariana heard the commotion first and then she felt it. Her pack mates were in a state of panic. Fortune was shouting and there were other voices. She and Shadow looked at each other before sprinting through to the kitchen.

'Do NOT ask me again! You are staying here!' Fortune was shouting and he slammed his hand down on the table as Ariana and Shadow burst into the kitchen. Fights-Eyes-Open was snarling at their Alpha, his shirt and tie loose at his neck.

'What's going on?' Shadow demanded. Ariana looked around to see Stone sitting at the table with her head in her hands. Flames was standing by the back door, his arms crossed over his chest and Wind Talker was talking rapidly at him.

'Where's Teri?' Ariana asked. There was too much noise in the room, no one heard her. She asked again, louder this time and she felt Shadow's warm hand on her shoulder, trying to calm her.

'Still your head and your heart, feel it,' Shadow whispered at her ear. Ariana's head snapped to him in frustration but she did as he told her and the room began to go quiet around them. She could feel Teri, the bond was still there, but she was far away, beyond the reaches of their telepathy. Ariana could just about tell that her pack sister was afraid. The rest of the pack felt panic, fear and anger and she caught a snatch of a thought from Wind Talker, the need for a plan to "get her back".

'She's been taken,' Ariana whispered and Shadow's hand on her shoulder tightened momentarily, telling her she was right.

Fortune looked at her for the first time since they entered the room, he sighed. Eyes was backing down, he paced the kitchen a few times then slumped into a chair opposite Stone.

'The southern perimeter is secure.' Shadow's Step spoke

softly into the silence. 'We were in Hepethia and didn't sense it until we crossed over.'

Fortune nodded solemnly. 'Where was she taken from?' Shadow asked, his voice still calm and quiet.

'Redfield,' Stone replied, lifting her head. 'I deliberately didn't take her into Crossway, we went north to patrol Northgate and Redfield. I thought that the Wrecking Crew would provide a nice buffer so that the Witches wouldn't get near Teri. I was wrong.' The Wrecking Crew were the pack to the north of the Blue Moon's territory, the rivals who marked their border so strongly. They too shared a border with the Witches.

'We ran the park, which I realise now was the mistake. I think the Witches may have fae allies there.' Stone's voice was heavy with responsibility and Ariana felt so sad for her. 'They appeared from the south and ambushed us. Teri lost control and ran, they chased her and herded her over into Fenwick.'

Ariana frowned, her mind racing across the territory trying to figure out the geography.

'But that means they came right up through St. Mark's,' she said softly, all eyes turned to her. 'They must have come right into the heart of our territory and tracked you north into Redfield in order to come at you from the south side of the park and to have avoided the Wrecking Crew. At least I assume we would have heard about it if The Wrecking Crew had got into a fight. They'd have warned us the Witches were coming. Right?' She looked around the room at the downcast faces of her pack.

'Not necessarily,' Fortune said sadly. 'But it is hard to keep a large scale fight quiet enough not to reach neighbouring packs one way or another, be it through howls carrying or through other communication. And you are quite right, we heard nothing from them. They will have heard Teri though. Shadow, go to the rooftops, see if you can find Sky Runner and liaise with the Wrecking Crew. Ariana, come with me, I need your tracking abilities. Stone, you're with us. Flames, Eyes and Wind Talker will stay here. See if you can summon some supernatural allies to help find her.' The pack stirred into action, Shadow was already gone when Ariana looked for him and she felt a little pang of disappointment that he had left without saying goodbye.

As everyone started heading in different directions Ariana caught sight of Fortune taking Eyes firmly by the elbow and muttering a warning to him.

'I mean it. I know you're worried about your family, but the best way to protect them is to stay here. If I get the tiniest hint of you disobeying me there will be consequences.' Ariana looked away, embarrassed that she had overheard and moved quickly down the corridor after Stone. Fortune was behind her in an instant and she glanced back to see Eyes disappearing into the basement.

Ariana stepped back out into the cool night air with Stone and Fortune. It was the first time she had been alone with these two pack mates and she felt nervous, almost like she had to prove herself to them, she knew Fortune was counting on her.

The rain was normal on this side of the veil, just another wet night in Caerton. She must have experienced hundreds just like this.

They moved into an alley a few houses down from the shop.

'I want you both to change. Stone, you scout ahead from the sky, Ariana, use your fox senses to pick up what you can. I'll stay in this form, a wolf and a fox together is an odd sight.' Fortune explained and Ariana gave a little smirk of agreement, thinking of the times she had seen him and

Shadow together. She did as she was asked, shifting smoothly into her fox form. Beside her, Stone twisted in on herself and disappeared upwards, she hovered above them, flapping her owl wings briefly before soaring away up over the rooftops.

Stone set off on the route she and Teri had taken earlier in the evening, Ariana glanced up to check which direction to go in and followed the silent owl gliding above. Fortune walked a short distance behind. Ariana soon picked up Teri's scent, though she had been in her human form and the scent was less pronounced than it would have been had she been in her cat form.

They retraced the route slowly, giving Ariana all the time she needed to follow the trail carefully. It was near the telecoms tower that she picked up the first foreign scent and she indicated to Fortune that she had found something. She wasn't one hundred percent sure, but she thought it was probably the same wolf that had tracked and bitten Teri the previous night.

'Can you trace it back to where it entered our territory?' Fortune asked her and she nodded. She set off at once. Following the trail towards Crossway. Where she thought it would lead them east she was surprised to find her nose turning south. With a small whimper she followed the trail, though it was growing cold now, too much time had passed since the intruder had come this way. Stone followed a little behind and Ariana picked up traces of guilt and frustration from her owl mind.

Fortune walked briskly behind and didn't speak when Ariana led them south. The trail was becoming increasingly difficult to follow, but she kept hold of it right to their border. The Witch had crossed over just south of Fenwick, trying to avoid the obvious places that the Blue Moon might expect an incursion.

124

'What about the rest of them?' Fortune looked out across the border, it was just another street in a vast city, nothing remarkable about it, but this was the point where the Blue Moon could go no further, an invisible line that Ariana knew instinctively not to cross.

She turned north and set off into Crossway, searching for the second breach, the place where the other Witches had followed their own tracker into enemy territory. Ariana knew it must have been closer to Redfield Park, it had to have been close enough to where Teri was so as to avoid detection before they reached her. So she ran quickly, but made sure not to leave Fortune behind. She skidded to a halt when she smelled it, it was overpowering.

At least half a dozen of them had been here, just south of the park. They would have made a bee line straight up the main road that came out at the south eastern tip of the park. They must have been seen, a big pack like that must have been seen by humans. She sniffed the air carefully, she put her nose to the ground and tried hard to distinguish the different smells. Soon it was clear that the strength of the smell came down to the number of intruders. They had been in their human forms here, she was sure of it, each individual had a more faint smell than the wolf who had slipped so stealthily into their territory before. That's how they escaped human attention too.

Fortune gave her head a scratch and she rubbed against his legs, enjoying the contact and his affectionate sign of gratitude. Stone gave a small hoot and set off towards the park. Ariana and Fortune followed her and Ariana kept her nose to the ground, waiting to come across some sign of where the Witches had changed.

It wasn't until they entered the park that she sensed it, in the cover of the trees that lined the green space in the middle of dense urban brick and smoke. She hated the smell, everything about it screamed "enemy", "intruder" and it grew overwhelmingly strong where they had shifted into their beast forms and attacked her pack sisters.

She snarled and Stone landed on the ground a few feet away, seamlessly shifting into her human form. Ariana smelled blood and dashed to where Stone was standing. Teri had been wounded in the attack, that was how she had lost control. She felt sick with rage, but she could feel that her pack sister was alive, for now.

Fortune stepped silently to her side and bent to touch the blood soaked ground, he sniffed the blood on his fingers and wrinkled his nose.

'We need to cover this,' he said, standing up and gesturing at the ground. Ariana started digging, burying the bloody earth under freshly turned soil. Fortune paced the area, examining every tree and stepped out from under the cover of the bare branches and into the open space of the park beyond. Ariana stood and watched the Alpha move carefully into the open.

The clouds above cleared and Ariana looked up to see the slip of a waxing crescent moon in the sky, a crooked smile on an invisible face.

She followed Fortune into the park, Stone just behind her. Cautiously they crossed the open field.

'We don't come here in Hepethia,' Fortune spoke softly. 'The fae that claim this park are mad, wild beyond control and as we have now seen, in league with the Witches.'

A gust of wind carried a flurry of dry brown leaves across the park towards them and Ariana caught the scent of a shifter. Her senses sharpened and she let out a short bark, catching Fortune's attention. The leaves swirled around them in an unnatural spiral and Fortune stopped still to watch them. A whisper reached out from the leaves, sending a shudder through Ariana, though she couldn't pick out any discernible words.

'You want permission to enter?' Fortune asked the disembodied voice. 'Granted.' He looked out across the park and Ariana followed his gaze as the leaves dropped to the ground around them.

Out of the dark cover of the trees on the opposite side of the park three figures emerged. The heckles on Ariana's back rose, but she knew the smell, it wasn't the Witches, this was the Wrecking Crew, or some of them.

A tall, wiry man with short reddish hair led them, he had stubble all over his chin and jaw and wore loose clothing. He was flanked by one male and one female, both of whom looked as hard as nails, though the female was painfully thin.

Ariana felt Fortune tensing up as they approached and could hear the rumble of a growl in his chest. Stone was equally rigid, her thoughts a tangle of aggression and apprehension. This was the first real contact Ariana had had with shifters outside her own pack, she couldn't feel their thoughts like she could her pack mates, she wasn't bonded to them. But she could smell them and read their body language just as well, she could smell the adrenaline and knew that these newcomers were anything but friendly.

'Fortune,' The Wrecking Crew's Alpha snapped, as the two groups drew level in the middle of the park.

'Rust.' Fortune returned the curt greeting. 'What can we do for you?'

'One of your bitches rampaged through our territory tonight,' Rust snarled, his eyes darting over Stone and Ariana. Fortune's chest puffed up and Ariana saw his fists curl by his sides.

'In case you didn't notice,' Fortune growled. 'Witches

invaded our territory and pursued one of our own. She was fleeing for her life.'

Rust let out a bark of laughter.

'Then your youngsters need to be taught to control themselves.' Rust's pack mates started laughing cruelly.

Stone lurched forward, growling and snarling at the skinny female. The Wrecking Crew took half a step back, pausing their laughter only for an instant before breaking into renewed jeers. Fortune held a hand out to tell Stone to back down, though Ariana could feel the anger rolling off her Alpha in waves.

'Get out.' Fortune's voice was barely more than a whisper but it carried the threat of a defensive alpha wolf on his own territory. The Wrecking Crew flinched and without another word turned and walked briskly from the park. Ariana felt the tension prickling over her skin and in the air around them for several long minutes as they watched the Wrecking Crew members leave and waited for all of their tempers to settle.

Fortune's fists relaxed, he turned and stalked past Ariana and Stone. The two of them fell into step behind him, not a word or direct thought was exchanged all the way back to the shop but Ariana felt the thirst for payback pounding in the veins of her pack mates.

Chapter Eleven

18th November

It was a restless night for the Blue Moon. They could all feel Teri's fear, and pain. Fortune paced the attic all night, Flames and Wind Talker had gone to the petrol station, having summoned supernatural allies to help protect the border. Shadow and Stone were patrolling while Ariana and Eyes were expected to rest.

Ariana couldn't sleep, she sat in the kitchen waiting for something to happen. She felt useless and confused, but her feeling paled in comparison to the frustration she felt from Eyes. He was taking it out on the punch bag in the basement. Ariana only caught fragments of unguarded thought and feeling, their human forms were the least communicative in so many ways. It was only when Eyes shifted into the monster and started shredding the punch bag that Ariana picked up more of the picture. A toddler, in yellow pyjamas with gorgeous curly hair, she was being put to bed by a beautiful young woman with long red hair. Eyes had a family. Ariana knew where they lived, she had smelled Eyes in Crossway on that first trip out with Shadow. If she had smelled him, so had the Witches. Tears welled up in her eyes and she rubbed them away with frustration.

As dawn broke Ariana's eyes were fighting sleep, the others were in mixed states of exhaustion. She couldn't feel much from Teri, she was still there so Ariana knew she was still alive, but there were no strong emotions coming from her. Ariana hoped that meant Teri was asleep, rather than unconscious or broken.

The pack sleepily assembled for breakfast, though it

seemed Ariana wasn't the only one with no appetite. Fortune burst into the kitchen, grim determination etched on his face.

'We're not going to sit around any more. I need intelligence from our allies, Flames and Stone. I need to know where she is being held and why they took her.'

'Blood,' Shadow's Step spoke softly from the corner by the back door. Everyone looked at him. 'The Witches value heredity above almost everything. Teri is from Fenwick, the Witches may consider her to be theirs by birth.'

Fortune rubbed his forehead and ran his fingers through his long hair.

'That sounds about right. Still, Flames and Stone, I need you to call in all favours from our allies. I want to get a message to the Witches too, let's see if we can arrange a negotiation for exchange. I want Teri back and if we can do it without open bloodshed, so much the better. Wind Talker, Ariana, you will help and observe. Shadow, I need you out on patrol.' Fortune turned to Eyes, a softer expression settling on his face. 'Eyes, I'm taking you home.'

The relief that washed over Eyes was palpable, his shoulders relaxed and he let out a huge sigh.

'Thank you,' he breathed.

The pack began to split up and Ariana took the opportunity to dash upstairs to check her phone. She got to her room and eagerly turned it on. A little ripple of disappointment passed through her when she found no messages from Rhys waiting for her. She shoved the feeling aside and checked her missed calls, at least a dozen from Ron at the dojo. The events of the last three days had consumed her entire life and everything that was normal before her first change seemed a lifetime ago.

She summoned some courage and made the call to work.

It only rang twice before a voice cracked with stress answered.

'Saint Mark's Self Defence Dojo.'

'Ron, it's Ariana.'

'Where the hell have you been?' her boss yelled. Ariana flinched.

'I'm so sorry. I've been in such a state. A couple of days ago I found out that my dad died.' She winced as she said the words. 'I've been back home to be with my mum. I'm really sorry for not calling sooner, I was just totally lost.' She had never got along well with her adopted family and didn't talk about them much. She felt guilty for lying to Ron and invoking such a tragic tale, but she couldn't very well tell him the truth.

'Of course,' Ron's voice softened, 'Of course, love, I'm sorry for your loss. I can grant you a leave of absence for a couple of weeks, if that's enough?'

'Yes, that should be fine. Thank you.' Ariana breathed a silent sigh of relief. 'I'll keep in touch and see you soon.'

'Take care Ariana. See you soon.' Ron ended the call and Ariana tucked her phone away in her pocket with a slightly shaky hand.

She shoved her guilt aside and ran back downstairs, just in time to fall into step behind Wind Talker as they filed through the door into the back of the shop and each stepped across the veil, unnoticed by any human occupants of the room beyond.

'Why do they never see?' Ariana asked as she stepped into the bizarre Hepethia version of the betting shop. The others looked at her quizzically. 'The humans? They didn't notice us crossing over.'

'Humans usually choose to ignore the things that their brain cannot comprehend,' Flames replied. 'But just in case,

131

we have a demon of obfuscation guarding the shop and concealing our comings and goings.'

'Oh, I see. That makes sense. So the humans who come in regularly have no idea about any of us?'

She was met with a slightly awkward silence, but only for a moment.

'They may suspect,' Stone volunteered. 'But no, they have no sure knowledge. Lily knows everything though and if any customer did ever see something they shouldn't and commented on it, I'm sure she could convince them to ignore it. She can be very persuasive.' Stone smirked.

Ariana nodded in silent acknowledgement and watched as Wind Talker and Flames-First-Guardian went about setting up the ritual. Wind Talker lit a fire in the fire pit and the room lit up with its warm blaze, the money on the walls fluttering gently. Flames cut his hand and let blood run into the fire, stoking the flames higher.

Stone walked around them in a circle, muttering a low chant, her steps seemed to leave the trace of a line behind her, forming a protective boundary around them, Ariana knew that it wasn't just a symbolic protection, it was a physical barrier.

Grins-Too-Widely slunk in through the door and sat just outside the circle, his head cocked to one side in the usual way, his peculiar grin too big for his face. She supposed that the fox must sense their rituals beginning, she wondered if there would ever be a time that he wouldn't come to observe.

Flames took a blood sacrifice from each of them in turn, catching their blood in the large goblet and returning to the fire. Wind Talker crumbled some herbs into the blood and slowly poured the mixture into the fire while Flames raised his hands over his head and clapped them slowly three times.

'We call upon the powers of the gods and all those that have dominion over tracking and surveillance,' Flames called out.

From out of the fire crawled a small creature, rather like a salamander, but its skin was made of gravel and it crunched as it crawled out of the fire pit and onto the floor before Flames. Behind it came what looked like a CCTV camera with strange legs like a spider, it had a small red light blinking in place of an eye and it made an electronic whirring sound as it moved robotically towards Flames.

'We thank you for answering our call.' Stone spoke calmly, but her voice was weighted with authority. 'We need you and your kin to find our pack sister. She was taken from us late last night by the Witches of Fenwick. We know she fled through Runmead, north of here, but after that we lost track of her.'

'Witches!' spat the salamander angrily. 'No friends of ours. We will look, but those shifters shun our paths and keep to the woods.'

'I know,' Stone sighed. 'But many of the nature fae are their allies and will not help us. Please do your best and we will continue to uphold our long standing bargain of keeping the roads clear and safe.'

'Done,' the salamander hissed and shuffled back into the fire, the surveillance spirit blinked its red eye and followed.

Flames cast his hands over the fire and it immediately died down, it didn't go out completely, the fuel still burned, but the ritual was closed and the fire responded by returning to its natural size. The circle faded from the floor.

'Will they find her?' Ariana felt sceptical.

'Perhaps,' Stone shrugged. 'They may find a way, or a sign for us to follow. Once we have news we will see about sending the Witches a message, but we don't want to play our hand before we know where Teri is, just in case we need to take further action.'

'You seemed to know just what to say to them,' Ariana mused.

'I guess I'm pretty diplomatic, yes. That's why Fortune asked me to help here. Teri is too, she has a certain way about her.' Stone cast her eyes down into the fire, weight heavy on her shoulders.

'Will we get her back? What if she should be with the Witches by right? What if she decides she wants to join them?' The questions tumbled out of Ariana before she could stop them. Stone put a steadying hand on her shoulder.

'One thing at a time. Let's find her first.'

One of the televisions suddenly stopped crackling with static and flared to life. The four shifters quickly went to it and watched as the image formed on the screen. The view was from a static CCTV camera, the image was black and white and somewhat grainy. Beyond the strange grey light from a street lamp was utter blackness, so it had to be out in the country, away from the lights of buildings. The rampaging bestial creature galloped across the screen, closely followed by two wolves and a fox. They all bounded across the road and disappeared into the blackness beyond.

The picture blinked away, leaving the screen black. Words formed on the screen, as if they were being typed, with the location of the camera that caught the action. It was right out in Fenwick, on the main street out of Caerton, the one Ariana had driven up with Rhys the night before she changed. Ariana's breath caught in her throat. She had been on Witch territory right before she changed. Had they caught her scent too? If she had changed that night she might be with the Witches now. What about Rhys? Would she have killed him in her frenzy? Would the Witches have killed him for witnessing supernatural activity? It didn't bear thinking about.

'Well, it doesn't give us much, but it's enough to confirm that they drove her up into Fenwick Forest. That's probably where they are holding her now.' Stone gave words to the group's thoughts. 'Let's update Fortune and see what message he wants to send.'

The four of them trooped back across the veil, seamlessly appearing and strolling through the door into the house at the back. They had been in Hepethia far longer than Ariana had thought, the day had grown late.

Fortune, Eyes and Shadow were all filing in through the back door as Ariana and the others reached the kitchen.

'It shouldn't have happened,' Shadow was saying. 'It was a shadow demon, our ally, it shouldn't have attacked her like that. I am telling you now, there is chaos and disorder among the spirits.' He fell silent when he saw the others and Ariana thought she caught a glimmer of apprehension in his face as his eyes passed over her. He had been talking about her run in with the shadow on the way back the night before, he was concerned and hadn't told her. Now was not the time to be petulant about it, however, and Ariana smiled as if she hadn't heard a thing.

She latched onto Fights-Eyes-Open, who looked grim and frustrated. She went to him and offered a friendly pat on his arm.

'Hi. Did you see your family?'

'From a distance,' he grumbled. 'Fortune told me I had to just check that they were okay, for my peace of mind, but not to go right up to the house and leave my fresh scent all over it. Which I know makes sense, but I really just want to be there to protect them myself.'

'This is why many of our kind walk away from our

135

human families, Eyes,' Fortune spoke softly and carefully. There was sadness in the Alpha's eyes and Ariana felt a wave of it pass through the pack telepathy. Had they all left loved ones behind them in order to live this life? Her family lived in another city and she had never been close to them, but she thought of Ben, and of Rhys. A lump welled up in her throat.

Stone walked abruptly back towards the shop without a word, Shadow set about feeding the pack, while Flames filled Fortune in on what they had learned. Ariana peered down the hall and watched Stone busying herself in the shop, it was closing up time. She gave Eyes another pat on the arm and what she hoped was a reassuring smile. Ariana sat down at the table and pulled out her phone. She had a message from Ben and she opened it hurriedly.

Where the fuck are you? I am worried sick. You were on death's door last time I saw you and now you've vanished. Call me, please.

Ariana stood and walked briskly from the room before the tears began to fall. She sat down half way up the stairs and sobbed. She hadn't thought of him until just a moment earlier, she had left him in the dark for days. The guilt clawed painfully at her insides.

I am so, so sorry. I am absolutely fine. I was pretty ill for a few days and basically shut the whole world out. But I am fine now. I am really sorry for causing you to worry. I totally failed to call into work too, I flaked out. It was so bad. Are you otherwise OK? Loads of love, A xx

The tears kept falling and her hands shook as she typed,

she had to keep going back and re-typing parts of the message. Just moments after she sent her message, her phone lit up with a reply.

```
Thank fuck. Glad you're OK. Work is a
bitch, as always, but I'm fine. Marcus is
taking me to Rome for a few days next week
for our anniversary. But when I get back we
are going for cocktails. ciao, bella xxx
```

Ariana smiled weakly and wiped her face.

```
Wow! Have a wonderful time. See you when
you get back xx
```

'Right,' Fortune's voice boomed out from the kitchen and Ariana hurriedly finished drying her tears and slipped back to the pack. 'Flames, I need you to summon a messenger, something substantial, to let them know we mean business.'

'We should all take part, it'll be easier to summon a powerful fae or demon with the whole pack there, bar Teri, obviously,' Flames responded.

'Fine.' Fortune nodded and indicated for everyone to cross over the veil. They filed down the hall and met Stone as she was bolting the shop door behind the last person to leave. 'Stone, join us please.'

The pack crossed over into Hepethia, which was becoming increasingly familiar to Ariana now. She was becoming accustomed to the static broadcasting from the televisions, the money fluttering on the walls, the eyes watching her and the strange silence that hung just beyond the shop like a soundproof curtain around them.

'We won't always do rituals here,' Wind Talker said softly at her ear. 'We sometimes have to go to where the right elements are, but this is the safest place.'

137

Flames-First-Guardian and Wind Talker rekindled the fire in the pit and Stone walked the circle, forming the protective boundary around them. Flames lit a black candle and walked around the circle with it, shielding the flame with his hand. As he passed her, Ariana noticed shadows dancing on him, on the back of his hand and on his face, everywhere that there were stark contrasts between the candlelight and darkness. The dance was unnatural, not the movement she expected to see from a flickering candle, the shadows themselves were alive.

'Come to us, demon of shadow, of movement in darkness. Hear our call,' Wind Talker called out and he followed Flames around the circle with the goblet and knife, taking blood from each pack member in turn. Ariana held out her hand and didn't even wince as he cut her palm. She knew by now that she would be shedding a lot of blood this way and that the cut would heal in seconds.

Grins-Too-Widely made his usual appearance through the front door, which always seemed to open for him of its own accord. Several small shadowy figures accompanied him; shifting, dark creatures, roughly the size of cats. They slunk around him, clinging to the floor and walls. They settled around the edges of the shop and watched.

Flames stood by the fire and held the candle over it, tipping it over so that the melting wax dripped into the fire.

'Essence of shadow, of flickering movement, I summon you.' Flames' voice reverberated off the walls, the command was clear and compelling. The shadows around the room shimmered and Ariana watched in awe as darkness was drawn out of every crevice and corner in the room. Out from under every fold of money on the walls, from behind each pack member, from under the fire pit, every shadow peeled away from the surface it was cast upon and seemed to be sucked in towards the centre of the circle.

Out of the fire rose a twisting black shape, constantly flickering and twitching. It had no face, no limbs, no discernible edges at all, it was just formless shadow. Ariana struggled to wrap her head around what she was seeing, it made sense even though it shouldn't. She could feel the power of it, it was stronger than any fae or demon that she had seen before and she felt drawn to it, even though it frightened her.

Ariana glanced around the circle. She could feel tension coming from Shadow's Step beside her and his eyes looked troubled.

'Shadow-of-Moonlit-Leaves,' Stone spoke, drawing everyone's attention. 'Thank you for answering our call.'

'Why do you summon me?' The demon's voice rustled, like leaves in the wind.

'Our pack-sister has been taken captive by The Witches of Fenwick and we wish to send a message to her abductors, calling for a negotiation.' Fortune spoke clearly and authoritatively.

'I am not your errand boy, dog, send your own messages.' The demon began to twist back down into the fire, but something caught its attention and it stopped its descent, although it still flickered. Slowly it rose out of the fire again and Ariana felt its attention turn towards Shadow's Step, standing next to her. 'You are of the darkness.'

'I am,' her mentor spoke softly, but his deep voice carried well.

'As are you.' The demon turned to her, shifting around constantly, dancing among the flames. Ariana felt her cheeks burn red, she didn't entirely understand.

'Yes,' she replied, trying to keep the doubt out of her voice.

'You would have me dance across city and forest to carry a message of peace to these Witches.'

'You are the shadow of leaves under moonlight.' Ariana let the words flow from her, though her eyes darted to Stone for confirmation that she was saying the right thing. Stone gave her a reassuring smile and small nod. Shadow took her hand briefly and gave it a squeeze.

'I am,' confirmed the demon.

'You can move unseen across the city, be anywhere you choose.' Shadow's Step took up the negotiation, much to Ariana's relief. 'You are powerful and command a host of lesser shadow demons under you. You are allied with the Blue Moon and I am the faithful servant of your kind. We know each other, you and I, though we meet tonight for the first time. If you carry this message for us, I will dim the lights of St. Mark's every night of every full moon from henceforth, so that you might grow in strength and influence.'

Ariana chewed her lip and carefully looked at him. How on earth could he accomplish such a thing? Then she remembered watching from the window of her flat as all of the street lights flickered out to mask the fight about to take place. She let out a slow, steady breath, unaware that she had been holding it.

The demon flickered, it seemed to rotate and look at each pack member in turn, reading them, deciding whether or not it could trust them.

'Very well. You will do this for me and I will take your message. What, precisely do you want me to say?'

Fortune and Stone hurriedly muttered together and seemed to come to a quick agreement.

'We cordially invite you, Witches of Fenwick, to

Redfield Park at midnight to discuss terms for the return of our pack-sister, Teresa Melrose.' Stone relayed the message.

The demon repeated it back in Stone's own voice.

'So mote it be,' Flames-First-Guardian said and clapped his hands.

The demon seemed to nod and it twisted down into the fire. The shadows spilled out from the pit and slithered back into their proper places. The boundary dropped and the lesser shadow demons outside the circle slipped away. A faint breeze lifted the notes on the walls for a moment and then there was stillness.

'Will they come?' Stone asked the Alpha.

'No,' Fortune said quietly. 'I don't believe they will. But we have to try.'

He strode across the room towards Ariana, crossing the veil right beside her, which sent a peculiar ripple through her body, as if she could feel the very fabric of reality moving as he crossed.

Chapter Twelve

At 11pm, The Blue Moon left the betting shop and made its way to Redfield Park, on the north-eastern border of their large territory. Shadow's Step and Speaks-With-Stone went in their animal forms, scouting ahead, the others as humans.

Ariana had her swords strapped to her back, their new magic hiding them from human eyes. Wind Talker and Flames both carried bags over their shoulders, packed with supplies and Fortune wore a huge war hammer on his back, imbued with the same magic as her swords, making it invisible to humans.

'I don't want a fight,' Fortune had explained as they all gathered their weapons and supplies back at the shop. 'I want a peaceful end to this, but we don't know what the Witches will do, if they come, so we need to be prepared in case it comes to blows.'

He led the way now, every bit the alpha; tall, broad and armed.

The pack gathered in the centre of the park and waited. It was a dry night, the sky was clear and Ariana looked up to see stars spread across the sky, a crescent moon hung high above, smiling upon the shifters that were so governed by her shifting form.

Shadow and Stone remained in their animal forms and made regular circuits of the park, Ariana watched them carefully, longing to shift form and join them.

Eyes grew restless as they waited, unable to keep still for long and paced across the back of their formation every now and then. Ariana could sense that he was itching for a fight and she had to admit to being curious to see what he could do.

She pulled her phone out of her pocket to check the time, it was 12.20am, the Witches were late. She heaved a sigh and put her phone away. Fortune turned to her and scowled a little.

'They're not coming,' he said in a hushed voice.

'No,' Ariana replied. 'No, they're not. What do we do?'

The sound of pounding paws across the grass drew their attention, Shadow raced towards them from the far north of the park and Ariana picked up a single word, company.

Her eyes darted to the tree line and the whole pack tensed up, eyes searching the darkness. But it couldn't be the Witches, unless they had come through Wrecking Crew territory, no, this had to be the Wrecking Crew. 'Will they enter our territory?' Ariana asked no one in particular.

'If they do, we fight,' said Fortune authoritatively. 'No warning, they've had plenty of those, they know the rules.'

Ariana looked at Eyes, his jaw was set, his hands clenched into fists.

Stone flew down from the black sky above and shifted form swiftly and seamlessly as she arrived at the assembled pack.

'No, we can't fight them,' she said quietly. 'If the Witches show up and we're in combat with another pack it will not only make us look bad, but they could flank us, or use the opportunity to slip past us. Cool heads, people, please.'

'Stone is right,' Flames spoke up. 'Eyes, Ariana, bring it down a notch. Even I can smell your adrenaline and in this feeble human form that's bad, very bad.'

Ariana took a deep breath and looked up at the stars and moon, focusing on their light to help soothe her heightened fight instincts.

Fortune stifled a snarl, but he nodded once to indicate his agreement.

'Fine. Stone, Ariana, you two with me. The rest of you

wait here.' Fortune led them towards the edge of the park at a brisk jog, one hand on the hilt of his hammer, the idea of a fight wasn't entirely out of his mind.

They reached the edge of the park and Stone led them to where she had caught sight of them from the air.

'Here, they're approaching from this way.' Stone indicated the street beyond the trees.

'Ariana, shift form, please,' Fortune whispered and she did as she was asked, dropping to all fours, her clothes and swords disappearing into her fur. She sniffed the air and smelled them heading towards the park, from downwind.

She caught sight of four of them, all in human form, walking briskly across the road that ran along the edge of the park, and entering the narrow band of woodland. They stopped suddenly, about five feet inside the tree line, right on the territory border. Ariana looked them each over carefully. They were all scruffy and covered in black grease, their clothes were smeared and at least two of them had it on their hands too. The Alpha was mostly clean and wore baggy jeans and a leather coat. The other two men wore overalls and big boots, the skinny woman that Ariana had seen the last time she encountered the Wrecking Crew was dressed in black leggings and a hooded top, also with big boots on her feet. Her long, thick hair was pulled back into a careless pony tail. They looked like they had just crawled out of a pit lane on a race track, except Rust. Ariana tried to focus her mind on Rust, she reached into his heart, digging, searching for that inner truth that must be there. She saw him watching the others work, felt his lazy boredom oozing from him.

Fortune indicated for Stone and Ariana to follow him to meet them.

'Rust,' Fortune greeted their Alpha, tension in his jaw. 'What can I do for you?'

'We got wind of your entire pack assembling in the park, thought we had better come and check it out. I'm sure you would do the same,' Rust replied.

'Perhaps. But this is our territory, it's our business what we do on it. It's no concern of yours.' Fortune kept his tone casual, though it was clear that a threat hung unspoken underneath it.

Rust snorted and shook his head.

'Fine. Fine, we'll leave you to your midnight stroll in the park.' He turned and his pack turned with him, they walked back to the road and then stopped. Rust glanced back over his shoulder, a glint in his eye. He looked like he was about to throw some dig back at them, then thought better of it and walked briskly away the way they had come.

Fortune growled and stomped back towards the centre of the park, Stone and Ariana exchanged worried looks and followed him.

'Waste of bloody time,' Fortune was mumbling as they rejoined the others. 'Right, Flames, I need our messenger here now. I want confirmation that the message was delivered, before we do anything rash.'

Ariana thought Fortune looked as though he wanted to be rash, but was reining himself in remarkably well.

Flames opened his bag and started digging through it, but before he could even begin the summoning, a gust of wind blew a flurry of leaves across the park and from out of the shadows stepped a beautiful, shadowy figure. It moved gracefully and was glinting with silver among its dark folds, like dappled light. Ariana felt the power of the demon, and knew it was Shadow-of-Moonlit-Leaves, here in its own environment it looked different, at peace, not scraped together out of what was available. She would even say it was beautiful. "Demon" didn't seem the right name any more and she wondered whether her perception of demons from her human life was entirely accurate in the real world.

'No need for all that.' Its rustling voice seemed to reach out across the darkness and halt Flames from rummaging in his bag. 'I am here. I delivered your message to their Alpha herself.'

'Did you wait for a reply?' Fortune barked impatiently.

'I did. What do you take me for?' The demon whipped towards him, like a leaf caught in a gust of wind changing direction. 'She sent this.'

Something thudded to the ground between the shadowy demon and Fortune. The Alpha bent to pick it up and Ariana moved closer. It smelled of Teri. Fortune turned it over in his hands, studying it closely and Ariana shifted back into her human form to get high enough to see, just as his fist closed around it. It was Teri's necklace, the one with the gibbous moon on it.

'What is this supposed to mean?' Fortune snarled.

'Why, the kitten has renounced Artemis, of course, and joined the Witches.'

Chapter Thirteen

19th November

Fortune tucked the necklace into the pocket of his jeans. Ariana watched him carefully, studying his hard-to-read face.

'Teri will be wanting it back.' His voice was barely a whisper and Ariana was sure she was the only one who heard.

'Thank you, Shadow-of-Moonlit-Leaves,' Stone spoke, her voice steady as a rock. 'We will ensure we keep up our end of the bargain. You may leave us.'

The demon swirled and folded in on itself, disappearing back across the veil, whipping up a small flurry of dry leaves in its wake.

'Fortune?' Stone turned to the Alpha, her face no longer a mask now that the demon had left. 'Can it be true?'

'No,' he replied with absolute certainty.

'What are we going to do?' Ariana asked, unable to hide the urgency in her voice. Fortune took a deep breath and thought for a moment.

'Flames, Eyes and Wind Talker, I want the three of you patrolling from here to the southern border. Stone, you come with me to Crossway. We're going to bang on the front door. Ariana, go with Shadow to the back door. Slip up into Fenwick Forest and find Teri. We'll draw their attention while you two slip in and fetch her. If she has been turned by them we will turn her back. She is our sister.' Fortune's voice was fierce and Ariana's pulse raced with the fire that had been ignited in all of them.

Fortune and Eyes embraced briefly in farewell, Ariana

found Stone's hand and gave it a squeeze and the pack went its separate ways.

Shadow's Step led her east, out of the park and towards Fenwick. He spoke hurriedly as they walked.

'Focus on Teri, on her feelings. She's still one of us, still connected to us. She can't have been turned. Use that telepathy to help locate her. We can do this.' He gave her shoulder a squeeze before dropping to the all fours as he shifted and running ahead as a fox. Ariana shifted form and followed him.

Ariana felt much more connected to her supernatural side as a fox, she could feel her own heartbeat, her senses were heightened and she was more attuned to her body. She was also vastly more attuned to the rest of the pack and she could feel Teri was still a part of her. She put her nose to the ground and began tracking Teri's very faint smell.

She had been driven north into Runmead, where they couldn't follow, so Ariana knew she would have to pick up the trail again one they reached Fenwick.

They reached the border in minutes and paused. Ariana smelled the Blue Moon's border markings and waited for Shadow to cross over first, he sniffed the border cautiously and led her to a narrow path along the side of a row of shops. He looked around before slipping around the side of the terrace and over into Witch territory. Ariana followed him slowly, and as they slipped through the darkness she could feel the presence of Grins-Too-Widely. She made a silent plea to him, asking for his protection from prying eyes, she had a feeling he could grant them that.

As she and Shadow reached the end of the alley they turned out onto a main road, swiftly crossed it and darted down a side street and into the deep shadows of the back gardens of Fenwick. Silently they slipped through the darkness, stalking their way past wheelie bins and garages, keeping to the shadows and away from the main road. Ariana hoped and prayed that the Witches didn't routinely patrol this route.

They took their time, working their way slowly through the area, coming in a wide arch north around Fenwick, towards the woods. Eventually Ariana caught the scent of the Witches, she paused and let out a low whimper to let Shadow know what she had found. He picked up the trail too and let her lead the way. She tracked it very carefully into the woods. She was starting to feel out of her element as she left the city behind, and trepidation threatened to overwhelm her. The trees were tightly packed, the darkness was oppressive and there was no hint of wind in this sheltered place.

She could feel Teri, she wasn't as scared as she had been, there was hope there and with the distance closed Ariana could pick up much more detail of her pack mate's thoughts and feelings, but she still couldn't tell exactly where she was. She could feel the physical pain and exhaustion from Teri, Ariana knew now without a shadow of a doubt that her pack mate had been tortured.

She got a mental image of the Witches from Teri's eyes and confusion filled her. Had Teri really been broken? It made no sense. She saw some sort of a ritual being prepared, possibly an initiation. Ariana came to a halt, something was very wrong. Shadow sensed it too.

They carefully picked their way onwards and the trees began to thin out as they approached a clearing. They could hear voices, and Ariana saw movement ahead. Teri was very close, but Ariana couldn't see her.

There was a crash a few hundred meters away, a tree branch falling, followed by shouts and yells and the unmistakable cacophony of a handful of people shifting into beasts too big for these closely packed woods. Shadow stood perfectly still, listening carefully and Ariana slowly inched her way through the under-brush, trying to pick up Teri's scent, but found nothing. She reached the edge of the clearing and saw a ritual set up, shimmering dust and coloured stones littered the floor, but the clearing was deserted.

There was a sudden rush of movement to Ariana's right, a raging monster charged past, crashing through the trees and sending branches and twigs flying. It was one of the Witches, she recognised the stench. Ariana became disoriented, seeing through Teri's eyes as well as her own, a bizarre double image that frightened and confused her.

The trees flew past her much faster than was normal. Teri was running and Ariana ran too, swift and silent, leaving Shadow behind. She ran from the woods, back to her original path through the back gardens of Fenwick. She was compelled to run, just as her pack-sister was.

Ariana picked up feelings of elation mixed with the kind of fear you get when riding a roller coaster. Her own body was filled with adrenaline, but she felt the same sensations from Teri, and as Ariana crossed the border back into her own territory double the fear and confusion overwhelmed her. She kept running but not towards home, she turned north and ran along the border, Teri was coming this way, straight through Runmead, Wrecking Crew turf.

Hope began to replace the fear as Ariana ran, she saw the stars through her pack mate's eyes and felt a glimmer of understanding. She decided to move deeper into Blue Moon territory and began to feel more secure. The moment Teri came sprinting into Redfield Ariana felt the soaring high, the relief and the victory and made a direct line for her pack-sister. Ariana rounded a corner and almost collided with the sleek cat coming the other way. They both shifted seamlessly into their human forms and embraced each other tightly, cries of relief and excitement exploding from them both.

'I couldn't believe it when I felt you in the woods!' Teri cried, releasing Ariana but still holding her arm tightly. Ariana was laughing and tears began to pour down her cheeks. 'I was already putting my escape plan into action, but when I felt you nearby I knew the stars were aligned and it gave me the courage I needed.' Teri held out a large, golden yellow stone in her other hand and tossed it into the air, catching it again. It glinted bright orange in the street light.

'What is that?' Ariana asked as the two of them set off at a brisk walk towards the betting shop.

'One of the stones from their ritual. I stole it.' Ariana frowned at her, theft didn't seem like Teri. 'As a token, you know, of my cunning escape. It stopped them completing the ritual too. I'll tell you all about it when we get back. We'd better hurry, they'll be after me and I can't guarantee they won't come right on into our territory looking for me.'

Ariana was confused and curious, but Teri was right, they had to hurry to safety.

As they were approaching the area where Ariana's dojo was located, Shadow caught up with them, galloping up behind them. He growled as he butted between them and nudged Ariana roughly into the wall of a building. She clung to the wall, afraid for a moment, until she felt the relief pouring from him. He turned on Teri and gave her a more friendly nudge and she dared to laugh a little.

Shadow's head whipped around, his nose in the air and he took a few steps away from them.

'What is it?' Ariana was immediately alert, something had caught his attention.

Out of the darkness a few meters away Grins-Too-

151

Widely came sprinting, crossing the veil and manifesting before them.

'Border breech,' he barked as he skidded to a halt beside them. 'They are coming in Hepethia, flee now or cross over to face them.'

We need the others. Shadow pressed the thought forcefully into Ariana's mind.

'Grins-Too-Widely, we cannot face anyone without help. Fetch Fortune and the others,' Ariana said hurriedly. The pack elder twisted on the spot and disappeared. Ariana had to trust that he was doing as she asked.

'What do we do?' Teri asked, fear filling her eyes.

Cross over. Shadow looked at them and then slipped into the shadows and crossed the veil. Teri and Ariana looked at each other in alarm before running after him. Teri was a step ahead of her and as Ariana's foot buckled Teri grabbed her arm and held her up.

'Thanks,' Ariana whispered, looking around her. Shadow was a few feet away, looking up and down the street. There were tall hedges on either side of the road, the houses beyond them were dark and close, looming overhead, dark windows watching the street. Parked cars lined the road, casting long, dark shadows. The cars themselves resembled huge, sleeping cats, panthers and the like, but made from metal. The closest opened a sleepy, yellow eye-like headlamp, blinked at them and then settled back to sleep.

Shadow slipped carefully out into the middle of the road and sniffed the air. Ariana and Teri followed him. He set off up the street, in the corresponding direction that Grins-Too-Widely had approached them from. They had been in Redfield and not far from Runmead, it wasn't the Witches that had breached their border. Ariana realised it at the same time as Teri and they exchanged worried looks.

Ariana's hand went to one of her dha on her back, checking that it was there. Her hand lingered near the hilt.

She heard them before she saw them, they were not taking any particular care to conceal themselves, loud footsteps and the occasional jeer between pack-mates carried easily through the eerie quiet of Hepethia.

Shadow shifted into his human form and held out a hand to halt Ariana and Teri.

The four familiar faces of the Wrecking Crew rounded the corner and stopped in a line across the street.

'That's the one,' the skinny female shouted, pointing at Teri.

'Your kitten crossed our territory again, Shadow, she needs to be taught a lesson,' Rust called down the street.

'She was fleeing the Witches, Rust,' Shadow replied calmly. 'She needed to make a direct line for safety.'

'That is no excuse,' Rust called out and the Wrecking Crew began walking towards them down the middle of the street. Rust was wielding a pipe with a jagged end, one of the other males had a flick knife.

Ariana's hand tightened on the hilt of her sword, she felt the adrenaline pumping in her veins and could feel waves of it rolling off the shifters striding towards them. Shadow growled, a warning to back down. Somehow he was still fox-like even in his human form.

'Give us the kitten, Shadow,' Rust snarled as he drew close. 'It'll be easier all around. It's only just, given the repeat offences. You know the traditions.'

Shadow reached over and gently tugged Teri closer to him, tucking her behind him. He lifted his chest and spat in Rust's face. Ariana sucked in a sharp breath of surprise. Rust blinked and for a moment Ariana thought he was going to back down, but he brought back his head and swiftly thrust it forward, head-butting Shadow hard.

Shadow staggered backward, paused for only a moment and then pounced. Ariana didn't have a spare second to watch him fight though, one of the grease monkeys was on her. He landed a punch to her face, sending her reeling backwards. He had looked wiry, but his strength was phenomenal.

She steadied herself and dodged a follow up blow, spinning behind him and turning him around. Her fist found the side of his head and sent him stumbling sideways for the briefest of seconds before he was on her again. She dodged two more blows before he managed to land an elbow to her back and she went flying forwards. Her eyes landed on Teri, she'd bloodied the face of the skinny female quite badly but was now being grappled by the guy with the flick knife and couldn't get free.

Ariana wheeled around, drawing her sword as she span. Adeptly, she ducked under her assailant and sliced right through his heavy boot and through his Achilles tendon, blood sprayed out onto the tarmac and he let out a strangled cry as he staggered sideways and dropped to his knees. Ariana drew back her blade and made to strike him with the hilt but a shout stopped her.

'No!' Fortune barked, racing up the street, his hammer in hand, Grins-Too-Widely and the rest of the Blue Moon with him.

Ariana stepped back and cast her eyes over the scene. Shadow and Rust were locked eye to eye, the pipe between them with all four of their hands on it. Neither of them let go or broke eye contact at the sound of Fortune's shout. Teri was limp, the knife to her throat, blood on her face.

Anger flared up in Ariana's chest and she felt her body shaking, she was going to shift. Her dha fell to the floor and she looked at her shaking hands as they curled into talons. But then there were arms around her, warm, strong arms and a soft voice at her ear.

'Ariana, listen to my voice. Ariana.' Stone had hold of her, her voice was calm, her steady energy reached into Ariana and slowed her heart rate. She took deep breaths and let her body go limp. The shaking stopped and the rage passed.

'Release her,' Fortune ordered, pointing at Teri. The flick knife guy looked to his Alpha before doing anything. Rust and Shadow had broken apart but were still eye balling each other warily. Rust nodded to his pack-mate, who reluctantly released Teri.

Teri stumbled away from him and Wind Talker rushed forward to catch her, the pair of them ending up on the ground.

'Fine,' Rust snarled. He looked at Teri and let out a bark of laughter. 'She's learned her lesson.' He strolled lazily over to where Teri was slumped and he leaned right over her, his nose millimetres from hers. 'You won't be rampaging through our territory ever again. Will you, bitch?'

Teri spat blood in his face. He flinched, but wiped it away calmly.

'Leave,' Fortune barked, the threat clear in his voice. 'You have had your justice, she will honour the boundaries to the best of her abilities. Let that be the end of it. If you linger on our turf, or initiate violence against any of us again you will feel the full force of our wrath.'

Rust straightened up and stalked away without a word, his pack falling into step behind him, injuries already beginning to heal.

Fortune saw them off while the pack gathered together. Shadow was at Ariana's side, Stone still held her, ensuring she was fully in control again.

'You did well,' Shadow told her gently.

'Thank you,' she smiled. 'Teri? Is she okay?'

'I'm fine,' Teri croaked. Wind Talker was helping her to her feet and Flames-First-Guardian passed her a handkerchief to wipe the blood off her face. 'I think I have a broken rib, but that'll heal soon enough.'

'Chew this,' Flames said softly, passing her a pinch of some herb from his bag. 'It'll help speed the healing.'

'We need to get back to safety, now.' Fortune said quietly, but firmly. The pack quickly pulled together and set off at a swift, quiet jog back to the betting shop. Ariana felt something stalking them on the way back, a demon just out of sight, not quite strong enough to take on a pack of eight shifters, but strong enough to consider it. She was glad to reach the safety of home.

Chapter Fourteen

Fortune was the first to speak, roaring at them and frightening Ariana for the brief moment that it took her to realise it was relief, not anger that he was expressing. He stormed over and caught both her and Teri in a tight embrace, dragging them inside and kicking the door closed in one fluid movement.

'Thank Luna you are both safe!' he cried. Ariana whimpered, hoping he would stop squeezing her if she submitted totally. He did let her go and turned to Teri.

'Are you all right?' he asked her softly, taking both of her shoulders in his hands. Teri nodded solemnly. Fortune tugged Teri's necklace from his pocket and placed it carefully over her head. She held it gently and smiled.

'Thank you,' she said quietly. 'I really hoped you would know it was a ruse.'

Ariana knew that Teri had much to tell them and that it wouldn't be easy. The rest of the pack moved in to welcome Teri home, Stone leaping in first. Ariana moved into a corner and breathed a heavy sigh of relief. Movement in the hall caught her eye and she nearly jumped out of her skin to see Grins-Too-Widely slipping silently into the kitchen.

The rest of the pack broke up and went quiet as the fox slunk into the room and sat down, cocking his head to one side. She got the impression that he was waiting for something. Flames-First-Guardian greeted their ally and asked the pack to follow him to the back of the shop. Dawn was just breaking and the shop was empty, so there was no need to cross the veil to hide their ritual.

He and Wind Talker cast a circle, Grins-Too-Widely walked the perimeter of it slowly. Ariana watched as

Flames led Teri into the circle and pulled a few of her hairs from her head. Teri hardly flinched. Flames burned the hair in a small bowl and then cut himself and Teri, mixing their blood in the bowl and then painting runes with the blood on Teri's cheeks. Sparks shot out from Teri and Flames, they darted around the circle, touching each pack member. Ariana stepped back in alarm, but Shadow placed his hand calmly on her back and nudged her forward again. She looked at him and his face was serene, reassuring. The rest of the older pack members were equally cool, though Eyes had flinched too so Ariana put her fear aside and put her trust in the ritualist.

She began to feel dizzy and shook her head to try and clear the fog that she felt building between her temples. She lost her footing and felt Shadow's warm hand steadying her, but she felt increasingly disorientated and her knees buckled. Around the circle the other young pack members seemed to be experiencing the same thing, she wasn't the only one on her knees and even Fortune was leaning over, bracing his hands on his knees. Blackness took over and Ariana let out a small cry of panic, but Shadow was there with her, steadying her and the fear abated.

She could see herself running, it was a memory and it wasn't hers. She was seeing the world through Teri's eyes and she could feel everything Teri felt as she ran in blind panic through Redfield Park and into Runmead, onto Wrecking Crew territory. She had run right into Fenwick and finally collapsed with exhaustion near the woods. The Witches encircled her and then knocked her out. Everything went black. When she awoke, Teri found herself in a dark basement and had been bound with silver chains, they burned her skin and prevented her from shifting. The agony lasted for hours, the Witches hadn't done anything else to torture her. Finally one of them came to Teri and questioned her about her family and her first change.

'You need to be with us,' she had stated plainly. 'You belong here. If you go back to the Blue Moon they will poison you with their lies, their lunacy.' She spat the word like it was filthy. Teri had listened to everything they said. They told her that Luna was insane and did not deserve to be worshipped, as the packs of Caerton thought she did. By renouncing her connection to the moon, Teri would become stronger and more in tune with her natural state of being. She wasn't chosen by an insane celestial, she was chosen by night itself. Teri stopped struggling against them, but not for a moment did she believe them.

They had released her from the chains and fed her, they treated her like one of the family and Teri let them believe it. She agreed to an initiation, she would forsake Artemis, or Luna as the Witches kept calling her. She would leave the Blue Moon and join the Witches. Three pack members took her back to the woods for the ritual and while they set up Teri had climbed into a tree to watch. Ariana looked down through Teri's eyes and saw the scene from above. The Witches drew circles with sparkling dust and placed bright gem stones around the clearing. Teri watched in wonder as green, blue and red stones of varying sizes were placed on the ground. A large topaz stone was placed in the very centre, it was polished and smooth, a perfect sphere. Light from the nearby fire flickered on it and it reflected the light beautifully. It looked like the sun, Teri thought and then it clicked into place; they had made a sort of orrery with stones to represent each planetary body in the solar system.

One young Witch stepped carefully over to the blue stone representing the Earth, she held a black pouch in her hand and opened it cautiously. As she bent to tip out the contents onto the floor something caught her hand and she leapt back with a growl. A tiny silver ball lay on the ground, just short of its intended mark next to the earth, the moon.

Teri knew what she had to do, but caution held her back. That was when she felt Ariana and Shadow nearby. Her pack had come for her and was approaching the clearing. Courage soared inside her, and determination not to let them walk into a dangerous situation. She climbed down from the tree and made a run for it. The young Witches were quick to follow her and Ariana's heart began to pound hard as she lived the memory of crashing through the trees. Teri circled around and cut back to the clearing. She ran into the empty circle and snatched the topaz sun from the centre, stuffing it into her pocket and hoping for the best, she shifted into her cat form and sprinted back into the trees. She dodged and weaved, leaving an erratic trail.

Ariana felt a jumble of memories, her own and Teri's all mixed together as they had felt one another on that run. Gradually Teri's memory began to fade, leaving Ariana exhilarated and clear-headed. She found herself lying on the floor of the betting shop and looking around saw the rest of her pack in similar states of disarray. Grins-Too-Widely walked slowly over to Teri and bowed his head to her.

'I am Weaver-of-Sky's-Loom now,' she spoke clearly to the pack. 'Let the fae know it and know that Artemis commands me, as a prophet and a bard.' A light shone from within Teri and Ariana watched in amazement as runes flared up on her skin for a moment and then faded to nothing. Grins-Too-Widely turned and disappeared across the veil as the pack rushed to congratulate Teri on taking her new name, Weaver. Ariana watched the space where the pack elder had been stood, elated for Weaver, but longing for a new name of her own.

Chapter Fifteen

Immediately after the ritual, Eyes had dashed away into a private room to call his wife. Ariana heard him talking on the other side of a door and passed quickly on her way to the attic, trying not to eavesdrop. It was clear that everything was fine at the other end of the phone, but Ariana knew Eyes would not rest easy until he could be back with them to guard them himself. Although Weaver was back with the pack they couldn't relax completely. The Witches might come back for her, or may even mount a full offensive against the Blue Moon. Eyes wouldn't feel that his family were safe yet.

Ariana curled up on a rug in the attic and slept all day, her aching body desperate to catch up properly now that her pack sister was home. Her sleep was troubled by bad dreams though. She dreamt of Rhys, dreams of longing and loneliness, and of the passion that she was so desperate for. There was a demon in her dreams too, weaving in and out of unrelated images, threading them together, although she didn't see the pattern until she woke. It was little more than a black shape, flitting at the corner of her eye, almost teasing her. She was still so new to this world, but she was coming to understand that demons weren't necessarily evil, they were neutral really, barely aware of morality, just like animals. She knew not to be afraid of this shadow in her dreams. In fact, she was compelled to find it.

She remembered how her dreams leading up to her first change had been a confusing jumble of worlds, how some things that had seemed like dreams had turned out to be psychic sleep walking into Hepethia. She wondered how much of her life she could trust now, what was still straightforward and what was touched by the magic she had only just learned existed.

When she was finally ready to face the world again Ariana joined the Blue Moon in the kitchen for another family meal. This was becoming a comforting and familiar ritual, and Ariana smiled on seeing her pack assembled and talking over burgers. She sat down between Shadow and Weaver, exchanging warm smiles with them both. Eyes seemed in better humour, chatting and laughing with Fortune, but there were dark circles under his eyes betraying the lack of sleep and deep worry that still plagued him.

'I need bodies out on patrol straight after dinner,' Fortune instructed, his mouth full of food. 'Be careful out there, everyone. Be vigilant and report back any slightly suspicious activity. Flames and I were running the borders all day and saw nothing, which is odd. I don't like it.'

Eyes moved quickly to their alpha's side as the rest of the pack began to move out but Fortune looked at him sadly.

'You can't return home, Eyes. We've been over this. If you reinforce your scent there they will get curious and they will track it right back to your family.' A growl rumbled in Eyes' chest and Ariana looked away in embarrassment. She felt sad for him, she could feel his frustration and knew there was nothing she or any of them could do.

Ariana followed Shadow across the veil. Grins-Too-Widely was waiting for them, sitting patiently with his head cocked to one side and that huge grin on his face. Shadow greeted him and led Ariana through the kitchen, which in Hepethia was warm and bright. The huge dining table filled the room, symbolic of the importance of meal times. A real stove burned against the back wall and the room was filled with the smell of cooking. Tiny motes of joy and family floated around the room, almost like Christmas lights. But there were small demons of worry sitting in the corners too. The tiny sprites here were not powerful, they didn't even seem sentient, let alone have names of their own. Ariana lingered to observe the room for a moment, before Shadow led her out through the back door. Grins-Too-Widely followed them outside.

The back street on this side of the veil was almost pitch black. The houses around them loomed ominously, the bricks were stained black and the windows were soulless and empty. Shadow and Ariana made their way up onto the roof via the fire escape and looked out across the territory. Ariana drew a sharp breath as she looked around. The dark sky rolled with heavy purple clouds and lightning flashed in the distance over the telecoms tower. The city was black in places and lit up like a fire in others, the contrast burned her eyes. Over in Northgate the factories were alive, literally alive. Giant monsters on the horizon, chugging plumes of thick smoke into the sky, they stirred and shifted with their heavy burdens. Ariana could even hear their moans carrying over the city towards her.

'Shadow?' She reached for him without taking her eyes from the factories. Her fingers found his hand and he twisted his fingers with hers and squeezed her hand.

'It's okay. I know it seems frightening, but by and large it is under control. The Blue Moon has held this territory for a long time, the demons and fae know us and know how to behave. But they can't change their natures, not easily anyway.'

'They look like they're chained down and trying to escape, but they're too tired to put up much of a fight,' Ariana whispered. Shadow chuckled and Ariana looked at him in surprise.

'That's almost exactly the situation.' He smiled at her and Ariana saw pride in his face. Ariana couldn't help but smile back. 'I'm going to run the northern border. I want you to stay here. Watch over the territory. Get to know how it looks from here. If you see anything to give you cause for alarm or if I'm not back in one hour I want you to cross back over and wake Fortune.'

Ariana nodded solemnly. She looked across the landscape again and wondered how on earth she was meant to tell normal from alarming. Shadow placed his hands on her shoulders and captured her eyes with his own amber ones.

'Don't worry, the others are heading for the borders now, they are the first line of defence. You will know if something gets past them, you will sense it.' His voice was soft and reassuring, but his words brought up a whole new wealth of causes for alarm. With one last look he shifted seamlessly into his fox form, ran to the edge of the building and leaped off the roof. Ariana dashed forward in time to see him dart into the shadows in the street below. Then he was gone.

'Okay Ariana. Don't panic. You're just on your own, in Hepethia, full of hostile demons and fae who don't know you. Nothing to worry about,' she muttered to herself.

'You're not on your own.' The voice made her jump and she spun around to locate it. Grins-Too-Widely was sat looking at her in his usual way in the middle of the rooftop. Ariana put a shaking hand on her chest and struggled to control her breathing.

'I'll keep you company for a while,' the fox said silkily, grinning at her all the while.

Ariana suppressed the discomfort she felt from looking at his freakish mouth as he spoke, the grin never faltered and the sounds that came out were a little bit wrong, a

165

symptom of the long life this former shifter must have lived. Ariana took a deep breath and cast her eyes across the territory again, trying not to look at the fox.

'Thank you. Can I ask, do we all become like you in the end?'

'If you survive, yes. Few do,' the fox replied. She could feel his eyes on her but couldn't look at him.

'Are you immortal?'

'No. Age may still end me, albeit very slowly.'

'How old are you?' Ariana's gaze snapped to the fox and he tilted his head this way and that, as if searching his memory for the answer.

'I do not know how to communicate that to you. The last time I took a human form was long before you were born and I was an old man then. Human measures of time mean nothing to me now. The seasons, the sunrises, it is all I know and all a blur, I cannot count them.'

Ariana couldn't imagine living so long and didn't feel like she would wish to end her days stuck in Hepethia in some distorted form. She shuddered at the thought and cast her eyes over the territory.

In the distance a black, winged shape swooped down from the tumbling purple clouds and took a dive into the dark city streets. When it emerged again there was something clutched in its claws and it disappeared back into the stormy sky. Ariana was startled and her eyes flicked directly overhead.

'Try not to worry. This place is well protected. We won't be troubled here.' Grins-Too-Widely spoke quietly beside her. Ariana nodded, she knew she could trust him, he was her ally. He may be difficult to look at, she doubted she would ever get over that, but she felt at ease in his presence. She thought about how he had protected and guided her when she ran to find Weaver and before that, when he had shown her the edges of the territory. The memory clawed at her, something didn't feel right. That was the night Weaver had been bitten, the first night. A deep frown creased her brow and she chewed the inside of her mouth, clutching at the details.

'You told me you would lead me to my new name. The night Weaver-of-Sky's-Loom was bitten. I think you were wrong, it was her that found her name following those events.' She looked down at him to see him gazing out across the city.

'I set you on the path. You have a short distance still to travel, but you will find yourself.' His voice was distant, as though his thoughts were really somewhere else. Ariana didn't like the cryptic answer.

'How will I know the path?' she asked, frustration causing her voice to crack.

'You will know. Follow your instincts. Your name is a reflection of your true self, who you are and who you will be, it is already inside you waiting to be found. Trust yourself. That is all you can do.' He was still gazing away from her and silently he stood up and took a step closer to the edge of the roof. She followed his gaze but couldn't see anything remarkable in his eye line. She felt frustrated by his advice, impatient to find answers and she let out a small snarl. Without a backward glance at her, however, Grins-Too-Widely stepped off the edge of the roof and disappeared into the night.

'Great. Just great.' Ariana leaned against the chimney stack and sighed. She waited, watching the sky and the streets below. She saw huge shapes lift themselves out of the streets and drop back down. More winged creatures swooped out of the clouds and the factories never ceased in their rhythmic groaning and lurching. Ariana let her thoughts roam over recent events, trying to put all of the pieces together, to make some sense of the chaos of the last four days. Her eyes began to feel heavy and drift out of focus.

A dark fluttering shape at the corner of her eye grabbed her attention, but the moment she looked for it it was gone. She stood to attention and scanned the roofs of the terrace leading away from her. There was nothing there. There was something familiar about whatever she had glimpsed, however, and she started walking carefully along the rooftop. She reached the end of the terrace but had seen nothing and she soon began to doubt herself. With a sigh she turned and set off back to the betting shop. As she approached she heard a noise on the fire escape and carefully she peeked over the edge. Shadow hopped nimbly up over the top rail and onto the roof beside her. She breathed a sigh of relief and stepped back from the edge.

'Are you all right?' Shadow asked. 'You look like you've seen a ghost.'

'No, nothing like that, I'm fine, thank you. Just a bit jumpy I suppose, from being here alone in the quiet.' Her shoulders gave an involuntary shudder and Shadow gave a nod of understanding.

'Of course. Let's go inside.' He let her go first, and together made their way back down to the ground and back across the veil.

All was quiet in the betting shop. Fortune was still sleeping. Weaver and Eyes were sat talking quietly in the kitchen when Ariana and Shadow entered. Stone, Flames and Wind Talker hadn't returned yet, but it was still early.

Ariana helped herself to some food while Shadow disappeared upstairs. Weaver leaned close to Ariana as she sat down beside her and whispered conspiratorially.

'Eyes and I are talking about making a break for it.' She flashed Ariana a wicked grin, but Ariana scowled at her.

She looked at Eyes, who was still looking worn down, his head in his hands and his eyes fixed on the table. He glanced up, apparently feeling her eyes on him and he shrugged.

'I'm sure we could take care of ourselves, the three of us,' he whispered.

Ariana couldn't quite believe what she was hearing.

'And do what? Go where? Eyes might be feeling cooped up and worried for his family,' she hissed. 'But you, Weaver, you just got back from being abducted and tortured. Why on earth would you want to go out there without... the others?' She crossed her arms and stared down the pair of them. 'I nearly said without a grown up then.' She huffed, feeling like a young teenager rather than a grown woman.

'It's not just feeling cooped up though, is it?' Weaver spoke softly and there was sadness in her eyes. 'It's Eyes' family being in danger and him wanting to protect them.'

Ariana tutted. Weaver had a point.

'It's way too dangerous,' Ariana sighed.

'Not if the three of us go together,' Eyes whispered urgently. 'The scents would be jumbled up together and harder to identify.' He looked at Ariana with such intensity and she could feel how desperate he was to be near his family. She felt herself softening.

'All right but it's a reconnaissance mission only. We get as close to your house as we can without getting close to the territory border and we watch the place for a while.' Eyes started to object but Ariana held a hand up to stop him. 'I won't budge on this. I know you want to see them, but you've spoken to them on the phone and know they are fine for now, so we guard them tonight, that's all. I won't have you leading the Witches right to your door.'

He opened his mouth with objections, but he promptly

closed it and gave one curt nod, an appraising look on his face. Weaver grinned and moved quickly to the back door.

'Let's go now, quickly while the coast is clear.' She held the door open and Ariana and Eyes dashed out into the cool night. Weaver closed the door and the three of them shifted form silently and set off running. It was the first time Ariana had seen Fights-Eyes-Open in his wolf form, his fur was grey, almost silver. Weaver was a stunning, black cat and Ariana took her fox form, as was becoming habit. She wanted to try changing into something else, but Shadow seemed to want to keep her ability a secret, even from the pack and she quickly pushed the thought aside in case one of the others caught hold of it through their pack telepathy.

Ariana thought about sending out her plea for protection to Grins-Too-Widely as she had done before, but quickly changed her mind. She didn't want to draw attention to their clandestine night wandering. The last thing they wanted was for the old fox to go straight to Fortune and tell him what they were up to. Instead she thought only of the night and the darkness and willed them to hide her and her young pack mates.

As she did so she glimpsed a flicker of pure black shadow chasing them, the same image in the corner of her eye that she had seen on the rooftop. Somehow she knew that the three of them would not be seen or heard. Her silent plea had been heard and they were protected from those senses at least, if not the most important one for their kind, the sense of smell was still against them. Eyes had been right about the mingling of their three trails, it would be confusing and more difficult to pick out any one, though their combined trail would be easier to follow.

Ariana led the others down back alleys, through gardens and down deserted back streets. They managed to stay cloaked in shadow almost all of the time and Ariana felt the influence of the powers she had invoked at work.

Soon they were drawing close to the neighbourhood that Eyes and his family lived in. The three odd animals slowed to a brisk walk and crept in the shadows towards his street. Ariana sniffed the ground and the air around them. There was nothing to cause any alarm. She caught images from Eyes' mind that showed her which house was his and just as she had insisted he came to a halt nearby but not too close. It was a wide street, trees and bushes lined the roadside and many houses had driveways and large gardens. Ariana could just make out a very nice looking black car in the driveway of Eyes' house.

The three of them settled down amongst some bushes on the opposite side of the street and about four doors down from his house. The street was quite well lit, which hindered their ability to hide, but it was late at night and the houses were all dark. There was a stillness in the air and it sent a small shiver of concern up Ariana's spine.

They sat there for what felt like hours. The occasional car swept past them and they hunkered down low to the ground to hide themselves from the headlights. Ariana was anxious, there was a nagging sensation in her gut that something was not quite right. The night was too quiet and she thought that one of the others would have come looking for them by now. She was just trying to communicate this to Weaver and Eyes when a sudden gust of wind blew a flurry of fallen leaves down the street towards them. All three of them jumped up, their heckles raised. The leaves blew right past them down the street, leaving a trail of dropped leaves in the wake of the wind.

We have to leave right now. Ariana thought and Weaver meowed in agreement. Eyes looked wistfully at his house and Ariana knew he was torn. Why come here to guard them if only to flee the moment something threatens them? She understood how he felt but every instinct told her to get away from this place, for the very safety of his family and for themselves. She led them up a small side road and back towards the betting shop, sticking to the small, unlit roads so that they could run hell for leather without too much fear of being seen.

Several times on the run back Ariana saw or heard this strange gust of wind, apparently blasting its way right through their territory, picking up leaves and debris from the road on its way and dropping it again in its wake. Like a mini tornado streaking through St. Mark's.

They arrived back at the betting shop just ahead of the wind. Shifting form mid stride Ariana burst in through the back door. The kitchen light was on and the rest of the pack were assembled waiting for them. Fortune burst forward and pulled her into the room. Weaver and Eyes slipped in behind her and someone slammed the door.

'Where the hell have you three been?' roared their Alpha, still holding Ariana roughly at the elbow.

There was no time for an explanation. The front door of the shop crashed open and the window pane rattled ominously. Shadow's Step was the first into the hall but the pack were close behind him. They jockeyed for a position to see from inside the small cash office and Ariana felt the veil shuddering with the influence of eight shifters and a powerful elemental all in the vicinity. The fae that had rampaged across their territory and burst into their headquarters manifested before them. It was clearly a wind elemental, it was a pillar of swirling air with debris trapped within its folds of mist.

Stone and Fortune were at the front of the pack, Fortune took an aggressive stance, but Stone, the pack negotiator raised a hand to calm him.

The elemental spoke, its voice nothing more than a whisper rushing through the air, but Ariana felt it go right through her, it echoed around the room and the words couldn't have been more clear.

'Keep the mewling wretch. We're finished.'

And as suddenly as it had entered their realm the elemental was gone, leaving the Blue Moon silent and every eye on Weaver-of-Sky's-Loom.

Chapter Sixteen

20th November

'Okay. Well that's good, right?' Weaver said quietly, looking around at the pack.

'Eyes,' Fortune barked. 'Get back to your family.' Eyes was out of the door before the Alpha had even finished. 'Everyone else, get some rest. It's been a long few days for all of us.' Fortune stomped up the stairs while the others lingered for a moment. Ariana felt unsettled by his abruptness. Could this conflict with the Witches be over so suddenly? She didn't quite believe it.

Weaver looked sheepish, Ariana sensed that she was embarrassed and just as unsure as Ariana was.

'Listen to Fortune,' Shadow said softly, patting Ariana on the shoulder. 'Get some rest.' He passed them and followed Fortune upstairs. The others drifted off. Morning had broken amid the chaos, so Flames went to open up the shop. Stone took Weaver up to the attic and Wind Talker decided to head down to the basement, having had some rest while Ariana and the others had been guarding Eyes' family. He cast her a dark look as he passed her, and her insides squirmed with guilt for excluding him.

She sat down at the kitchen table and pulled out her phone. This new life was exciting and terrifying, but more than anything else, it was pulling her away from the things she had wanted for so long. She looked through her old messages from Rhys with a sense of longing, she needed him in her life, she missed him so much.

> Hi. How are you? Life has been manic here. Really hope to see you soon, love Ariana xx

She rested her head on her arms on the table and closed her eyes, exhaustion starting to take hold of her. Just as she started to drift off to sleep, her phone buzzed on the table and startled her. She grabbed the phone and opened the message.

```
Hi, so glad to hear from you. Pretty
manic with work myself. Yeah, would be good
to meet up soon xx
```

Ariana smiled and thought about when and where to suggest meeting. Her life was so unpredictable now. How could she possibly make plans and keep them? Frustrated, she punched a brief reply into her phone.

```
OK, I'll be in touch soon and let you
know when I'm free xx
```

She stood up, shoved the phone into her pocket and went to her little room to sleep.

21st November

Something resembling normal life began to take shape over the next day. Ariana slept a lot during the day and found herself up at night, like several other pack members and she supposed that this was normal in a family of largely nocturnal animal shifters. Lily slept in a room of her own, away from the pack and dutifully worked in the shop, as she had done throughout the chaos of Weaver's abduction. She asked few questions and yet seemed to know everything.

They were sitting together for their evening meal. Stone and Fortune jostled around them preparing and serving a tasty fish and pasta dish. Lily leaned in close to Ariana and gave her a friendly smile.

'We're both different, Ariana,' Lily whispered carefully. Ariana regarded her closely and then glanced around the kitchen to check that the rest of the pack were not eavesdropping.

'How do you mean?'

'Well, I can't change at all yet and you, well, there's more to you than a scruffy urban fox.'

Ariana was taken aback.

'I don't, I can't imagine, I mean that's just... what are you saying?'

'Well, I was only mildly suspicious, but your reaction just confirmed it. What is it? What is so different about you?' Lily asked, her voice full of excitement.

Ariana looked around anxiously again. No one was paying them the slightest bit of attention.

'I seem to be able to shift into a cat too, maybe other things but I haven't tried. It's been total chaos and when I found out I wasn't normal it freaked me out. Shadow knows, so it's not a total secret or anything and I really want to talk to Fortune about it.'

Lily's eyes went wide.

'Can you show me?'

Ariana grinned and nodded. The two young women slipped away quietly and snuck down into the basement. Ariana had tried hard not to think about her unusual ability and with everything that had happened since she changed it had been easy not to dwell on it. Now that she had the chance she was excited to see what she could do. Lily took a seat on the bench and watched expectantly.

Ariana shook out her limbs and concentrated hard. She knew she could shift into a cat, so she tried that first, willing her body to take the shape of a small, grey cat. She felt everything crunch and shrink and shift, then looked up at Lily watching with wide eyes.

With a shake and some serious focus, Ariana made herself stretch and change into a beautiful dark grey wolf. She turned a few circles in the cold basement, trying to catch sight of her own tail and Lily erupted into peels of laughter.

Ariana let out a low bark of elation and then concentrated on the black and white, shuffling form of a badger, a moment later she was compelled to dart for the shadows under the stairs, drawn into the darkness by her new badger instincts.

She emerged and focused all of her will on the form that she thought would be hardest to achieve, being the only flying animal among the usual shifter forms, an owl. She had no idea if she could do it or if she would be able to fly if she managed it. With great force of will, Ariana made her body change. She pictured a snowy owl and felt her limbs creaking and straining to take that form. With a delighted hoot she flapped her wings and managed to take off and flutter slightly awkwardly up off the ground and over Lily's head. Lily clapped and cheered as Ariana flew around the small space as best she could with such limited room.

She landed clumsily on the floor and decided the time had come to really push the boundaries. She knew now that she could take any of the five shifter animal forms, but what about something else? There were countless species of animal on the planet. She had seen her hands become lion paws during her first change and with a sudden burst of lion's courage, she pushed outwards with her wings and little legs and directed the image of a proud lioness to the forefront of her mind.

It was by far the hardest change she had attempted, it

actually hurt a little as all of her bones and muscles shifted with crunching, scraping sounds. Lily watched with a hand raised to her mouth as Ariana changed shape.

Ariana felt very strange, so much heavier than in any other form, and so powerful. She prowled around the basement, trying to focus her thoughts and keep them ordered. It was hard, her animal brain was stronger in this form, her instincts stronger. Just as the badger had sought out the darkness, the lioness wanted meat. She took a few steps towards Lily but stopped in her tracks when her eyes locked onto the girl. Lily was stood on the bench, pressed against the wall. She stank of fear and her eyes were wide in terror.

Ariana let out a whimper of an apology and backed off. A moment later a noise on the stairs grabbed her attention and her head snapped towards the intruder.

Fortune and Shadow stood near the top of the stairs, their eyes wide.

'What the hell?' Fortune barked and Shadow placed a steadying hand on his shoulder.

Ariana shifted quickly into her human form, her heart was pounding and she was sure the Alpha could hear it threatening to leap out of her chest.

'I'm sorry,' she stammered, looking down at the ground. 'Lily, are you OK?'

Lily nodded, still visibly shaken up. She slowly stepped down off the bench and took a few cautious steps forward.

'That was just incredible,' she said after a moment's pause. 'I can't believe you can do that!'

Ariana felt relief wash over her and the two girls laughed and embraced one another.

'What was that?' Fortune snapped, jogging down the stairs to them. 'How did you do that?'

He caught hold of Ariana's shoulders and looked at her,

turning her this way and that and inspecting her eyes, hair and neck. Ariana let him and stifled a giggle.

'I don't know. I just can. I think I can be anything.'

Fortune looked severely at Shadow.

'You knew,' he stated accusingly.

'I did,' Shadow said softly, stepping down off the last step. 'Or I suspected. She shifted into a cat on the first morning we spent down here.'

'Why didn't you tell me?' Fortune released Ariana and turned on Shadow, his chest puffed out and his voice barely more than a snarl.

'We were a bit distracted,' Shadow stated simply, remaining perfectly cool. 'I was going to tell you, when the moment was right and when I had had chance to look into the matter myself first.'

Fortune spun away and paced the basement, his eyes flitting between the three of them. Lily looked nervous, but Shadow stayed calm and collected, he was obviously very sure of his place. Ariana didn't know what to think. She caught a glimpse now of how her difference might scare other shifters and she realised that might be very dangerous for her.

'I'm sorry, Fortune,' she whispered. 'I should have told you. It wasn't Shadow's secret, it was mine.'

'No,' Shadow said quickly. 'I urged you not to mention it.'

'It doesn't matter,' Fortune snarled. 'What matters is figuring out what you are, why you are and how to keep it from the other packs.'

Ariana flinched. She was a shifter. Wasn't she? His words cut like a knife. She knew she was a little different, but hadn't doubted her species before.

'I'm a shifter, just like you. Artemis made you one way, when she turned you under a full moon. Well, she's made

179

me another way. I don't know why. But we're more alike than we are different.'

She tried to pull herself up to her full height, which wasn't a patch on Fortune's, but it was all she could do. He stopped pacing and looked her hard in the eye.

'What else can you do?' he challenged, his tone benevolent, and she grinned in response.

'I don't know. But it will be fun to find out.'

The next two days were filled with more training with Shadow. She tried out lots of different animal forms with him, both in the basement and outside in Hepethia where she had more room. She flew over the buildings as a hawk, sprinted along the street as a jaguar and played on the fire escape as an orangutan. The birds were hard work, flying didn't come easily and it was necessary for her to spend a few minutes getting used to it each time. The bigger mammals were hard to shift into, and definitely seemed to take over her rational human mind more easily than other forms.

The rest of the pack ambushed her about it and had spent a long time questioning her after she had emerged from the basement with Fortune, Shadow and Lily. Wind Talker didn't seem remotely surprised and speculated on other possible occurrences of this phenomenon among shifter kind. Weaver gave Ariana a knowing wink that told her she had known all along.

Despite the fuss everyone made over her, Ariana felt that she had caught sight of what ordinary pack life would be like.

Fortune ordered a new punch bag for the basement to replace the one Eyes had shredded a few nights previously, though Ariana had a sneaking suspicion that Eyes had paid for it, and as soon as it was delivered a queue formed to try it out. There was also some much needed down time for the whole pack. Most of them slept for long stretches, but there was time for a little mundane maintenance too, chiefly shopping.

The betting shop kitchen housed a huge double freezer and it needed restocking with the meat on which their large pack was inclined to feast. On the Thursday morning Ariana went with Stone and Weaver to collect their order from the butcher. They received some odd looks from the customers and the butcher himself as he bagged up package after package of meat. All three of them left carrying several bags packed to bursting with steaks, burgers, sausages, bacon, minced meat, chicken, pork, liver and even some disturbing offcuts and specific body parts that Flames had requested, which Ariana was certain couldn't be for eating.

That night Flames called the pack to join him in the shop for a ritual in honour of the newest members. It had only been a week since Ariana's first change, though it seemed like a lifetime.

It was the first time Ariana had seen Eyes since their escapade to his house, he had returned home to his family and was spending as much time with them as he could in order to make up for his absence in the preceding days and nights. They grinned at each other on sight, a shared camaraderie between the two of them and Weaver from their unauthorised adventure and the trouble they had been in afterwards.

'So I heard a rumour that you're a little different,' he said as they made their way into the shop and across the veil.

'It's true,' she replied with a wicked grin. 'Sorry for not telling you right away, it was all a bit weird when Shadow and I first established it and then Weaver got snatched.'

'It's fine, I'm not remotely offended. I understand. So you can be any animal you want?'

Ariana nodded and Eyes gave her an appraising nod. 'Very, very useful.'

They both laughed and gave each other a friendly nudge.

'Ariana,' Flames interrupted. Her attention went to him as her laughter subsided. 'I'd like you to help me cast the circle, please.'

'Of course,' she replied, a little surprised.

He passed her a smudge stick and invited her to walk around the circle with it, while he and Wind Talker opened the ritual. She was happy to be involved and took on the task with enthusiasm, even though it was quite mundane. She walked around the room waving the smoking stick of herbs as the rest of the pack formed a circle. Flames made a circle of red sand on the ground just behind the feet of the others and Wind Talker lit candles. In the middle of the circle was the fire pit and a selection of tools, including Flames' large knife with a bone handle, and several protective amulets.

Flames held up the bone knife in one hand and a selection of macabre items in his other, including two eyeballs and something red and stringy that looked suspiciously like sinew.

'I open this rite by invoking protection fae to us, see that we are not disturbed this night. All hail to Luna, we ask that you watch over and bless this pack, The Blue Moon. We invite our ally, Grins-Too-Widely to join us.'

The fox slunk into the shop and sat down next to Fortune in the circle. Once the room was suitably smoky Ariana placed the smudge stick next to the fire pit and took her place in the circle. Flames gave her an encouraging nod before continuing.

'We welcome our newest pack mates to the circle, Wind Talker, Fights-Eyes-Open, Weaver-of-Sky's-Loom and our newest youngster, Ariana.'

Ariana felt a little pang of jealousy and frustration that she was the only one without a shifter name, her plain old human name, unusual as it was, sounded so wrong in that list. Stone stood next to her and gave her hand a squeeze, apparently picking up on her feelings, which Ariana tried to put aside.

'We honour the waxing moon, Luna's face grows brighter and the time of the half moon comes again. We ask for balance, fairness and justice at this time. The growth of our pack is a blessing. But it has been a troubling period and we are thankful for the respite we have been recently granted, and ask that we enjoy more peace and stability in the days to come.'

Across the circle a small chuckle escaped Fortune's throat and the rest of the pack smiled and stifled laughter of their own. Undeterred, Flames continued.

'We celebrate the safe return of Weaver-of-Sky's-Loom from captivity and honour her new name. Let the world know that our business with the Witches is not concluded, justice will be sought, but patience will be the victor. There is no peace between us but let quiet days and nights be ours.' Flames passed a small bowl to Wind Talker and took the bone knife to his own open palm. Blood trickled into the bowl. 'My blood, the pack's blood, is shed to keep us whole and sacred. We honour our power and our duty. We are Luna's subjects and we spill our blood in her name.'

As he spoke, Flames cut Wind Talker's palm and allowed the blood to flow into the bowl. Wind Talker then took the knife and went around the circle, cutting each pack member in turn and mixing their blood together. He came to Ariana last and gave her a reassuring smile as he opened a vein on her palm, she tilted her hand so that a few drops of her blood ran into the bowl.

Wind Talker returned to the centre of the circle and

passed the blood to Flames. He held the bowl up over his head, dipped the assorted bits of animal into it and then threw them onto the fire, which hissed and spat angrily. Ariana saw strange movements in the flames, shapes that resembled various animals and humans twisting over and around each other. It was sort of beautiful and infinitely fascinating, if a little morbid.

'We give thanks to Luna and all of the fae present and close this rite.' Flames tossed some sand onto the fire and it went out with a loud hiss. Smoke billowed out and then dissipated. The pack broke into lively discussion but Ariana watched Flames as he carefully transferred the pack's blood from the bowl into a small brown vial and tucked it away into the satchel across his shoulder. She knew how potent their blood was and supposed that mixed together it would be even more so, but she couldn't help wondering if he had some specific purpose for it in mind.

Fortune ushered everyone back across the veil and through to the kitchen, where he set about cooking up a feast. Ariana and Stone helped and in no time the pack was sitting down to generous helpings of spaghetti bolognese, and Fortune fetched a few bottles of mead from the basement.

The pack sat around the table sharing jokes and stories. Weaver told the story of how she had escaped the Witches, painting vivid pictures with her words and Ariana grinned every time Weaver added a little embellishment here or there. Storytelling seemed to come so naturally to Weaver, she became so animated with it and it made Ariana very happy to see her pack-sister so comfortable and happy.

Stone helped ensure no member was left out, each of them taking a turn to entertain the others, though she seemed to instinctively know who was least comfortable taking the limelight and respected them completely, chiefly

Flames-First-Guardian, who hardly spoke except to add his deadpan humour to other people's stories.

The pack grew quiet and listened attentively to Shadow's Step speak in his soft, lilting voice.

'My grandfather was a respected elder in his village in India, his true nature was known and he was deeply venerated. The culture there at that time was very different to here and now, shifters were known of and celebrated, they protected their families and villages fiercely. He was known as a nāga, a snake skin shifter, they don't seem to exist on this island.'

He gave Ariana a little smile and she returned it, thinking of his cobra form and her potential to take a snake form too. 'My father came to Britain during the late days of the Empire, having just escaped being drafted into the military to fight in the Second World War due to being too young. He worked as a serving boy to a wealthy family in Caerton. He had never changed, but when he married another immigrant from his new community he had shared the stories of his family with her and I was raised in full knowledge of my lineage. My father couldn't have been more proud when I did change, and I protected my community as he would have done in India, though with much greater emphasis on secrecy and keeping my nature from becoming known in Caucasian circles.'

Shadow was vague about dates, but Ariana guessed that her mentor was about fifty now, though he looked much younger.

When he finished his tale there was a lingering quiet around the room. Eyes broke the silence at last, fixing his steady eyes on Fortune.

'Tell us about your first change, Fortune.' His face was serious but full of yearning and Ariana had to admit that she was curious to know about the Alpha's history. She knew he was older than the rest but not by how much. Flames let out a gruff bark of laughter and took a swig of his drink. Fortune ran his finger around the rim of his glass, his eyes glazed over.

'Well, there's nothing quite like the dropping of bombs to scare a young pre-change shifter into changing.' Weaver and Ariana both took a deep breath of surprise and glanced at each other. Lily was sat next to Ariana and she shuffled in her seat uncomfortably. The rest of the pack were silent. Fortune glanced up before looking back to his glass and continuing. 'The change can happen at any time. Puberty is not uncommon. But for others it is later.' His eyes flicked back to Fights-Eyes-Open, who was by far the eldest of the four newest shifters. 'Often it happens at a time of great stress or trauma. I got the double, I was fourteen and it was the Blitz. It was a terrible time for Caerton. The port here was a big target, military ships were built here and it was a major import venue for Britain's food supplies. So we got hit pretty hard.

'I was not raised by my kin, I grew up in an orphanage and knew nothing of our world. When I was twelve I ran away and found work in a factory making shell casings. Despite the air raids and the city being blacked out, the factories couldn't shut down. Just like today, they ran all night, it was far too expensive to shut down the machines and start them up again in the morning, so we worked through the air raids. One night we were hit. The west side of the building collapsed and the screaming began. The lights went out and the fire spread quickly.

'I was just a child really, I was terrified and I changed right there in the chaos and blood and flames. Artemis chose a full moon for me, so I shifted right through the wolf and into the beast. I must have slaughtered a dozen men, women and children on my rampage through the wreckage, but at last I found my way out into the open and ran. I made it half way across the city before my limbs gave way and I found myself naked and covered in blood, sweat and dirt in the shadow of St. Mark's church. The Blue Moon found me and took me in.' He picked up his glass and knocked back the last of his mead.

The room was utterly silent and Ariana had tears streaking down her face. He had told the story without a single crack in his voice, not a tear shed or a trace of a frown, no sign of pain or weakness at all, which Ariana found all the more moving. She didn't know if it was simply the passage of time that had eased the pain out of the memory, or if he was just a skilled expert at hiding it, but either way she felt for him deeply.

She looked around at the pack, Flames and Shadow had clearly heard the story before, but kept a respectful silence. Eyes looked pained but not surprised and Ariana wondered if Fortune had already told him some of the tale in private. Weaver was shaking a little. Stone was sat next to the Alpha, her face was cast down but Ariana thought she saw a streak of a tear on her cheek and she couldn't help but notice Stone's fingers lightly brushing against Fortune's hand resting on the table. His fingers twitched and for the briefest second he returned the affectionate gesture before yanking his hand away and clearing his throat.

'More mead!' Flames cried and started refilling everyone's glasses. The rest of the pack followed his lead and lively conversation began to flow again. Ariana joined in but Fortune's story echoed in her mind. It put her own first change into perspective and she felt a sense of release.

In the early hours of the morning Stone announced that she was going to have a quick look around the neighbourhood before sleep and Ariana volunteered to go with her. Stone didn't object and they left together, walking out into the cold night. They walked in silence for a minute or two, Ariana wanted to talk to Stone about Fortune's story and the subtle exchange she had witnessed. It probably wasn't any of her business, but she couldn't deny her curiosity.

'Fortune's story was really moving,' she said at last. Stone kept walking, staring straight ahead. 'It really put my change into perspective for me,' Ariana continued. Stone still didn't respond and Ariana began to feel a little foolish. 'Had you heard him talk about it before?'

'Yes,' Stone sighed. 'Yes, he's talked about it with the pack and privately to me too. When I first joined the Blue Moon he was in a bad place and needed to talk things through, I was the first female to join the pack in decades. There are some conversations men can only have with women. You know?'

Ariana nodded and waited for Stone to go on.

'He bottled a lot of it up for a long time.'

'And that made the two of you very close, didn't it?' Ariana asked, sensing that she was right.

'Yes.'

'Stone, do you love him?' Ariana was grinning, hoping to tease out a confession. But Stone stopped walking and glared at Ariana.

'No,' she snapped.

Ariana's smile faded and she felt as though Stone had thrown cold water in her face.

'Sorry. I didn't mean to assume anything,' Ariana stammered.

'No, it's all right,' Stone spoke with more softness and set off walking again. 'I should explain, you weren't to know. Once I would have said yes. Once, so would he. There is still love there, but it is like that between brother and sister.' Stone stopped again and took hold of Ariana's elbow gently. 'Shifters aren't supposed to fall in love with their pack mates. It's wrong, it's like incest, or bestiality, or both. I don't know, it's just strictly forbidden by our kind. We can breed with shifters from other packs, humans and those humans with shifter blood. But not our pack mates. It's important for our survival, it's genetics. Do you understand?'

Ariana frowned. This revelation came as a surprise, but as she thought about how she felt towards her pack mates she understood. In a very short time they had become her family. She had never been close to her own family and had hardly spoken to them since she moved to Caerton, her pack were the brothers and sisters she had never had. The idea of forming a romantic attachment to any of them was deeply unsettling now that Stone mentioned it.

'Yes, I do. That makes sense.' They set off walking again, but Ariana mulled over exactly what Stone had said. 'But it happens sometimes. It nearly happened with you and Fortune?'

'Yes. Nearly. But we never even spoke of it with each other and this is the first and only time I have ever or will ever speak of it with anyone.' There was a trace of threat to her voice and Ariana understood completely.

'Of course,' she whispered.

They finished their walk around the block in silence and returned to the betting shop. It was dark and quiet inside and the two made their way upstairs to join the others in the attic. Ariana decided to stop by her room to check her phone on the way and let Stone go ahead without her. She felt so sad for Stone and Fortune, such a tragedy to have love denied to them like that. It made her think of Rhys with deep longing. She had felt that, she had come so close to what she thought could have been a true love and had felt it slip away from her. She sat on the bed and looked sadly at her phone. No new messages. With a heavy sigh of resolve she typed a message to Rhys.

```
I need to see you. I miss you. Xxx
```

It was far too early for him to be awake, so Ariana left her phone in the room and went to join the pack upstairs.

Ariana's sleep was disturbed with dreams of Fortune raging through flaming rubble and a sense of deep longing. A black shape flitted through her dreams, it seemed almost familiar, but too illusive to be certain. Whatever it was, it stalked her and troubled her enough to keep her tossing and turning and waking to the black attic and soft breathing of her pack-mates. Fortune and Stone slept on opposite sides of the room, Ariana noticed, and she went back to sleep thinking of lost love and loneliness.

Chapter Seventeen

23rd November

When she awoke it was still only early in the morning and the rest of the pack was still sleeping. She went back to her room to check her phone and her face lit up when she saw that there was a message waiting for her.

```
I miss you too. Are you free for lunch
today?
```

Her heart pounded and she quickly replied.

```
Yes. Where's good for you?
```

She tapped the side of her phone while she waited for a reply.

```
There's a café just around the corner
from work, The Spoon. Is that OK for you?
How about 12.30?
```

Ariana grinned and confirmed eagerly. She knew the place, it was where she used to have lunch with Ben, a whole other lifetime ago. With a sigh, she headed for the house bathroom to freshen up. She took a shower and gelled her hair, then dressed in her usual clothes and headed for the kitchen to make breakfast for everyone.

Cheerfully, she fried bacon, sausages and eggs. She ate her fill while she kept on cooking vast quantities of food. Gradually the pack joined her and she served everyone with a big grin on her face. Weaver took a plate of food with a knowing glint in her eye and Ariana caught her arm as she started to turn away.

'What? What was that look for?' Ariana whispered. 'Did you see something?'

'No, I don't need to. Love is all over your face.' Weaver smiled warmly and sat down to eat.

Fortune took his food with a mildly suspicious look and he watched her carefully while he ate slowly. Finally everyone had food and Ariana sat down next to the Alpha.

'I was hoping to go into the city today, to see a friend.' She wasn't asking his permission, exactly, she fully intended to go, but she wanted him to give his blessing. She waited patiently while he chewed slowly and thought it over.

'That's fine. But get off the bus in China Town and walk the rest of the way, okay? Don't go to the station. That's claimed territory.'

'Sure,' she grinned. 'I'll do that, thanks for the caution.'

'And Ariana,' Fortune took her arm firmly as she stood to go and wash up the pans and plates. 'Be careful with this friend of yours.'

'I'm not going to tell him anything I shouldn't.' She was a little surprised at Fortune's serious tone and a little offended that he would show so little trust in her.

'It's not that, well, not just that,' he sighed. 'It can be hard to maintain friendships with humans after the change. You're different now, remember that.'

She nodded in acknowledgement and moved to the sink. She refused to let Fortune's serious words dent her excitement about seeing Rhys and she went about washing up, daydreaming about Rhys.

An hour later, Ariana practically skipped to the bus stop, she felt elated at the prospect of seeing Rhys and was happy to be doing something normal for the first time in a week. It was a taste of her old life, which, if she paused to think about for a moment, she was missing. She was no longer free the way she had been, she answered to her alpha and she had obligations that were so important they had to come before every other thing in her life. She had seen already how this life could challenge relationships from the way Eyes was kept from his family, but she had to believe that it didn't have to mean the end of everything she knew.

She did as Fortune had said and got off the bus a mile before reaching the bus station, in the heart of bustling China Town. It was yet another wet day in Caerton, and the streets heaved with heavy traffic. Ariana made her way south, reaching the city centre just after noon. It was such a dramatic change of pace to St. Mark's and she looked at everything with new eyes and new heightened senses.

She remembered what Shadow had said about how powerful the demons and fae here were and she looked at everything with awe. The buildings seemed bigger and older than she remembered, the streets seemed busier, the cars louder and the people seemed almost alien to her.

She walked past a shopping centre and glanced at the wet entrance steps, remembering Fortune sitting there, hooded and strange, watching her have coffee with Ben. It seemed an age ago. Now he was her dearest brother and her whole world was different. She crossed the road and shoved the maudlin thoughts from her mind as she entered the café opposite.

The café was bustling inside, determined not to sit outside in the cold and rain she found a small table in the back corner and got comfortable.

She was only waiting a few minutes when Rhys walked in. She sensed him before she saw him and looked over to the door in time to see him wiping rain from his face. He was just as gorgeous as she remembered, tall and athletic, dark and brooding. He took a quick look around to locate her and when his eyes found her the world seemed to slow down for a moment, then he made his way over to her through the crowd. She leaped up and smiled broadly as he drew her into a tight hug.

'Hi,' she breathed into his shoulder, drinking in his musky scent. 'I've missed you.'

He released her and sat down in the chair opposite, smiling his amazing smile.

'You look really well. Glowing I'd say,' he said with a curious edge to his voice. 'Have you done something different with your hair?'

Ariana reflexively patted her unruly mop and stifled a laugh.

'Thanks. New mousse,' she fibbed and felt a satisfied feeling settle in her stomach that he had noticed her altered appearance but didn't seem too bothered by it.

'How have you been?' he asked, leaning across the table. Ariana noticed that he was wrapped up against the cold and it occurred to her that she should probably start doing the same if she wanted to blend in, though she didn't really feel the cold all that much any more.

'Erm, busy,' Ariana stammered, laughing at the understatement.

Rhys nodded grimly in apparent understanding.

'Me too,' he stated solemnly.

They ordered coffee and food and Ariana found herself desperate to know his thoughts. She had glimpsed the depth of power that was available to her, and it occurred to her that it might be possible to gain the kind of telepathy that she had with her pack to use with others. She sighed and tried to think of something to say.

'What is it?' Rhys asked, frowning and starting to smile at the same time.

'Nothing,' she shook her head. 'I'm sorry for not keeping in touch while I was ill and being so crap this week.'

'Don't worry about it.' Rhys reached across the table and offered her his hand. She took it and he squeezed it gently. Ariana felt a tiny spark go through her, a glimmer of hope. She was frustrated at how little she could tell him about her life and wondered how they could possibly have a real relationship now. She chewed her lip while she thought frantically of ways to step around the secrets that filled her life.

'I've made some new friends recently,' she offered as a compromise. He raised a curious eyebrow and Ariana realised she couldn't leave the statement hanging there, she was going to have to construct a careful embellishment. She thought for a moment. 'Just some people in my neighbourhood. We met in my local pub last week.'

'Oh, right,' his voice was full of caution.

She took a drink to delay more of a response. What could she say? Was there anything she could say that would keep her pack's secrets safe and divert Rhys away from this subject?

'So, work has kept you busy then?' Ariana asked, diverting the conversation smoothly onto Rhys and she worked hard for the rest of their lunch to keep it that way.

As they got up to leave Rhys took her hand and held it as they left the café. Ariana grinned to herself as she followed closely behind him out of the busy café and into the wet street. It was beginning to feel easier and as he pulled her into one of his warm hugs she felt that surge of hope again. She breathed deeply against his knit sweater, taking in his scent, feeling his heart pounding against her ear. She felt his reluctance to pull away as he slowly did so but she couldn't help smiling, he was smiling too, but it was a sad smile of goodbye and longing.

'I'm going to be really busy at work this week, probably next week too. But I'll keep in touch by text message and we can try and meet up again soon. I promise.' He still had hold of her hand and he caressed the back of it with his thumb, sending a warm shiver up Ariana's arm. She managed to nod slowly, the tingle still rushing through her as he gently let go of her hand. 'Bye,' he said softly and leaned close to kiss her cheek.

Ariana's breath became shallow and she felt a wave of intense longing. She didn't want to just be friends with this man, every fibre of her being wanted him and it took all of her will to let him walk away from her. Something felt very wrong and sad about their parting and as Ariana made her way back to the betting shop she had a terrible feeling that she would never see him again.

Darkness fell quickly over the city later that afternoon. The nights were drawing in and the rain was relentless. The attic above the betting shop was developing a strong smell of wet animal hair. That night the pack ate together as usual, though Ariana felt somewhat more sombre than she had done at breakfast. After the meal they went their separate ways. Fortune took Ariana's arm as she started to follow Shadow towards the basement.

'No. I want to take you out.' He released her arm and moved towards the back door. Ariana followed him, a nervous knot forming in her gut. They crossed the veil into Hepethia and Fortune led Ariana outside into the street. Across the road a darkness demon slithered out of sight into the shadows of the building opposite. A shiver crossed Ariana's spine as they started walking. Fortune led them silently north towards Redfield Park. The rain pounded on the street and Ariana was soaked to the skin within a few minutes, but she didn't complain.

She felt eyes on them from the shadows and the buildings towering over them, she felt as though they were being followed and kept glancing over her shoulder, but if there was was something there it was staying hidden. Fortune walked just ahead of her, seemingly confident but ever watchful. She didn't know if he could feel the same things she felt, if he did he was giving no sign of it. She quickened her steps to draw level with him and glanced into his face.

'There's something tailing us,' she whispered.

Fortune inclined his head down towards her, a grim expression on his face.

'Yes, there is,' he stated solemnly. Ariana looked around again, she caught movement out of the corner of her eye but it was gone the moment she tried to latch onto it. She turned and walked backwards, casting her eyes across the road, looking for signs of whatever was following them. The road was slick and wet, deep puddles had formed at the edges of the road and in dips in the pavement, the pouring rain thundered on the wet surfaces causing big splashes with each giant drop, and the spray filled the air.

Ariana focused on a puddle by the side of the road about twenty meters behind them, the movement of the rain on the surface didn't look quite right, something moved in the spray and she stopped still, grabbing hold of Fortune's arm to alert him. He stopped beside her and she pointed to the rippling movement in the rain. Ariana bent down and squinted into the darkness, trying to get a better look at whatever it was. The swirling spray moved suddenly towards her and Fortune and she leapt into a feral and defensive stance. Fortune took a step back and Ariana kept her eyes fixed on the elemental moving closer through the spray. It was without form, but it moved through the rain and spray and the water bounced off it and rolled down its indistinct sides.

She didn't know if it was hostile or not, it could have been a messenger, so she remained defensive but waited. The elemental stopped in front of her, she could see its height now as the rain bounced off it just higher than her own head. A sudden movement caught her eye but not in time and she felt the impact across her face, an ice cold slice to her cheek and she stumbled sideways.

Rage mounted inside from her gut and she let out a roar as she shifted form, growing in height and sprouting thick fur all over her body, her muscles stretched and strengthened, her face became a snout and her teeth were long and sharp. Her clothes had melded into her body, but her swords remained strapped across her back, the straps had stretched around her enlarged torso. She stood shaking in the pounding rain, she was the beast she feared. But she was fuelled by the impulse to defend herself, so the fear abated and she struck out at the illusive fae. She hit only air and rain and she stumbled forward into the space that the rain elemental had occupied only a moment before.

She spun around and sniffed the air, but the rain disguised any hint of a scent the fae might have had. Ariana centred herself, fighting the beast in her chest and subduing it enough to still herself and focus on her surroundings. Fortune stood on guard a few meters away, but looked calm, watching the scene carefully, also trying to locate the fae.

The next hit landed across Ariana's back, a whip of ice sliced through her fur and skin, stinging and causing her to take a reflexive step forwards away from the pain and its perpetrator. She twisted and reached out her arms, catching the invisible fae in her grasp, probably somewhere around its middle, and with a roar she wrestled it to the ground but it slithered from her grasp like water escaping through fingers.

She leapt up and snarled but was promptly knocked back to the floor by a solid blow to her shoulder. Thinking quickly she jutted a leg out and spun quickly around, knocking the fae over and where it landed the puddles sprayed up, revealing its form on the road. Like lightning she pounced on it and ripped with teeth and claws. Again, the elemental seemed to leak away from her and she groaned with frustration when she could no longer feel it under her thighs.

A cold sensation crept over her and she felt the creature covering her, moving all around her and then it was gone, the fae had passed over and around her and reformed behind her. Spinning around, she drew both of her swords. The rain bounced off the blades, making an almost musical sound, and they looked so small in her hands now that she was transformed into a great, hulking Agrius – half human and half bear. She lunged at the elemental with her blades outstretched and felt them slice through something, pulling it apart. With a roar of satisfaction she leapt again and struck out with her deadly blades but it evaded her. She knew it was injured and allowed herself to pause, waiting for a sign of its location.

There was a sound nearby, the sound of water trickling down a drain and she focused her sharp eyes on the spot the sound was coming from. She could make out its hunched form in the spray of the rain, it quivered with its injuries and the puddle beneath it was growing too rapidly.

With a final burst of fury Ariana bounded over to the elemental and went in for the kill, driving her swords into its middle and slashing outwards, ripping the creature into pieces. She felt the cold essence of its being all over her as it disintegrated under her attack, ice chips flew as she ripped it apart and they stung her as they showered over her face and body.

She was still roaring when she felt Fortune's presence behind her and instinctively she leapt to turn on him, but as soon as her eyes came upon him she felt calm wash over her and the rage began to subside.

Ariana, Ariana, calm down. It's Fortune, your Alpha. Shift down. His voice was inside her mind, and slowly her form shifted back to human. She stood shaking from the adrenaline coursing through her. She could feel the spirit matter lingering on her body, it was more than water, there was something of its being, like blood, still on her skin and clothes and she felt a jumble of emotions about the kill. Fortune gently placed his arm around her and pulled her to him in a warm embrace.

'Let's get back,' he whispered against her hair and he led her silently away.

Ariana sheathed her swords and Fortune slung an arm over her shoulders.

Ariana was intensely satisfied that she had made her first kill, her blood pounded in her veins and she knew she had done her job, done what she was born to do. But she was frustrated at herself for being caught off guard and for not being able to contain and subdue the elemental on her first strike. She also felt a strange sense of remorse and sadness, as though something precious was gone from her now that she had fought for more than competition and personal satisfaction. She had felt the rage in her, just as she had the first time she changed. It frightened her and she felt again that she had lost a part of herself to the beast. She had killed now, albeit a supernatural being and not a human. The human law would not care and in terms of supernatural law she was in the right, but she had a sense of sadness about taking a being from the world, a being that had as much right to exist as she did. She let that gnaw at her on the walk home and she knew that Fortune would be picking up some of it, but he did not say anything and she was thankful for that.

As they entered the house and crossed the veil again Fortune released her and watched her carefully for a minute.

'You did well, your training is coming along nicely,' he said softly.

'Was that a test?' Her eyes flicked up to meet his as she sat down at the kitchen table, dripping water on the floor from her sodden hair and clothes. Fortune tossed her a kitchen towel from a nearby drawer and she began to dry her hair.

'It doesn't matter if it was or not. Every time you step out there you have a job to do and you did it tonight. Demons and fae have to be subdued and controlled. If they step out of line, including attacking us without provocation they have to be put down.' He sat down opposite her and they held each other's gaze for a long moment before Ariana shook her head a little with relief.

The two of them sat and talked, they went over the brief fight and carefully analysed it. They celebrated her victory and Ariana soon felt good about what she had accomplished. They were still dissecting it when the pack entered late in the evening from their patrols and training sessions.

'Ariana made her first kill,' Fortune cheered as they entered and she was met with lively congratulations. Shadow patted her firmly on the back and leaned over her shoulder to congratulate her solemnly.

'I'm proud of you.' His words shot to her heart and she choked back the threat of a sob of gratitude.

Fortune patted Shadow hard on the shoulder and grasped his hand and arm to shake and congratulated him on training Ariana so well.

'You should take her to meet your friends, Shadow,' Fortune said with a sly grin on his face. Ariana looked between her two mentors, curious. Somehow the idea of anyone having friends outside of the pack seemed very odd, but she remembered that Weaver had other friends too, that she had been prevented from seeing after she was bitten. Shadow regarded Fortune carefully for a moment and then nodded.

'I'm meeting some of them tomorrow night. We have an event the night after and have some preparations to discuss.' He gave Ariana a reassuring nod and a small smile on seeing her puzzled expression.

Fights-Eyes-Open sat down next to her and leaned in close.

'So? Tell me about it?'

Ariana laughed.

'Honestly, I probably didn't do as well as I should have. Have you gotten into a fight yet?' she asked in a low voice. Eyes grinned and nodded.

'Fortune took me out a week after I joined the pack too. I think he's been rumbled.' Eyes chuckled, Ariana sighed and glanced across at the Alpha as he talked animatedly with Flames, Stone and Weaver.

'I thought it was a test.' She shook her head and suppressed a small laugh. 'Afterwards, it just felt like he stood back and let me deal with it.'

'Was it a rain elemental?' Eyes asked shrewdly, taking in her wet appearance. Ariana nodded. 'With me it was a derelict building construct. Big hulking stone thing with wires and cables sticking out of it. I tried crushing it by knocking a wall down on it but that made it stronger. I

202

literally had to rip it to pieces.' His eyes lit up as he remembered the fight and Ariana smiled at him, loving the energy buzzing from him. She recognised him as a kindred spirit, he fed off the thrill of the fight, thrived on it. 'Fortune will have tested you in a different way,' he said suddenly, his wistful expression changing back to his shrewd one. 'You're not just about brute strength. You're like Shadow, cunning. I bet a rain elemental was quite an elusive challenge for you.' He grinned at her and she laughed in response.

'You could say that. I can't say I'm eager to come up against any kind of water elemental again.'

'Wait until you have to fight fire,' Flames-First-Guardian spoke softly right behind her and she whipped around in her chair to look at him. His eyes had that far-away glaze that she was becoming accustomed to and she didn't probe more deeply into his comment. She turned back to Eyes.

'You know, you don't look like the brute force type.' She cocked an eyebrow and tugged at the lapel of his suit jacket. Eyes chuckled.

'Looks can be deceiving.' He winked at her and she giggled. Fights-Eyes-Open was of a medium build, but she could tell he was strong beneath his smart clothing.

'Why do you wear a suit?' Curiosity piqued and Ariana couldn't help asking. 'What are you when you're not a werewolf?'

'A barrister.' They both laughed but she knew he was serious. She had a sudden mental image of him in court, smart, articulate and passionate. He had the big house and the nice car. It all fit. Their laughter subsided and she wondered how easy or difficult it would be for him to go back to work now.

'Have you been to work since you changed?' she asked

quietly, unsure she wanted to know the answer, fears about her own future gnawed at her as she asked.

'No,' he said, shaking his head. 'But I need to go back this week. I took annual leave and my time is nearly up. It'll be interesting to say the least.' He gave her a quick smile and she tried to return it.

Their lives really weren't their own any more, but she was encouraged that she wasn't the only one who was willing to try.

Ariana allowed herself to enjoy the attention of the pack, the requests to recount the fight and the way the pack rallied around her. She was relieved though when Stone drifted away to get some sleep as it gave her a window to do the same. She didn't sleep with the pack that night, she slept in her little room, cradling her phone in her hand, hoping for a message from the outside world. She dreamed of the rain and of the elemental she had destroyed. In her dream it didn't slip through her fingers, she was fierce and in control, she remembered all of her training. She was perfect.

Chapter Eighteen

24th November

The next evening, after another hard day of training and uneventful patrolling, Ariana boarded a bus with Shadow. They sat in easy silence. Throughout the day Ariana had asked him questions about his friends and where they were going, but he had been vague in his responses and kept telling her that she would see for herself. She had given up asking and now sat looking out of the window of the bus, curious and a little impatient.

Their bus skirted the northern edge of the city centre and turned west, crossing the river and heading into Old Town. Caerton was a very old city. Once a Roman fort had stood here, then a Viking castle. Old Town still held the remains of the Norman castle and town, built over the Viking one. The city's oldest museum was located here and some major tourist attractions, such as the Dungeons and the city's premier theatre. It also housed a few narrow Tudor streets with cobblestones and some quirky independent shops selling everything from traditional sweets to bespoke wedding gowns.

The bus stopped just around the corner from the museum, on the main road that was jammed with traffic. Ariana followed Shadow quickly and quietly through the bustling streets of late night shoppers. The road was still a little wet, though it hadn't rained all day. She wondered if that had anything to do with her destroying a rain elemental the previous night. She watched Shadow carefully as they went. His eyes were so sharp, looking everywhere at once, and she quickly stopped watching him and followed his example. She cast her eyes around, looked carefully into the deep shadows around doorways and alleyways. They left the busy main road and walked briskly up a dark side street. There were cars parked on either side and visibility was poor, so Ariana tried to use her other senses but found it frustrating, they just weren't as sharp in human form as in some of her animal forms.

'Can you tell me where we're going yet?' she whispered. She was unsure why, but some instinct told her to keep a low profile. Shadow glanced at her.

'This is the territory of The Watch. A very old pack. We are on vaguely friendly terms with them and they know we are coming, but it pays to be prudent.'

'Are they the friends we're meeting? The Watch?' she asked and he shot her another look.

'One of The Watch will be there, he offered to host, the other is coming in from Fenstoke.'

'But that's on the other side of the city centre.' She frowned. 'Why didn't we meet in the centre on neutral ground?'

Shadow stopped walking abruptly and turned to face her, a trace of impatience on his dark face.

'The city centre isn't exactly neutral, no one claims it so it's neutral in that sense, but it is rife with urban demon activity. It's not a safe place, Ariana. Not for any of us. We meet on claimed ground so that someone is in command of the elements there.'

'I see,' Ariana answered meekly. She felt a little chastised and foolish for asking so many questions.

Shadow set off walking again and she followed quickly and silently.

After a few minutes Shadow slowed slightly and grasped an iron railing to his right. He turned and jogged up some steps leading to a tall, narrow house in the terrace of townhouses. There was a small brass plaque by the large, wooden door, but Ariana couldn't read it in the dark. The door swung open and Shadow produced a slip of paper from his pocket. A hand emerged from the shadows to take the slip and a moment later the door opened wide to admit them.

Ariana followed Shadow inside and past the be-suited figure that had admitted them. Shadow led her into what appeared to be a small and secluded private club, reminiscent of an old gentleman's club, but no one batted an eyelid at Ariana's presence. There were a few people sat in comfortable chairs around small tables and a fire blazed in a large grate at one end of the main room. Shadow led her through the lounge and into a small private room. There was a fire burning in here too, one low table sat before the fire and deep sofas sat on either side of it. She felt Shadow relax as they entered the room and found two men deep in conversation. The men looked up as Ariana and Shadow entered and broad grins erupted on their faces.

'There he is,' the younger of the two called as he rose to greet Shadow. He drew him into a brotherly embrace and Shadow's face lit up with warmth and energy. The older man grasped Shadow's arm with both of his hands in a sort of old fashioned hand shake.

'Sorry we're late,' Shadow said with a smile. 'Not right of me to keep an old dog waiting.' He nudged the older man with his fist and the three of them chuckled.

This was by far the most animated Ariana had ever seen her mentor. These two new shifters were fascinating. She felt instantly submissive to them, the elder of the two exuded power and authority, this was his territory and she knew it. He looked far older than any other shifter she had yet seen and knowing how old Fortune was despite appearing to be no more than fifty, she guessed that this ageing shifter was into his tenth decade or more. He wore loose clothing, a wooden staff propped against the sofa he had been sitting in when they arrived had to belong to him. He had long, messy grey hair and scars on his weathered face. He was dressed like an ageing biker had the look of the wolf about him, like Fortune.

Shadow took her arm and brought her closer to the fire, a wide smile lighting up his normally serious face.

'This is Ragged Edge,' he said, indicating the old man. Ragged Edge extended a hand and she took it, his grip was firm and commanding. He shook her hand and eyed her carefully. The warmth he had shown Shadow was gone. His shrewd eyes were narrow and serious, but she sensed caution behind them, not hostility. 'Don't let the staff fool you,' Shadow said, a mocking smile etched on his features. 'It's no walking stick.' Shadow sat down and spread his arms out over the back of the sofa. Ragged Edge chuckled, it was a low and gravelly sound deep in his chest.

'Pleased to meet you,' he said quietly, a hint of warmth creeping into his gruff voice.

The other man nudged him aside. He couldn't have been more different. He was tall and broad with skin the colour of black coffee and several piercings in his ears. He looked about Ariana's age, though that didn't necessarily mean much.

'I'm First Strike,' he said. He grinned and grasped her hand. She couldn't help but smile back.

They each took a seat by the fire, Ariana ended up next to First Strike and felt a little flustered. He was warm and charismatic and she found him extremely attractive. But Rhys popped into her head, and a gnawing sensation travelled quickly from her gut to the rest of her body. She blushed and averted her gaze, focusing on Shadow's skin, glowing in the firelight.

The three men got down to business, Ariana tried to

follow the conversation but much of it went over her head, with references to names and places she didn't know.

'The barrier will keep humans out, of course and it will be totally sound proof,' Shadow said, very matter-of-factly.

'What's the radius?' First Strike asked, leaning forward on his knees.

'A hundred feet, that should encompass the venue and a little beyond,' Shadow replied.

'How many do we need to cast it?'

'Three,' Ragged Edge replied. 'We're well prepared.'

Ariana allowed the conversation to wash over her. It was clearly nothing to do with her and she allowed her mind to wander.

Suddenly she was aware of the drop in conversation and saw that Ragged Edge had turned to her and was watching her carefully. She felt herself growing uncomfortable under his gaze.

'Shadow's Step has told me that you have a gift for combat,' Ragged Edge said slowly and thoughtfully. Ariana shifted her weight and nodded once.

'He tells me that too. I've always trained, before I changed I was a martial arts instructor.' She smiled with pride and saw Shadow give her a quick nod of encouragement. First Strike stirred beside her and she glanced at him, he was grinning.

'What do you think of what you can do now?' he asked, a sly look in his deep brown eyes.

'It's awesome,' Ariana returned his broad grin.

The four of them talked for a while about Ariana's background, how she was adjusting to life as a shifter and her passions. She felt a little like she were being analysed and wasn't really sure what to make of it all, but she tried to answer their questions openly.

'Where are your family?' Ragged Edge asked, sipping his whiskey.

'On the south coast. I grew up there but moved to Caerton when I was seventeen. I haven't really seen my family since. We were never close.' She didn't mind talking about her family, though didn't know why they were asking. Ragged Edge simply nodded.

'Do you think it's possible that any of them might relate to what you're going through now?' First Strike asked carefully, a change in tone from him. Ariana was surprised by the question and paused to give it some thought.

'No, I don't think so. But I was adopted. I don't know anything about my birth parents. I never felt close to my adoptive family because I always felt different from them. Now I know that wasn't just because I was adopted.'

'We should examine her lineage,' Shadow spoke softly to Ragged Edge, but didn't try to prevent her from hearing, she frowned at him as he spoke.

'The Scroll Keepers could help there,' First Strike said quietly, barely above a whisper.

'Excuse me, but why does my lineage matter?' Ariana had images flashing through her mind of elite groups among the shifters who were obsessed with heredity, like the human aristocracy and the Witches. The three men looked at her, Shadow barely hiding a smirk, First Strike grinned at her and Ragged Edge just stared at her thoughtfully.

'Does it matter to you?' he asked carefully. Ariana frowned and thought for a moment.

'It hadn't occurred to me before. I'm not an elitist or anything, I couldn't care less about a person's family when it comes to rank or leadership. Do we have more potential with stronger blood? Is it a biological thing? And I mean really, not in a "Divine Right of Kings" way.' Her thoughts flickered to the absent heir to the throne of Caerton, but she squashed the thought down and turned her focus back to the present moment.

Ragged Edge smiled and almost broke into a throaty chuckle.

'I don't know much about biology, but I'm not really sure the normal rules apply to us. It's not about power or leadership or potential. It's about heritage. Caring where we come from and the deeds of our ancestors. Do you care about that?'

'Honestly, I haven't had time yet to even think about it. I guess, now you mention it, it is weird. I understand a bit about the shifter trait in our blood and that some of us change and some don't, so my biological family must have a history of it and yes, I would like to learn about that. I never used to think it was important, but my views have changed recently.'

'Well then,' said Ragged Edge, standing up. 'Come with Shadow to the gathering tomorrow and meet the others. You have promise, Ariana, and I think you will be accepted should you choose to join.'

Ariana stood up with the others, confusion filling her as Ragged Edge shook her hand again.

'I'm sorry, but join what?' she asked cautiously.

Ragged Edge looked quickly between her and Shadow and then smiled warmly.

'Why, Odin's Warriors, of course.'

The elder shifter placed a heavy hand on her shoulder and gave her one last long look, like he was studying her, reading her. She thought of the ability Shadow had taught her and became uncomfortable under Ragged Edge's careful consideration, wondering if he was doing that to her. She wondered what he would glean from her soul.

First Strike opened the door and the four of them filed

out through the club, drawing the wary attention of the other members, who looked up from their strong liquor and stalled their conversations to watch these four strange characters stride through the stuffy lounge.

Ariana thought it a very odd place for shifters to meet, but supposed there must be reasons for it. Ragged Edge could easily have been a member of the club for decades.

They stepped out into the cold night and said their goodbyes. Ragged Edge set off one way up the dark, tree-lined street and First Strike walked with Ariana and Shadow to the other end of the street before taking a right where they turned left.

Ariana and Shadow moved quickly through the streets of Old Town. Ariana's head was still spinning from the bizarre meeting with Shadow's friends. She was annoyed that he hadn't told her anything about them or why they were meeting them and resented being assessed like that without her knowledge. What if she didn't want to join this group? She knew nothing about them. Shadow had promised to talk to her about it when they got back to the betting shop, so for now Ariana was silently stewing over it.

When they arrived back at the shop the rest of the Blue Moon were busy with their own tasks. Shadow took Ariana to the kitchen and started to get food out to cook for the pack. Ariana stood and watched him as he started chopping meat and vegetables. She leaned against the tall freezer and crossed her arms over her chest.

'Well? Are you going to tell me what that was all about?' she asked him, a touch impatiently.

'What is there to say?' he asked, not looking up from his work. He tossed her an onion and she grudgingly joined him at the worktop and began chopping.

'What if I don't want to join Odin's Warriors?' she mumbled.

'You will,' he chuckled and they glanced at each other, Ariana reluctantly smiled back. 'You won't be able to resist now you know they exist. The fight will call to you, from your very blood and you'll be drawn to others who feel the same.'

Ariana watched him carefully for a long moment. She thought of the way Eyes had been drawn into his thoughts when they talked about fighting.

'Is Eyes a member? Or will he be?'

'Maybe. That's for him and Fortune to talk about. I suspect Fortune has other ideas for Eyes though,' he said softly, throwing chunks of beef into a pan. Ariana frowned but didn't say anything. It wasn't the first time she had felt that each of the older Blue Moon members were steering their protégés toward something. Maybe that was normal among their kind though, there were a lot of things about their society that were different from what she was used to and every day she was sacrificing a little of her old life and her old expectations. She wasn't in control of her own destiny, but she realised now that she never had been. Her whole life had been steering towards this change and this life. She didn't know what she was meant for now but she felt it was something important.

'I need you to tell me more about them. I think I know what you mean about being drawn in a certain direction, but I am still a rational being and I still need information to base my decisions on, Shadow. I can't promise I will always follow you, I might want different things to you.'

He stopped chopping and looked at her.

'I know,' he sighed. 'Just as in human society, shifters each have their own interests and talents. Some of it is in our blood. Weaver was born a prophetess and she can't

213

change that, but that's not all she is. You were born to fight, you've always known that, so was Eyes but you won't necessarily both feel it pulling you in the same direction. You're drawn to the dark places, to the silent kill. Eyes is, well, he is a born leader. Like Fortune. Odin's Warriors attracts both kinds and everything else in between, but we're spiritual at heart. I can't really tell you much more, you have to see for yourself.'

Ariana was intrigued. One of the things about her martial arts that had always called to her was the inner peace and stillness it gave her, the focus she had learned from years of meditation and the ability to listen to her spirit. It wasn't something she really talked about much, but it had always been present in her life and it was something she had applied to other areas of her life too.

She was a no nonsense kind of person, she didn't articulate herself that well all of the time and she didn't think this was something she could or should share with anyone. Had someone else tried to tell her they felt those things before she might even have dismissed it as hippy crap, despite sharing those feelings herself. But Shadow telling her this now made so much sense and different cogs of her life suddenly clicked into place and were finally turning together.

'Ariana? Ariana?' he was saying her name softly and she realised that she had drifted into her own little world for a moment.

'Hmm?' She slipped back into the present moment and took a deep breath. 'I was just thinking about how that made sense. The spiritual thing. Are there other groups then?'

'Well, not really in the same sense, not organised groups as such, but we each have other friends among our kind.'

'Who are the Scroll Keepers?' Ariana asked, going back to her chopping.

'They're record keepers, basically, they do a lot of research into bloodlines and shifter history. There aren't many of them now though, there doesn't seem to be as much appeal in that course for many young shifters,' he said with a sad sort of smile. 'Flames is one of them, though. We'll talk to him about looking up your line.'

Ariana stifled a snort of surprise, causing Shadow to look up from the cooking.

'Sorry,' she said, trying not to laugh. 'That just caught me off guard. But I suppose it makes sense. I guess it's a fairly solitary calling?'

'Yes, mostly.' He was trying not to smile but the corners of his mouth betrayed him and soon they were both laughing as they finished frying the meat and onions.

'Ariana,' Shadow broke the laughter with a return to his quiet and serious voice. Ariana stopped laughing. 'The pack comes first. We may have other contacts and friendships outside of the pack, but we're family and we always come first.'

'I know,' she put her hand over his and looked into his eyes. 'I know that. I feel it.' She smiled and to her relief he returned it with a smile of his own.

'Well that's okay then.'

The pack assembled briefly for a meal and Ariana told Weaver all about meeting Ragged Edge and First Strike. Weaver had never met them and listened with interest. All too soon Stone was whisking Weaver off, Fortune left with Eyes and Flames took Wind Talker out. Ariana sighed, longing for a time when their training would ease off and the youngsters could all spend some more time together.

Chapter Nineteen

25th November

It was gone midnight and Ariana was starting to get tired, having spent the day training and an evening out across the city. But her mind was buzzing and she slunk out through the back door for some peace and quiet in the still night before turning in. She climbed the fire escape and went onto the roof to look out over the city.

Her eyes adjusted quickly to the darkness and she looked over the territory, pausing to peer into dark corners and the shadows between cars. It was as though she were automatically tuning in to the territory, the way Shadow had been teaching her to.

A movement half a block away caught her eye. Just a glimpse of a shift in the shadows, but it had her attention. It was the same shifting in the corner of her eye that she had been experiencing for a few days. Stepping to the edge of the roof and peering over she tried to focus on the movement, but her dull senses weren't up to the task and with a sigh of frustration she shifted into the form of a wolf. She ran along the edge of the roof, just above the guttering, all the way to the end of the terrace and leaped down onto a garage roof and down to the ground. She set off running after the mysterious shadow.

She caught the scent of an intruding shifter. For a split second she contemplated going back to alert Fortune, but knew that she had one chance to track down the intruder. So she put her nose to the ground and set off. The trail was incredibly hard to follow, it was a much lighter scent than she was used to and she lost it a few times, only picking it up again when the wind made subtle shifts in her favour. It was male, so it couldn't be one of the Witches and it wasn't a familiar scent from the Wrecking Crew either.

The trail led her to the southern edge of St Mark's and the boundary of Blue Moon territory, but it didn't cross the border into China Town. She followed it up a dark alley to another fire escape like the one at the betting shop. She shifted silently into her human form and climbed the ladder deftly. She came out onto a flat rooftop with high walls and a small cabin in the centre with a door into the building. Deep shadows were thrown across the roof by the orange street lamps just below roof height. She could feel the presence of the one she had been following, though she could no longer smell him in her human form.

Her heart hammered in her chest but she summoned her courage and called out.

'Hey. Who's there?'

A movement behind the cabin got her attention and a slick, dark grey wolf padded out, his nose to the floor in submission. He shifted before her into a tall, slender young man with long black hair tied in a loose ponytail, his clothes were dark and loose and he wore a pendant on a leather strap around his neck. He raised his hands and stepped into the light.

'Hi. I'm sorry to alarm you. I crossed into your territory in pursuit of...' He stopped and looked at her hard for a moment, a small smile of wonder crept onto his face. 'Huh.' He dropped his hands and cocked his head.

Ariana took a defensive stance and watched him carefully, she felt a strange sense of connection to him, a glimmer of trust and warmth, but she didn't entirely trust the new feeling.

'What?' she snapped at him, narrowing her eyes.

'She's called to you,' he whispered, stepping closer to her again. 'You're on the path.'

Ariana twitched, confused, to say the least.

'What are you talking about?' she hissed at him.

'Pursuit-of-Midnight-Solitude, she's called to you, hasn't she?' He smiled, but faltered seeing her confused expression. 'Oh. You haven't answered the call yet.'

Ariana planted her hands on her hips and scowled at him. She did not appreciate being spoken to in riddles.

'Look. You can't just run across other people's territory,' she huffed at him, impatiently.

'I know. Fortune knows me, he gave me permission to cross your territory when I need to. Check with him. I swear. You must be new to the Blue Moon. My name's Hunter.' He took another step towards her and Ariana twitched nervously. He held up the pendant around his neck so she could see it in the light. It was a circle with a hole in the middle and there were small runes carved into the metal. She squinted to see them clearly, cursing herself for not having paid enough attention to the runes Flames-First-Guardian was always using in rituals. It was the written language of their kind, but there had been no time yet for her to study them.

Deciding to save face rather than admit she couldn't understand his apparent free pass, she relaxed.

'Okay. So what is this Pursuit-of-Midnight-Solitude?'

Hunter smiled and Ariana couldn't help but smile too.

'I think she'll be making that clear to you soon.'

Ariana flung her arms up in exasperation.

'You aren't going to give me a straight answer are you?'

Hunter burst into a warm laugh.

'No.' He looked down in mock sheepishness with surprising schoolboy charm. 'It's against the rules. I can't show you the path, you have to find it for yourself. But I can tell you've been called. You feel it too don't you?

We're on the same journey, you just haven't let yourself follow the path yet.'

Her conversation with Shadow rang in her ears, about being called by her blood and suddenly she wasn't sure she was meant for Odin's Warriors, but that didn't feel right either. Did it have to be one thing or another? Could she have two things calling her? Something else tugged at her memory too, Grins-Too-Widely had spoken to her about her path. He'd used that word, path, just as Hunter had.

'Are you all right?' Hunter asked softly, he took a few steps towards her. She startled a little but quickly regained her composure.

'Yes, fine, thank you.' She didn't know where to look.

'You know what I'm talking about now, don't you?' he whispered. She nodded and closed her eyes as the pieces began to fall into place in her memory. 'Good,' he whispered in her ear.

Then he was gone and she opened her eyes with a start, just in time to see him disappear over the side of the building. She ran forward and leaped up onto the high wall with ease, but by the time she had got her balance and leaned over to look down into the street he was lost into the shadows.

She searched the street below for him but he was gone. Ariana jumped back down onto the roof, propped her elbows on the wall and stared out at the night. The shadows she had seen in her dreams and those demons that had disappeared suddenly on her catching sight of them now felt as though they were taunting her, inviting her to follow. In Hepethia a darkness demon had even grabbed her, perhaps to drag her into the chase, or possibly just to claim her as its own. She wasn't sure, but she did know now that it wasn't all coincidence.

As if on cue, movement caught her eye a few car lengths

away and the shadows seemed to blend and shift around something. It was Pursuit-of-Midnight-Solitude. She knew it. She felt the elusive being calling to her, begging her down from the roof. It was three storeys, she was not about to jump as Hunter had. She ran for the fire escape, descended swiftly and shifted back into her wolf form in the dark alley, before sprinting out into the street.

Hunter's scent was gone already, Pursuit-of-Midnight-Solitude left no scent either, but she felt her call and followed it. The shadows seemed to dance before her, teasing her and she pursued the spirit relentlessly across St Mark's, unsure whether it was a demon or fae. It took her all over her territory, past her flat just a few blocks away from where she had started, up alongside the river and into Northgate where the factories churned and hissed. The shadows here were deep and dark and Pursuit-of-Midnight-Solitude led her right into them. Ariana felt the shadows clinging to her, hiding her from prying human eyes, she knew her scent would be light, almost impossible to track, just as Hunter's had been.

The chase took her east into Redfield and then south, past the looming telecoms tower and back into St. Mark's. She was led down back streets, through gardens and through the underpass that enabled pedestrians to cross the huge roundabout where the two dual carriageways that crossed north Caerton met. The lights in the underpass were out and it was pitch black. Ariana raced through, soaking up the darkness and when she emerged on the other side her fur had absorbed it and turned a darker shade of grey.

Ariana knew that she wouldn't ever catch the spirit, that wasn't the point, the point was the chase, the quest, embracing the darkness and running in the night. It was thrilling and everything she had been excited about since she first knew what she truly was.

Eventually it led her home to the back yard of the betting shop, where Shadow's Step was sat waiting for her on the step in front of the back door. He smiled as she strode into the yard, resuming her human form with a wild grin on her face.

She could feel the most important words of her new life pulsing through her. She felt the call of the night, Pursuit-of-Midnight-Solitude had spoken to her as she ran and called her by her true name.

'Are you all right?' Shadow asked, still smiling knowingly.

She nodded, breathless from her run.

'Yes,' she managed to say at last. 'I met someone.' She threw her head back and looked at the cloudy sky. Light rain fell on her face.

'You've changed.' Shadow stood up and stepped towards her. She looked at him with a broad grin that wouldn't go away. She felt something brush against her legs and looked down to see Grins-Too-Widely slinking past them. He sat down and looked at them, they returned his gaze.

'Did you enjoy your run, Stalker-of-Night's-Shadow?' he asked and she laughed.

'Yes. How did you know?'

'I know your spirit,' he seemed to shrug before twisting and disappearing back across the veil.

'Stalker-of-Night's-Shadow?' Shadow raised an eyebrow.

'Yes. That's my true name.' She felt warmth spread from inside her and her skin glowed suddenly in the darkness of the back yard. She looked at her hands in amazement and then lifted them carefully to her face. She felt the runes flare up on her skin, they faded just as quickly as they had appeared. The marks would be invisible, but they were there on her spirit, the runes that represented her true name. Stalker smiled, finally she felt whole.

Chapter Twenty

That night Stalker-of-Night's-Shadow slept with the pack, though Stone and Flames weren't there. Beside her, Weaver was restless all night and Stalker got flashes of images of her nightmares through the pack telepathy, though by morning she couldn't remember anything about them.

Stalker's own dreams were a chaotic jumble but she recognised Pursuit-of-Midnight-Solitude for the first time and knew that she had been seeing her in her dreams for days. The thread that tied all of her dreams together was her hunt for the night spirit and at last she was able to welcome the Path of Night into her soul. She dreamed of being buried alive with no light or sound, and of chasing the night as an ancient fox with only one tooth. It was prophecy, she felt it in her bones. She knew she would always dream like this now, Pursuit-of-Midnight-Solitude would tease her relentlessly and she would be drawn out into the night to hunt for her all her life. The quest would never end, it was the hunt that mattered, not the kill. Hunter had secured permission to enter other packs' territory because of the lure of the path and Stalker may have to do the same.

When she awoke the next morning she didn't feel rested at all. It seemed that her packmates felt the same, they had picked up her anxiety and adrenaline. But the excitement over her finding her true name overrode the sluggishness and they were quick to offer their congratulations.

'I like it.' Eyes gave her a big brotherly hug and a wide grin. 'Very evocative.'

Over breakfast she recounted some of her revelation to the pack, though for some reason she held back on parts.

She didn't mention Hunter, something inside urged her to hold her tongue, so she described tracking an unfamiliar scent to the rooftop on the southern edge of their territory and having an epiphany about the Pursuit-of-Midnight-Solitude and then chasing it home.

'It's been bugging me since I changed, flitting in and out of my dreams and my peripheral vision when I'm awake. I'm just glad to know what it was all about really,' she explained over her toast and bacon. 'This doesn't stop me being able to join Odin's Warriors, does it?' she asked Shadow quietly, as the others tidied the breakfast things away. He shook his head.

'No, not at all. I'm sure you will have room in your life for them both.' He smiled affectionately and she grinned back at him with relief. 'I'm looking forward to introducing you to the others tonight. It should be an interesting gathering.'

Stalker didn't probe for more, she simply accepted that she would learn all she needed to when they got to the gathering.

That afternoon she sat down to learn to read runes with Shadow's Step. She would need to know them for rituals and recognise markings of territory and so on. But learning them was hard and relatively dull. Shadow had tried to make it easier and more entertaining by making it a card-pairing game. She had to match the rune with the amusing cartoon.

'Probably the single most important rune is this one,' Shadow said, passing her a card with the simple combination of strokes on it.

'Wolf?' she asked, knowing the answer, she had come across it earlier.

'Yes, but it has other nuances, often "savage wolf", "werewolf" and also "Berserker", another name for Odin's

Warriors. It can mean any of these, so you'll need to pay attention to context.'

Stalker looked at it carefully, committing it to memory. She looked up at Shadow.

'So tell me about Odin. Isn't he a god?' She recognised the name from Norse mythology but didn't remember any of the details.

Shadow stood up and pulled his black jeans down a bit over his left hip, exposing his hip bone. She squinted and saw a black tattoo of the rune, almost invisible against his dark skin.

'The patron of Odin's Warriors, obviously. Some believe him to be a god, others see him as a very powerful fae. We pledge loyalty to him. In return he makes us stronger, faster and better able to use the ferocity of the beast without succumbing to it entirely. He grants us even faster healing and gives each of us an additional animal form, my cobra for example. I'm not sure what will happen with you. We are his warriors, Berserkers.'

'Will I meet him tonight?' she asked in awe.

'No. He doesn't manifest in this realm lightly. I've never seen him. But I've felt his presence in combat a number of times.'

Shadow smoothly handed her the next set of cards, returning to her lesson, though she was bursting with questions. Grudgingly she turned her attention to the work and the afternoon passed slowly as she struggled to get to grips with the ancient runes.

As the sun set the pack gathered briefly for food and then departed, like a deep breath in and out again. Stalker and Shadow's Step set off for their evening with Odin's Warriors. They took two buses, crossing the city and heading south-east into Barrow Market. They walked quickly through an ageing industrial area and made their way towards an abandoned warehouse.

The night was almost silent around them until they were no more than a meter from the huge sliding doors that formed the main entrance of the warehouse. Suddenly Stalker could hear noises coming from inside; raised voices and the banging of drums, as if she had passed through an invisible sound-proof barrier.

Shadow pulled open the sliding door, spilling firelight out into the dark street. They stepped inside and Shadow slid the door closed again. It was a vast space, almost empty, but metal bins containing fires were dotted around, and a large open bonfire took up a large portion of the middle of the warehouse. Stalker glanced up and saw open shafts in the high ceiling, releasing the smoke out into the night. There were a dozen people laughing, shouting and singing around the fires in smaller clusters. Someone was pounding a drum and chanting and a few faces turned their way as Shadow and Stalker entered the space. Stalker recognised Ragged Edge and First Strike among the gathered participants and she smiled in greeting to them.

First Strike was standing close by a striking woman. She was exceptionally tall and lean with pale skin and bright red hair that fell almost to her waist. She wore a long, loose skirt and huge combat boots, a red vest on her upper body clung to her muscular frame, red and black tattoos covered her arms and chest, across her back were strapped two long swords.

Stalker tried not to stare, and on looking around the rest of the room found herself not knowing where to look as everyone displayed similar bold appearances; with tattoos and weaponry on display everywhere. First Strike himself was topless, his massive upper body was decorated with several dozen tattoos, which had been covered by clothes last time they met.

Shadow led her towards Ragged Edge, who sat perched on a bench, leaning on his staff. He looked exactly the same. Next to him was another mature-looking shifter, he wore ceremonial robes of some kind. They were deep burgundy with delicate gold embroidery at the hems, in what Stalker thought looked like Viking patterns. The robes looked as old as the man in them, fraying slightly at the edges but well cared for. The man had greying hair tied in a neat braid that hung half way down his back and his skin was leathery. He had a thick beard to match his long hair, which was also braided. Propped up next to him against the bench was a scythe, which Stalker tried not to gawk at.

The two grizzled old shifters stood to greet them. Shadow grasped each of their forearms in turn and respectfully bowed his head. He held out a hand to Stalker as if displaying her and she stepped forward tentatively.

'This is my pack-sister, Stalker-of-Night's-Shadow. I bring her to you as a daughter of the fight. I have seen her spirit and it yearns for the fire of Odin.' His voice was strong and confident, but as low as ever. Stalker tried to lift her head and puff out her chest with pride, but she couldn't help but feel submissive to these two ancient shifters, and it took great effort to hold her head high.

They bowed their heads to her. Ragged Edge smiled encouragingly and stepped closer to her, taking her arm the way Shadow had taken his moments before in a formal gesture of greeting, she guessed it was their way of saluting one another.

'I like your new name,' he whispered, it was a low, throaty rumble in her ear and she grinned at him with gratitude.

'Thank you,' she spoke softly, shaking slightly with nerves.

'This is Red Scythe.' Ragged Edge held his hand out to the robed elder, who in turn took her arm. 'He is our leader. The strongest of us.'

Stalker mentally assessed the two old warriors and decided that Ragged Edge must be senior in years and perhaps past his best fighting days, she guessed he served as an advisor, maybe he had been the leader in decades past. She would have to ask Shadow.

Red Scythe didn't smile, he looked at her for a long and silent moment, the general noise of the room seemed to dim around them. Stalker felt deeply uncomfortable, he still held her arm tightly in both of his hands and looked deep into her eyes.

'You have come to us on a most joyous night, Stalker-of-Night's-Shadow,' the elder spoke at last, releasing her arm. His face softened. 'I hope you enjoy the celebrations.'

With that he moved away from her, leaving her a little confused and curious as to what he had seen in her eyes. He didn't seem displeased, whatever his judgement of her had been. Shadow placed his arm gently around her shoulders and led her smoothly away.

'I think he likes you, but it's not always easy to tell,' he said with a chuckle at her ear.

She felt relief wash over her and resumed scanning the other occupants of the room. She looked longingly at the array of swords, axes and hammers strapped to people and about their person.

'I wish you had told me about the armoury. You've been teaching me how to use my new body but now I see all these folks with even bigger weapons than mine and I'm beginning to feel you've been holding out on me.'

'You need to get used to what your body can do first. Isn't that a principle in your martial arts?' he replied gently.

Stalker knew he was right, she'd had to master judo and bando before progressing to banshay with swords, but still felt annoyed with him and only grudgingly gave him the satisfaction of agreeing with him. After all, it was her swords that had enabled her to defeat the rain elemental that Fortune had put her up against. She just didn't know how to use them in her savage beast form yet, she had been clumsy that time.

'Shifters use these weapons when they're in that beast form, don't they?'

The Agrius form still frightened her and would until she had better control of herself when taking it.

'Yes,' Shadow replied. 'Some shifters use weapons in that form. That's why you see a lot of very large weapons.' He gave her a wink and her lips cracked into a smile.

The sliding door flew open then and a huge cheer rang out through the assembled shifters as two newcomers entered. Stalker looked around at everyone in surprise, the two men in the doorway were grinning, the elder one guiding the other into the warehouse with a hand on his back.

First Strike bounded forward with a huge tankard overflowing with mead, he gave the younger man a warm embrace before thrusting the tankard into his hand.

'Congratulations Fire Talon!' he cheered, more to the room than the newcomer and the crowd echoed the salutation. First Strike led Fire Talon into the room and the door was closed behind him. As they moved into the room people crowded around them and all shook hands with Fire Talon, thumped him on the back and ruffled his hair. Even the women in the group offered these brotherly gestures of welcome and Stalker watched with bemused curiosity, an outsider but in no way unwelcome.

'Well? It's been three days, tell us what it is.' Red Scythe spoke, his voice ringing over the jubilation with authority.

'A girl!' Fire Talon replied, beaming from ear to ear. 'She's beautiful, perfect.'

Stalker grinned with the realisation that this shifter had just become a father.

Drinks were passed around the group and Stalker happily took a glass of beer from the red-headed woman. The two of them stood quietly, looking over the celebrating crowd.

'You must be Shadow's new packmate,' the red-head spoke. She had a melodic voice that almost rang like a bell, yet it was full of authority.

'That's right. Stalker-of-Night's-Shadow.'

'Crimson.' The red-head offered her hand and Stalker shook it. 'I'm First Strike's Alpha.'

Stalker nodded her head submissively, acknowledging the woman's seniority.

'Your territory is Fenstoke,' Stalker recalled, hoping to impress.

'That's right. Just north of here. My pack, The Hand of God, have always had a good relationship with Crimson Dawn's Blood.' She tilted her glass towards the be-robed elder. 'Red Scythe's pack. This is his territory.'

'Of course.' Stalker nodded in agreement and tried to take in all of the information. She was going to have to get Shadow to draw her a map and label it.

'Gather around,' Red Scythe's voice boomed out across the cavernous warehouse, echoing off the metal walls. A loose circle was quickly formed around him, also encompassing the large fire and Fire Talon, who still looked as pleased as punch and clutched the huge metal tankard of mead in one hand.

'We are gathered here tonight to celebrate the birth of Fire Talon's first-born and the continuation of his line,' the elder spoke in his commanding voice. Around him the circle seemed to solidify and Stalker noticed that several members of the group were stamping their feet firmly in unison, she could almost see the ripples of energy flowing out from each of their feet, forming an energy barrier around the circle. A shiver went up her spine. The crowd was chanting, a low rumble at first that she couldn't quite identify, but it soon grew louder and Red Scythe lifted his arms, looking up at the tendrils of smoke from the fire beside him snaking up to the open vent above.

'Blood. Life. Fire. Blood. Life. Fire,' they chanted, and Stalker found herself joining in.

'We beseech Freya and all of the Vanir to bless this child with lifelong happiness, health, luck and fertility,' Red Scythe called over the rising chant.

Fire Talon was swaying, drifting into some sort of trance. The elder supported him and walked him closer to the fire. Taking out a sharp knife, Red Scythe held Fire Talon's arm out over the fire and cut into his flesh. Blood dripped into the flames, with no reaction at all from the new father.

'May this blood be shed in the name of Odin, as a sacrifice for the gifts granted by the Gods upon this shifter and his progeny.'

The crowd began to get restless. Stalker could feel the adrenaline coursing through the circle, and someone to her left started to shift form.

'I close this circle and thank Odin for his ever-lasting protection! Let the feast begin!' Red Scythe shouted and the crowd erupted, many people shifting forms suddenly, as if unable to control themselves any longer. Stalker felt fired up too, but without a tangible or spiritual connection to the group she didn't react as strongly as the others. Roars went up through the crowd, a few small fights broke out, where adrenaline had spilled over, but gradually people started regaining control and shifting back to their human forms.

A greasy guy came forward, dressed in loose, dark clothes, he had long blond hair, a goatee and tattoos on every visible inch of skin. He lead Fire Talon to a chair and pulled off the new father's top. Another chair appeared and this grungy-looking shifter went about adorning Fire Talon with new ink, right over his heart.

Platters of food were brought out, a hog on a spit was placed over one of the fires and alcohol flowed freely. Stalker had lost Shadow but she began to mingle a little with some other familiar faces, gravitating towards First Strike and Crimson.

'What will happen to the baby?' she asked Crimson quietly. 'Who will raise her?'

'She will stay with her mother. Fire Talon will protect them if necessary, but he won't be able to be close to them. For their protection,' she replied.

Stalker nodded sadly, thinking of Fights-Eyes-Open.

'Do you think the mother knows what Fire Talon is or what their little girl could be?'

Crimson sighed and looked over at Fire Talon sadly.

'I hope for her sake no.'

'What about us?' Stalker asked tentatively. 'Female shifters. We can have babies too, right?'

Crimson tilted her head and looked into Stalker's eyes.

'We can and we do. Some give up their babies, others bow out of pack life for a time to bring up their child away from the dangers of our kind. I have heard of shifter communities out in the countryside who all live together with those who have turned. But they don't last long.'

'What happens to them?' Stalker was compelled to ask, though she didn't want to hear the answer.

'Enemies slaughter them, or they turn on each other. We are pack animals, certainly, but we don't gel well with humans.'

There was sadness in Crimson's eyes and Stalker wondered what life experiences the beautiful shifter was drawing on.

Stalker thought of Wind Talker and Lily.

'Some packs keep human kin close, though,' she said, not mentioning any names.

'Yes, of course. Normally once a child is through the most vulnerable years they will be raised by their pack.'

Stalker nodded. Crimson's words made sense. A baby must be quite a burden for a shifter mother or father. She could easily imagine how difficult it would be to have to care for a small child with all of the dangers of this life around. She couldn't imagine ever choosing to try.

A short while later, Stalker found herself in a small and serious circle, feeling quite out of place amongst some of the most powerful shifters in Caerton. Ragged Edge, Red Scythe, Crimson and Shadow's Step stood around her, casually observing the revelries of the younger shifters.

'I notice Fury hasn't joined us tonight,' Shadow observed and the others murmured in agreement.

'I hear there was an altercation between your packs recently,' Red Scythe noted, with a sly wink.

'Nothing too much out of the ordinary,' Shadow said seriously. 'You know how it is between the Blue Moon and the Wrecking Crew.

Stalker's ears pricked up and she tried to discretely sip her drink and listen attentively.

'Indeed,' Crimson said. 'I recall similar tensions a few decades ago between the Hand of God and the Glass Wolves. When Theodore was first Alpha and a while before my tenure began. It got quite nasty at times.'

'I had an interesting message from Theodore the other day,' Red Scythe mused, stroking his jaw. 'Something seems to be even more amiss than usual in the city centre. You know his pack mops up a lot of that mess when it overspills into Burnside.'

'Has he had a vision?' Shadow asked, an edge of curiosity to his voice.

'Not that he shared with me,' Red Scythe replied. 'He just said that the urban demons were in utter disarray. Have any of you noticed anything?'

'The darkness demons,' Stalker piped up, forgetting her place. The others looked at her curiously. 'They're behaving strangely, aren't they?' she asked, looking pointedly at Shadow.

He cleared his throat and looked awkwardly around the group.

'Yes. There was that one that grabbed at you in Hepethia. I didn't wish to trouble you with it at the time. But yes, that was a bold and unusual move. Darkness demons can usually be counted on to be cautious.'

'Ragged Edge, could you speak with your patron? I would assume he would know if any of his underlings were unhappy.' Red Scythe looked pointedly at the other grizzled old shifter.

Ragged Edge made a strange grunting sound deep in his throat and shifted his weight about.

'I will see what I can find out, of course. It is a city-wide matter, I see.' He knocked back the last dregs of his drink and strode away to find a refill. Crimson drifted away to speak to someone else and Red Scythe was approached by two slightly intoxicated younger shifters who seemed intent upon having his attention.

'What did he mean about a patron?' Stalker asked Shadow.

'The King-of-Glass-and-Steel, the embodiment of Caerton in Hepethia is an ally of the Watch.'

'Oh wow,' she said, awestruck. 'I knew the Watch were old and powerful, but that's incredible.'

'Not everything old is powerful though, be cautious of that assumption.' Shadow finished his drink, gave her a sad sort of smile and drifted away. Stalker felt uncomfortable at his words. She watched him pick at the hog roast and thought about the discussion she had been very privileged to be included in. It was a glimpse into the city's politics, pack rivalries and a hint of the way in which cooperation was hesitantly sought. It seemed that cooperating was not a strong trait in shifter-kind, if these alphas and betas had been anything to go on.

The celebration continued into the small hours of the morning, finally Shadow gave the word for them to head back to St. Mark's. They said their goodbyes to the dispersing crowd and made their way out into the cold night. They walked quickly, talking in low, excited voices about the night's events. The buses had long since stopped running, so Shadow led them on a direct course out of Barrow Market, across the city centre, just skirting the edge of Burnside, which was claimed by the Glass Wolves, then north through China Town and into their territory. It was a long walk and Shadow moved quickly, constantly vigilant. Stalker was a little drunk, but her senses quickly sharpened as the wind whipped around her hair and face. As they crossed onto their own territory Shadow finally looked directly at Stalker, an expectant smile playing on his lips.

'So?' he asked with eagerness in his voice.

'When can I join?' she asked, grinning up at him. He gave a satisfied nod and returned her grin.

'I will make the arrangements.' He placed a brotherly arm around her shoulders and they walked home in easy silence.

Chapter Twenty-One

26th November

That night, Stalker-of-Night's-Shadow dreamt of Odin's Warriors. She saw fire and glorious battles, she saw herself wielding her dha and she saw celebrations of new life. She awoke feeling sweaty and restless.

The rest of the pack were still sleeping as she crept from the attic, again there was no sign of Flames. Weaver was tossing and turning, images of fire flashed through her nightmare. Stalker wondered where the elusive ritualist slept as he was so seldom with the pack. Eyes, she knew, would be with his family and she envied him a little.

She made her way down to the basement and went a few rounds with the punch bag to work off her excess energy and satiate the feelings of frustration building within her. By the time she was done, the rest of the pack had assembled and were eating breakfast. Stalker fetched her phone and checked her messages while she ate a breakfast of bacon and eggs. Rhys had sent her a text message the day before asking how she was. With a satisfied grin she replied.

```
Good thanks. You? Would really love to
see you again soon. Let me know when you're
free xx
```

Shadow told her he would be out all day making preparations for her initiation into Odin's Warriors, so Fortune asked her to do some rituals training with Flames-First-Guardian. Flames ambled into the kitchen mid-morning and Stalker followed him to the basement.

The excitement of the previous night felt like it had

happened to someone else and she longed for night to come around again, when she would really feel alive and completely in tune with the shifter within.

Her increasing familiarity with runes was a big help in her training session with Flames. He gave her some notes to copy and got her to cast a circle, carving runes for the elements at each of the four directional points of the circle, all of which she could now do. He was very pleased with her and decided to teach her the rite that enabled shifters to will their clothes and weapons to change with them.

'It is a fundamental rite, one all of us must learn early as a platform for others,' he said in his solemn tone. She remembered what it had involved from when he had performed the rite on her and that familiarity helped her to grasp what was involved.

The rest of the day was quiet and Stalker decided to take a little down time. Flames said it should be okay for her to take a walk over to her flat to pick up her post and check on things. She went to her room first and checked her phone. There was a new message from Rhys and her heart skipped a beat as she read it.

Yeah I'm good, thanks. Miss you loads. Really busy with work though, hopefully see you next week. That OK? R xx

She let out a slightly disappointed sigh, then tapped a quick reply.

Yeah. Shame it can't be sooner, but I'm sure I'll survive ;)

Stalker tucked her phone away and set off for her flat.

As she walked, her phone buzzed in her pocket and she drew it out eagerly.

```
Me too. It's hard ATM. I'm sorry :(
```

Stalker read the message a few times and tried to decide how to reply.

```
Don't worry about it, she wrote, I
understand, I'm swamped myself.
```

What she really wanted to say was that she needed him, she wanted to ask if he was still interested in her at all. But she had never been that girl; the needy one, she was always guarded in her emotions. She had had relationships before, but they hadn't lasted because of her inability to open up. But she was also straightforward, she didn't do games and she didn't like to waste her time.

```
But Rhys, I do need to know if I'm
wasting my time here. I like you, a lot,
and I just need to know if you feel the
same, because this feels like a brush off.
```

She hesitated before sending the message, but with a resolved breath, she sent it. Stalker was a block from her flat when his reply arrived.

```
We really need to meet up and talk in
person. Let's not do this by text xxxxxx
```

She frowned, unsure what to make of his words. She knew there was no point continuing the discussion and she put her phone away.

She arrived home and found her flat in much the same state that she had left it in the previous week when she came to collect some of her things. There was a pile of post waiting for her and the food in her fridge had gone off, so she spent time cleaning that up, taking out her rubbish and doing laundry. When her precious home was clean and tidy she left with a reluctant heart. She missed her space and wondered about moving back soon. But the truth was this wasn't her home any more, her home was the Blue Moon Betting Shop, with her pack. She knew that she just felt a little homesick because she had been to her flat, she hadn't missed it at all until she was there.

When she arrived back at her new home the rest of the pack was buzzing around, the shop was still open and fairly busy so Stone and Lily had an additional human helper in there. Fortune seemed on edge having this other person in the shop, so close to the pack. The poor young man seemed on edge too and Stalker thought about the vibe she got from shifters who were older and more powerful than her. It must be ten times worse for humans to be around that energy, and she felt sorry for him.

Fortune assembled the rest of the pack in the kitchen and quickly dished out tasks for the evening, it came as a nice surprise that Fortune planned to take her and Eyes out together patrolling the territory on the other side of the veil, in Hepethia.

The three of them left the building by the back door and crossed over. Fortune and Eyes shifted into their wolf forms, so Stalker joined them in the form of a dark grey wolf. The three of them set off at a steady run towards the southern border. Stalker ran up front, scouting ahead using her heightened senses, the others followed a short distance behind. She negotiated the twisting streets, learning how to not fall for their tricks and dead ends and actually get to where she intended to be. As she approached the border she slowed down to sniff carefully around the mystical boundary that she could sense. There was nothing, no sign of a neighbouring pack, just as Shadow had told her. It was as if the Blue Moon had drawn an arbitrary line and chose to claim no further.

Fortune and Eyes caught up with her and she nodded her head in the direction of the border. Fortune let out a low bark and she picked up vivid images in his mind. She saw China Town and got a sense of the unknown from him, a big mystery for all the packs of Caerton, not just the Blue Moon. China Town stood unclaimed by any shifters that they knew of, their kind could pass through unhindered and there were no traditional territory markings. It worried Fortune, she felt it rolling off him. China Town stood between St. Mark's and the unclaimed city centre with its wild and unpredictable urban demons.

Stalker felt a pang of worry, her flat was on this boundary.

Fortune sent her warm vibes of reassurance and she looked at him carefully, he gave her a friendly nudge and they set off along the border, towards the river. All was quiet as they moved through the strange streets, Eyes took up the rear and Stalker continued to lead the way. Stalker never felt safe in Hepethia; there was a constant feeling of being watched, and the sure knowledge that at any time the demons and fae might decide to strike out against their controllers.

Fortune ran ahead of her suddenly and led them a block or so deeper into their territory. The street looked like any other on this side of the veil; not so different from in the human world, but the buildings felt taller, darker and like they were alive, shifting and groaning slightly. There was the feeling of too many people squeezed into the residences and there were fae. The fae and demons weren't on the street, but she could feel their presence behind closed doors, for now.

They walked on, towards the river a few blocks away

and their western border. Across the river was St. Catherine's, a particularly rough neighbourhood of Caerton. As they approached the river, several vehicle demons roared past them from the bridge and into St. Mark's. They would have been normal cars and trucks, but for the snarling teeth on their grills and their eyes for headlights. Stalker snarled as they passed and she felt Fortune's heckles rise.

Eyes growled too and was eager to pursue them but Fortune kept them focussed and led them to Red Bridge. The river here was very wide and there was a small island in the middle, which Red Bridge crossed like an overpass, with vast red pillars holding the huge structure up over the island. It looked much like the bridge in the human world, the Blue Moon seemed to have recreated it in Hepethia and she wondered why.

Stalker could hear the riot before they reached the riverbank. As they came to a halt looking out across the river she was shocked by what she saw. It looked as though the opposite bank were a seething mass of life, industrial demons worked tirelessly, vehicles raced along the roads, there were sirens blaring out across the river and on the bank ugly, twisted little goblins were trashing the place. They tipped cars into the river, tore down walls and chanted indistinct jeers as they caused chaos.

Demons gone wild. Stalker understood that no pack claimed St. Catherine's and this is what happened when shifters failed in their duty. The Watch held Old Town to the south of St. Catherine's and she was vaguely aware of a pack to the north on the coast but knew nothing about them. The area had long had a gang problem and she guessed that was the nature of the goblin creatures she could see and hear.

China Town doesn't look like this, Stalker thought, pushing the thought into Fortune's mind.

No, it doesn't, he replied.

Several more demons crossed the bridge and passed them, curving south and rampaging into China Town. Fortune calmly moved towards the bridge, which was a huge structure of metal and concrete, the road section of it was four lanes wide. Fortune shifted into his Agrius form and stood right in the middle of the road just before the bridge. Stalker and Eyes took up position just behind him.

She could feel power exuding from her Alpha, anger bubbled under the surface and a strong instinct to restore order at their border. Eyes shifted into the Agrius and Stalker followed suit. She felt the rage within her, the adrenaline pumped and the power that made her what she was threatened to spill over, but she took deep breaths to keep it under control as they stood and waited.

She saw the biggest demon yet coming. It was tearing across the bridge towards them, a jumble of car parts and darkness with sparks flowing off its back like metal being dragged along the ground. It rolled and tumbled over itself, with no grace but a lot of energy and force. Stalker readied herself and felt Eyes do likewise. Fortune calmly grasped his hammer just under the head and slid it from its strap, smoothly taking hold of the hilt. A moment later the chaos demon was closing on them.

As the demon thundered off the bridge Fortune lifted his hammer in one fluid movement and swung the weapon upwards, smashing it into the demon and sending it reeling off on a tangent. Fortune swiftly sheathed his hammer and he jumped up onto the demon's back. His huge claws erupted from his hands and with a terrifying howl he dug them into the mass of the demon. Eyes bounded over and tackled the thing, slashing with his claws and ripping with his teeth. Stalker watched for a second, trying to decide what to do with herself. The demon was huge, the size of a large goods lorry, and it had barely slowed down with the impact of two large shifters. She marvelled at the strength and speed of her packmates and took a second to admire them.

Stalker looked around, quickly taking in the surroundings. She had to pen it in fast and the only hope of doing so was to drive it into a small car park half a block away that was surrounded by tall buildings. She looked up and saw power cables running across the street above her, without hesitation she bounded to the nearest building and climbed the face of it, clinging to window ledges and guttering until she could reach the cables anchored high on the corner. She grabbed hold of the two cables and yanked them from their tether hooks. Sparks flew out and she pointed the torn ends away from herself as she let herself drop, fearlessly, back onto the street two storeys below. She chased after the chaos demon and her packmates. She drew level with them and thrust the sparking cables into the demon's side. It yowled in shock and changed course, just as she had hoped. She was able to steer it into the walled car park, where it finally ground to a halt and proceeded to shake off the fleas that were Fortune and Fights-Eyes-Open.

The three shifters regrouped and faced this demon, blocking its way out onto the street. As one they leaped at it and each attacked it, pulling at the solid bits they could get hold of and yanking them out, throwing them aside. The demon roared in pain and twisted around, trying to shake them off, but they were too quick for it and kept too close for it to lash out at them with the cables that whipped out from its dark depths.

Stalker dug her way through a lower section and found a

hollow behind an old tire, she threw the tire aside and reached into the dark innards of the creature. It felt cold and a sickly sensation crept up her arm as she groped for something, anything she could get hold of. Their only hope of destroying this thing was to literally turn it inside out. Her feral talons grasped something, a wisp of something tangible and she clutched desperately but her Agrius hand was too big and clumsy to get hold of it. Knowing what it might cost her, she shifted into her human form, still holding onto the side of the demon, one arm deep inside it. Her dexterous fingers located the flimsy thread inside it and she quickly caught it and held it tight in her hand, then pulled. Her arm emerged from the black hole in the side of the demon, caked in thick, dark ichor and in her hand was a string of fleshy sinew and she felt bile rise in her throat. But she clung to it and yanked hard, pulling the stringy substance out through the hole.

The demon lurched and screamed, twisting towards Stalker, trying to reach her with its limbless form, cables whipping around and catching her across her back. But she held fast and kept pulling until she felt tension in the sinew, she tugged again but it was held fast. With a grin, Stalker braced herself against the demon's side, wrapped the sinew around her arm as if coiling up a rope or hose then shifted back into her Agrius form. She felt her strength and power fill her body again and with a mighty roar she leaped down from the creature, still holding its innards in her feral, clawed hand.

There was some resistance as she jumped but it gave under her strength. The demon dropped to the floor, howling in agony. Her packmates were at her side, both pulling on the cord with her and together they heaved the demon's heart and lungs out through the hole in its side. The demon shook uncontrollably and made terrified curdling noises for a moment. Then it was still and silent, aside from the clanging sounds of bits of it falling off, no longer held together by its life force.

Fortune and Eyes howled and roared in victory. Stalker stood breathless and shocked, staring at the wreckage. Hastily she dropped the flesh from around her arm and backed away. Eyes thumped her on the back and tried to drag her into the celebration, with a deep breath she let go of the shock and allowed the pounding in her veins to take over, freeing her enough to join in with the victory howls that would also warn demons across the nearby river not to cross into their territory again.

She felt alive in that moment, raw power pounding through her body and her head swam with the cacophony of emotions surrounding the kill; pride, exhilaration, power and that same strange sense of guilt that she had felt with the rain elemental. Just enough rational thought remained to allow the trickle of hope that she would learn to live with that guilt.

Chapter Twenty-Two

27th November

Stalker slept deeply that night, exhaustion overtook everything else and she slept soundly with just the right amount of dreaming for her to awake fully refreshed late the next morning. She was still buzzing from the fight and the pack was still talking about it when she found them in the kitchen getting ready for lunch. Fortune couldn't praise Stalker highly enough for her part in the fight and after an hour she was beginning to feel embarrassed by it.

'You should have seen it, Shadow,' Fortune's voice boomed, full of pride and exultation. 'She used the terrain, she knew just what to do.'

The Alpha grabbed her and gave her a tight squeeze, then patted her hard on the back. After he released her, he grasped Eyes and took him by both shoulders, looking seriously into his face. 'You did great, Eyes, I'm proud of you.'

Shadow sat with her for lunch and respectfully steered the conversation in a different direction, much to her relief.

'I've arranged everything for your initiation into Odin's Warriors, it will be tomorrow evening. The first part will take place on Watch territory, the second back at the warehouse, since we already have security in place there. We don't normally meet in the same place too frequently as it draws attention to us, but this should be fine, it's an out of the way spot.'

Stalker nodded along, eager to know more about what would be involved.

'The initiation can be very demanding, so take it easy

today. Will you be all right to help Stone in the shop this afternoon?' he asked, watching her carefully.

'Yes, that's fine,' Stalker replied, taken a little by surprise, but she supposed that she would need to help out in the shop from time to time and needed to be shown the ropes.

'Take tonight off too. You've earned it.' Shadow smiled warmly and squeezed her hand before moving away.

Stalker needed no more encouragement. She reached for her phone and quickly sent Rhys a message.

```
Are you at work?
```

She waited for the reply, which came a moment later.

```
I'm on my lunch break but will be back at
work until 6pm. You up to much exciting?
```

Stalker nearly choked on her food and had to stifle laughter that threatened to break into hysterics.

```
Exciting doesn't quite cover it.
```

She replied, not wanting to lie but hoping to keep it suitably vague. He didn't reply and Stalker went reluctantly with Stone into the shop.

The afternoon was slow and dull, she and Stone were alone in the shop and there weren't many customers. The televisions blared horse racing commentaries to a single old man in an anorak and over the course of the afternoon he and only a handful of others came in to place bets. Stone kept apologising for how slow it was, but Stalker put her at ease and tried not to seem ungrateful for the rest or the time with Stone. She soon got the hang of taking the bets and filling in slips.

At 5pm they closed up the shop and Stone showed Stalker how to bag up the money and stow it securely in the safe, which was looking pretty well stocked. Stalker didn't want to know how much profit the shop made, she knew it was enough to keep a pack of eight housed and fed and she had a strong suspicion that business wasn't entirely on the level. There was the distinct lack of winning bets that day and she could hardly imagine Fortune sitting down to fill out tax returns or Flames taking these bags of money into a bank. She decided not to dwell too much on the details and to just be thankful for the income.

Stalker found Fortune working out in the basement with Eyes. They were both stripped to the waist, Fortune was pounding the punch bag and Eyes was lying on the bench lifting weights.

Feeling relatively confident, she approached the Alpha. He stopped what he was doing when he caught sight of her and gave her a broad smile.

'Hi,' Fortune greeted her warmly. 'How's it going?'

'Fine. Seems it was a quiet day in the shop, but I think I've got the hang of it.'

'Oh good. I know it's not thrilling, but we all just need to do our bit to keep it ticking over.' Fortune seemed genuinely apologetic. Eyes racked the weights and sat up, he nodded to her in greeting and she returned the gesture.

'That's okay, I understand and I'm happy to help. I do want to go back to my job though. It's my passion, teaching kids. You never know, it could help identify young shifters before they change too.' Stalker knew she was clutching at straws.

Fortune gave her a slightly indulgent smile and nodded.

'We'll work it out,' he replied.

'I have a big day tomorrow,' Stalker went on, getting to the reason she had approached him. 'I'm kind of nervous about it so I was hoping it would be okay for me to go and blow off some steam tonight. You don't have anything you really need me to do, do you?' She already knew the answer, she was still strongly in favour for her contribution to the fight with the chaos demon.

'That's fine. Are you meeting your old friends?' he asked, returning to the punch bag.

Stalker swallowed hard and nodded, making an affirmative noise in her throat. Fortune dropped his fists from the bag and looked at her carefully.

'Stalker, that's fine. I'm not going to stop you seeing the people you care about. You know already that it might be hard to maintain those relationships, you don't need me to lecture you on it and it's up to you if you want to try. Believe me, I do understand.'

She felt Eyes shift uncomfortably to her right, where he had resumed lifting weights, and she suspected that their Alpha had had some similar words to say to him on more than one occasion. She knew that Fortune more than likely knew that she had feelings for someone. At times her feelings had surfaced very strongly and she thought that it was likely her pack mates had sensed them through the pack telepathy. She hadn't talked about Rhys to any of her pack, nor had any of them asked about him. Everyone seemed to respect the boundaries that each member had, it seemed to work well. Their telepathy connected them to one another so strongly that it was essential to allow one another some mental privacy sometimes.

'Thank you,' she answered quietly and turned to leave.

'Be careful though, please. If you're crossing other packs' territory take public transport and be respectful,' Fortune called as she climbed the stairs.

'I will,' she said, pausing only briefly.

Without another word to anyone she dashed out into the

dark evening. It was dry for once and she walked quickly to the bus stop down the street. She was desperate to see Rhys; she felt an uncontrollable force drawing her to him and her heart felt lighter with the prospect of seeing him.

She felt sexy in her skinny jeans, asymmetrical purple top and velvet jacket, she had also donned a thick scarf and winter boots in order to blend in, though she didn't feel the cold at all.

When she arrived in the city centre it was already nearly 6pm and she ran to the Central School of Martial Arts. As she burst into the foyer there was a group of students leaving. She took a seat in the reception and waited for Rhys to appear. The woman behind the desk watched her carefully but was busy with a member of the school so left Stalker alone.

A few minutes later Rhys came jogging down the stairs to the side of the reception, his fleece done right up under his chin and some papers in his hand. His eyes went straight to her and he paused for a second before striding across the reception to meet her. His face set in a serious expression.

'Hi Ariana. What are you doing here?' he asked, giving her a slightly awkward one-armed hug. Stalker felt a nervous knot form in her stomach and she doubted whether turning up like this was the right thing to have done.

'I just thought I'd surprise you,' she said as he released her and she tried to smile.

'Consider me suitably surprised. I just have a bit of paperwork to do, can you wait a few minutes?'

She nodded and he disappeared into the office behind the desk. The receptionist scowled at Stalker but she shrugged it off and went back to her seat in the window. Rhys soon emerged with his jacket, he had a brief conversation with the receptionist, who continued to frown at Stalker, then made his way over to her.

'So. We should go have a chat, I guess. There's a half decent pub down the road,' he suggested.

'Pub sounds just the thing. Do you need to eat? I could do with dinner.' Her heart was hammering in her chest, her gut squirmed. She was scared of what he might say, he seemed so grim.

'Dinner is an excellent suggestion,' he replied and Stalker felt a little relieved that he had agreed to eat. This wasn't going to be a quick, goodbye drink.

They walked in slightly uncomfortable silence to a nearby pub that served excellent food. It was fairly busy for a Tuesday evening but they found a small table in a quiet corner and ordered some food.

Stalker sipped her drink and waited for Rhys to speak. He stared at his hands for several long minutes.

'It's been a crazy couple of weeks,' he said at last and let out a huge sigh. He looked up at the ceiling and ran his hands through his hair. Stalker let out a light snort of laughter. He had no idea how crazy her life had turned and if he caught a glimpse of it he would be forced to block it from his memory in order to protect his sanity and her secret.

'Tell me about it,' she whispered. Rhys looked at her carefully.

'I'm sorry you felt I was giving you the brush off,' he said at last. Stalker felt her stomach turn, she didn't know where to look. 'It's hard to explain, something has changed recently.' His voice died away, like he had run out of appropriate words.

Stalker sighed and rubbed her temples hard with her fingers. They had all warned her, she had seen the way humans were on edge around shifters and was afraid it would change things with Rhys. Last time she saw him she had hoped it would be okay, but now that hope lay in tatters. She had been falling in love with him when she changed and now she wanted him on a very primal level, she wanted to claim him, but he was pulling away.

'Yeah,' she said at last. 'Things have definitely changed, since I was ill.'

He nodded slowly.

A waiter interrupted them suddenly with their food and the pair of them sat silently staring at their plates, neither seeming to have much appetite now. Eventually Rhys picked up his fork and started picking at his food. Stalker did the same. She'd ordered the steak and she took her time chewing it.

'Ariana?'

It had only been three days since she took her new name, but already it felt strange to hear someone calling her Ariana, a name she had lived with for nineteen years. It was a duality she would have to get used to if she wanted to keep anything of her old life, and she did still feel strongly that she must try to do that. She remembered what Shadow's Step had told her that very first night, that she would need to keep her friends close in order to remember who she was and prevent herself being lost to the darkness. She wondered how long it had taken for Shadow to lose everyone that he had been close to before he changed and whether Odin's Warriors provided that function for him now, with their emphasis on fire and life.

Rhys put his fork down and reached across the table for her hand. She let him take it and looked into his dark eyes.

'Yes?'

'I'm sorry. Let's try to enjoy our dinner.' He released her hand and went back to his meal.

Stalker felt confused and sad and reluctantly picked her

way through dinner. They barely exchanged words, but she kept catching him looking at her in the most peculiar way. There was so much longing in his face and she noticed the way his knee kept bumping against hers under the table. She got the impression he was just as confused as she was and she began to wonder if they were feeding off each other and creating a problem out of nothing.

Eventually they finished eating and split the bill. They made their way out of the pub, which had grown quiet, and stood awkwardly outside for a moment.

It was still early in the evening by Stalker's standards and the sky was almost clear. A swollen belly of a moon approaching full shone overhead, and Stalker drank up its bright light.

'I'm heading this way.' She pointed up the street towards the north road up into China Town, a soft smile lingering on her lips from the sight of the moon.

'Sure. I'm heading home.' He indicated over his shoulder, in the opposite direction.

Stalker longed for him to take her in his arms and invite her back to his home, but he stood with his hands shoved into his pockets, looking nervous. 'See you soon, Ariana.'

Her name sounded wrong on his lips and she felt a stab of regret, she wished with all her might that she still felt at home with that name or that he could know and use her new one.

'Yeah, I do hope so,' she replied softly. His eyes were so sad. He took a sudden deep breath and a step back.

'Safe journey home. Bye.' He turned abruptly and strode away, leaving Stalker standing alone in the street feeling sad and confused and more than a little hurt.

She looked up at the moon again for some restorative energy. Friday would be the full moon, her first full moon as a shifter and she wondered what the day would have in store for her.

Chapter Twenty-Three

28th November

The following morning Stalker was woken early by Shadow's Step to begin their preparations. Fortune wished her luck before heading out for the day and Shadow cooked her a big breakfast.

'You'll be fasting for the rest of the day, so eat plenty now,' he told her, placing a plate full of bacon, toast and eggs in front of her. She tucked in eagerly and tried to focus her attention on the upcoming events, and away from Rhys.

'Talk me through the day,' she requested between mouthfuls.

'We're meeting Ragged Edge this afternoon to begin the rituals. He will test your stamina and discipline and perform a purification ritual,' he said, sitting down opposite her with his own breakfast.

'Why Ragged Edge and not Red Scythe? Isn't he the ritualist?' Stalker asked, her curiosity piqued.

'They both are. It's required for the elders of Odin's Warriors to be well versed in rituals. Ragged Edge used to be the leader, but his prime fighting days are behind him and now he's the chief advisor.'

Stalker nodded, she had been exactly right and felt pleased that her ability to read people was developing well.

'Is that unusual?' she asked. 'For one of our kind to get so old they can't fight any more?'

'Yes. But it's also considered taboo to say such things out loud, Stalker. Mind who you voice that to.' He smiled knowingly at her and she felt embarrassed even though it was just the two of them present. 'Ragged Edge certainly can fight, don't let his advanced years or appearance fool you. That walking staff of his is all for show, he can walk just fine without it and it's a lethal weapon in his hands when the need arises. But he's past the point of going out looking for a fight. It would be a huge dishonour to suggest that he couldn't defend himself well if required to.'

Stalker listened, captivated.

'Generally speaking, shifters live hard and die young, though I'm sure you've noticed we do age more slowly than humans so in theory we could live comparatively long lives if we kept out of trouble. It's rare for anyone to touch a hundred years though, I can think of only a handful in Caerton who are older than Fortune, Ragged Edge is by far the eldest.'

'How has he managed to live so long? Was he just that awesome in his youth?' she asked.

Shadow chuckled.

'He was, and still is, a force to be reckoned with.' His smile lingered and he seemed lost in thought for a moment. Stalker watched him carefully but kept a respectful silence. She felt there was so much more to tell but somehow knew she wouldn't hear it.

'How long have you been one of Odin's Warriors, Shadow?' She spoke softly, breaking gently into his reverie.

'Hmm. A long time, it must be coming up on thirty years. I wasn't anything like as newly changed as you are, it took me a while to find my calling. You've taken to this life so easily and found your place so naturally. I envy you.' He smiled at her and she felt all warm inside. She had her moments of fear and doubt, but she did feel born to this life and as though the world finally made sense to her. She was glad that her perception wasn't wildly inaccurate and was thankful for the reassurances of her mentor.

'Can I tell you something?' she asked him tentatively. She wanted to know that her doubts weren't going to be a problem for her or anyone else and that they would fade with time.

'Of course.' He leaned across the table and listened attentively.

'Both times I've participated in killing now I've felt something afterwards, kind of sad, like remorse or something.' She didn't want to look at him. 'I love the fight, it's amazing. I love what my body can do and I love the feeling of power, but I can't help feeling guilty. Is that normal?'

'Completely. It's normal to feel that way at first,' he smiled softly and patted her hand. 'We're not stone cold killers, in fact killing humans or our own kind is strictly forbidden, unless its self defence.'

'Oh.' Stalker was surprised, though with a moment's reflection she realised she shouldn't be, what he said felt right in her gut.

'We kill demons, elementals and whatever else poses a danger to us or the human world because we have to. Protecting the world from the harm they can do is our responsibility and our sole reason for being. We are predators and they are our prey, just as the fox kills the rabbit, and in time you will learn to feel that way. But it is important that we respect and honour the lives we take.' He stood and cleared away the breakfast things while Stalker considered what he had said. She knew he was right and decided there was no hurry to cast aside her feelings.

'So, what will these stamina and discipline trials involve?' she asked, changing the subject.

'I don't know. There are a selection of options and Ragged Edge could choose any of them for you. Typically they involve physical and mental tests, you might have to walk across hot coals. Once he had an initiate swim across the estuary with weights tied to him.'

Stalker's jaw dropped.

'You're kidding, right?' She knew he wasn't.

'No. But I know that your initiation will take place on Watch territory in Old Town and then at the warehouse in Barrow Market this evening, no where near the coast.' He winked at her and she felt some relief, though the prospect of walking on hot coals didn't thrill her either.

'Who was it who had to do the swimming?' she asked out of curiosity.

'Fire Talon,' Shadow replied. 'The young father you met the other night. He is a member of the Storm Riders, the pack that holds the territory on the coast north of St. Catherine's. They're, well they're all very heavily influenced by the sea and the weather, so it was fitting for him.'

Stalker noticed some hesitation in his voice, some barely concealed negativity. And she called him on it.

'What? What was that about?'

'The Storm Riders keep to themselves mostly. Fire Talon is one of us and he's a fine warrior and good man, I like him. But his pack are... well they're a little odd.'

'Right,' she said mockingly. 'Because Flames-First-Guardian and Wind Talker are so normal.'

Shadow laughed and nodded emphatically.

'You're absolutely right. We really can't judge.'

They laughed together and conversation turned back to her initiation. Shadow's Step explained that when they got to the warehouse there would be a purification ritual involving all of Odin's Warriors, followed by a ritual combat for Stalker.

'Who will I have to fight?' she asked nervously.

'A volunteer,' he replied. 'It could be anyone. Well,

almost anyone, myself, Ragged Edge and Red Scythe are prohibited from stepping up. Them because they are the group's elders, and me because I'm your mentor and your petitioner for entry and have a conflict of interests.' He grinned at her. 'Don't worry, you'll be fine. You're ready for this and it's not a fight to the death or anything.'

'What happens if I lose?' She didn't want to go through all of the rituals and tests only to be bested at the last hurdle and refused entry on the basis of one bad fight.

'It doesn't automatically exclude you from joining. A decision will be made based on your overall performance.' He watched her for a moment as she struggled with the idea of failing. 'Don't worry. I'm sure you will do well. It won't be easy, they wouldn't be trials if they were easy, but I know you and I know you can do this. Though discipline may be an area that lets you down.' He scowled mockingly.

Stalker sulked but knew he was right, she was undisciplined at times despite all of her martial arts training; she was wilful and spontaneous. But she was dedicated to improving herself and was extremely competitive. She had applied herself to martial arts training since she was a young girl and risen to be one of the best in the country, so she knew she could accomplish anything if she set her mind to it. So it was with that determination that the two of them set out to meet Ragged Edge in Old Town at midday.

Shadow led her to a secluded old house away from the hubbub of the lunchtime rush, it had Tudor accents but had clearly been renovated at some point, and was surrounded by a well tended garden with high walls, affording it a great degree of privacy.

Ragged Edge met them at the door and greeted them warmly.

'How are you?' he asked, placing an arm around her shoulders and leading her into the dim, narrow hallway.

'I'm nervous, but excited,' she replied and Ragged Edge released his arm from her shoulders and gave her a gentle pat on the back.

'That sounds appropriate,' he smiled. She felt strongly that she was going to grow to be very fond of this grizzled old dog, who already felt much like a father or grandfather to her. 'We're going to cross the veil.'

Shadow squeezed her shoulder reassuringly.

Ragged Edge picked up his staff from behind the door. He pounded the floor with it twice and then disappeared in a twist as he stepped across the veil.

'Where are we anyway? Is this his house?' Stalker whispered to Shadow.

'Stalker, we may be on vaguely friendly terms with some members of the Watch but we certainly don't lead each other right into our places of power or personal abodes, that would be beyond foolish,' he chastised her. 'Come on, he'll be waiting for us.'

With a huff of resignation, Stalker closed her eyes and calmed herself. She took a deep breath and focussed on feeling the delicate veil that separated the human world from Hepethia. She could sense it ripple around her at her will and with an edge of excitement she stepped eagerly. She felt the world twist at her navel and her foot landed awkwardly, her eyes flew open and she found herself in Hepethia, swaying slightly with the dizziness that often accompanied crossing the veil. Ragged Edge stood before her and offered a hand to steady her, which she took gratefully. He was smiling warmly, no trace of derision or disapproval.

'Thank you,' she whispered and suddenly Shadow was at her side.

She looked around and saw that the house looked almost exactly the same, just a little darker. Ragged Edge led them immediately outside into the garden, which was equally well cared for on this side and almost identical to its human world counterpart. The light was different and the shadows seemed to twitch and shimmer, but otherwise it seemed normal. Before them was a coffin-sized wooden box and a very deep hole in the ground. Stalker felt a wave of nausea and panic rise hard and fast in her chest as she realised what was going to happen. Shadow took her hand and squeezed it.

'You'll be fine,' he whispered at her ear.

'Your stamina and discipline trials have been combined. You will be entombed for six hours, or until you give in to the beast and claw your way out,' Ragged Edge spoke in a commanding tone. 'You may call upon whatever reserves, powers or affinities that you feel may help you.' His voice softened and he gave her a reassuring nod as he held his hand out to indicate that she should step into the box.

'Six hours? What about oxygen?' she asked, the alarm evident in her shrill voice.

'The box is enhanced to provide unlimited air to breathe,' Ragged Edge explained.

Stalker swallowed hard and looked imploringly at Shadow. She didn't want to do this. Every fibre of her being screamed against it and she seriously considered making a run for it. Over Shadow's shoulder the light shifted and caught her attention, a flicker of darkness where there shouldn't have been any and she recognised Pursuit-of-Midnight-Solitude. The panic abated and she felt comforted, she knew that she would not be alone in the black.

With a slightly more confident smile she walked to the box and climbed inside.

'Good luck,' Shadow said softly. He watched her from the edge of the pit, the worry clear on his face and it was her turn to give him some reassurance with a nod and small smile.

Ragged Edge closed the lid and hammering began as he and Shadow nailed the coffin shut. Stalker took some deep breaths and closed her eyes to listen to the rhythmic knocking of metal on nail and wood. When she opened her eyes there was just a tiny hint of light creeping in through the crack around the rim of the box and she allowed her eyes to adjust. Moments later, however, the whole box moved and she felt herself being lifted and then lowered into the pit.

As the first few thuds of earth hit the lid of the box she felt her pulse quicken and dust rained in on her. She just about had enough room to lift her hands to her face to cover it from the falling dirt and she coughed hard against it.

The tiny slither of light disappeared and the sounds of earth being shovelled in on top of her grew more distant. The panic took hold of her and she started to shake. She was being buried alive. A scream rose in her throat and threatened to break out through her clenched teeth but it became a strangled throaty sound as she battled the fear with her will.

She closed her eyes and drew some shaking breaths, willing her muscles to unclench. Her jaw remained resolutely locked even though her body was starting to relax and she let her breath out through her lips with a soft "whoosh" sound. A few more breaths and relaxing humming sounds finally released the tension from her face and she lay quietly in the dark.

After a while she couldn't tell if her eyes were open or not and the silence was deafening. She had no sense of time or place and she drifted in and out of awareness. She could feel the darkness around her, it should have been oppressive but she felt at one with it and knew that Pursuit-of-Midnight-Solitude was protecting her.

'They aren't going to dig you out, you know,' a silky voice whispered at her ear. Her eyes popped open and she twisted towards the voice. It was pitch black but she knew a demon was with her, probably a fear demon.

'Go away,' she hissed.

'You will lie here forever, you will suffocate soon and then you will rot here,' the voice went on. Stalker began to shudder. 'Do you know what the fae of earth and demons of decay do to fleshlings who die in Hepethia?'

Her heart thumped hard in her chest as the voice taunted her. She started to give in to the doubts and her body trembled with fear. Stalker lifted a hand and touched the wood above her face, pressing her palm against it. It was warm, it was real wood, cut from a living tree, it was part of the earth, part of where she was now and so was she. That word the demon used was meant to be derogatory, but "fleshlings" was the word she clung to. She was a flesh being, he was a demon. She was a part of the world and could interact fully with it. He could not. He was trapped here in Hepethia, forbidden to cross over into the world of flesh and any attempt to do so would be met with deadly, shifter force.

She smiled, hoping he could see then closed her eyes and returned to her meditative state.

As the time passed, Stalker began to feel cramping sensations in her legs and arms that shook her from her peaceful meditation. Her right leg jerked reflexively and thumped against the side of the box, the sound completely broke her focus and she was brought crashing into the present. Her leg twitched again, this time her foot slammed against the end of the box and she felt it splinter.

'No!' she yelled and tried to get control of her limbs. She knew that if she broke out of the box it was over and she would not ruin this test because of stupid muscle spasms. Her leg betrayed her and broke into a full cramp and she screamed in agony and frustration. Her knee jerked up towards her chest and the box shuddered, spilling dirt in through the narrow cracks. There wasn't room for her to double up the way her body was reflexively trying to and it took all of her self control to force her leg to stay straight. She pushed back against the end of the box, trying to simulate standing on her cramping leg, the way she would relieve the cramp if she were free to move.

It wasn't working and she groaned with the stress of the situation. She stamped her foot hard, knowing it might splinter the box further, but hoping that she could stamp out the cramp without inadvertently breaking out of the box and bringing the test to an end.

With a few hard stomps and some ominous cracking noises the cramp abated and the box remained intact. Stalker's calm was shattered though and she felt increasingly claustrophobic. She shifted her body around uncomfortably and tried to focus her breathing again, but the damage was done and the discomfort only continued to mount.

Stalker exclaimed in frustration, growling, snarling and thumping on the lid of the box. She refused to give in, she refused to tear her way out, though she knew full well that she could do so at any time if she shifted into her Agrius form.

With a great effort she reined in her frustration, breathed deeply and concentrated on embracing the darkness, eventually she was able to grow still on the outside, even if her mind continued to race and her pulse remained elevated.

Those last minutes or hours, she had no idea how long, took an age to pass but pass they did. She heard the sounds of earth moving above and muffled voices began to break through. She fought the urge to cry out for help, she knew that she had to hold it together for those last few moments and as the lid was ripped up from above her and fresh air rushed over her it was all she could do not leap from the pit.

She grasped Shadow's extended hand and he pulled her up, she scrambled hurriedly from the pit and into his arms without so much as a whimper, though she shook all over. It was dark, night had fallen and thick purple clouds rolled overhead, obscuring the nearly full moon from view. The eerie sounds of Hepethia could be heard quietly in the distance and yet everything seemed loud and bright to her.

'It's okay. It's over. You did so well,' Shadow whispered in her ear.

'Is she all right?' Ragged Edge spoke softly somewhere nearby, Stalker couldn't move her head but she heard the genuine concern in his voice.

'I'm fine,' she murmured, trying to find her normal voice and failing. She cringed at the crack and waiver that she heard in it. 'Just give me a minute,' she managed to say in a more controlled tone.

Shadow stroked her hair and she breathed deeply. It was over. She had survived and she had kept control over the beast. She couldn't know for sure how her performance would be judged, but as far as she was concerned, she had passed the first test.

Chapter Twenty-Four

Stalker was given a few minutes to compose herself before Ragged Edge led them back across the veil and out of the garden into the quiet street. Stalker became acutely aware that she was filthy, Shadow and Ragged Edge were also dirty from digging her out of the ground and she looked around to check that they wouldn't be seen. She couldn't understand why the two men didn't seem concerned.

A short distance from the house Ragged Edge unlocked a dark grey mid-sized car, the sort you wouldn't look twice at because of how common they are and he opened the back door for her. Looking inside Stalker saw that the seats were covered with plastic sheets to protect the upholstery and she managed a strained laugh at the planning that had gone into this day.

They drove in silence across the city, Ragged Edge at the wheel, his staff propped up next to him in the foot well of the passenger seat. Shadow sat next to Stalker on the back seat, holding her hand. Her heart had returned to its normal rhythm and she was beginning to feel calm again after the entombing ordeal, though her throat ached and she was desperate for a drink of water, or preferably a nice stiff shot of vodka. The darkness of the night wrapped around her and brought her comfort so that by the time they pulled up outside the warehouse in Barrow Market she was ready for the next step.

They approached the warehouse and entered through the large, sliding doors. The warehouse looked somewhat different on this occasion, there were no flaming barrels and the assembled members of Odin's Warriors were still and quiet as Stalker entered, flanked by the elder and her mentor. In the centre of the huge space there were two rows of hot coals glowing red. The only light in the room was coming from a string of blinking decorative lights that hung from pillars and poles in a circle just above head height. Red Scythe was standing next to the coals, holding his impressive namesake in one hand.

Ragged Edge led her forward, every eye was on her and she felt incredibly uncomfortable. Red Scythe grasped her hand and forearm in greeting and she returned the gesture. The rest of the group formed a circle around them and she quickly found Shadow among them. He had a serious expression on his face and was avoiding looking at her, that worried her.

'We are assembled here tonight for the initiation of Stalker-of-Night's-Shadow into Odin's Warriors. She has been nominated by Shadow's Step and has already completed a trial of stamina and discipline,' Red Scythe spoke in his authoritative voice and it echoed around the large empty warehouse. She looked at him and tried to read in his eyes if he knew somehow what had happened in Ragged Edge's garden, but she couldn't tell.

He moved away from her and walked around the outside of the circle of assembled shifters, casting a ritual circle. 'We call upon Artemis, mother of shifters; Odin, Allfather; and the Valkyries, sisters and judges of the chosen of Odin; to observe and protect the rite of purification.'

Various assembled members began stamping their feet as they had done the last time Stalker witnessed one of their rituals and again she could actually see the ripples that spread out from their feet as energy built to form a protective barrier around them.

Red Scythe returned to her side and took her hand in his.

'We ask that our sister be cleansed of doubt, fear and loneliness. That emotional equilibrium be restored

268

following her trials today and that her spirit be judged here tonight by Odin.'

Stalker's eyes darted to Red Scythe in alarm. She felt suddenly scared of being judged and was certain for a split second that Odin, the god of war and death, would manifest before them and tear her to shreds himself if he disapproved of her. But she saw the fire and warmth in Red Scythe's eyes and remembered what Shadow had told her about their patron remaining a distant observer rather than active participant in their lives.

The impressive leader of Odin's Warriors walked her over to the burning coals and indicated for her to stand between the two rows. She wondered if he was going to ask her to walk on them and instantly judged that as deeply unfair, she had already completed her trial of stamina. However this did not seem to be his intention, as he stepped away from her and lifted a large jug of water from the floor in the centre of the circle. He held it up high as if offering a toast, then approached the coals again and tipped the water over one row and then the other.

Steam hissed up from the embers and surrounded Stalker, the heat was only just bearable and she held her breath as the steam swirled around her and made her skin prickle. She tried to relax and take deep, cleansing breaths and as she did so she could feel the tension ebbing out of her body. She became aware of fae within the steam reaching into her as she breathed in and retracting again as she breathed out, taking with them her negative energy, leaving only calm and confidence within her. She knew that no matter what happened next, she would now have much finer control over her inner beast, just as she had developed a profound connection to the shielding power of darkness when she answered the call of Pursuit-of-Midnight-Solitude.

Standing there in the cleansing steam she had a sort of epiphany, a deeper understanding of herself, of what she could do and of her connection to the world around her. Grins-Too-Widely was able to keep human eyes from seeing her as she navigated her territory and connected her to her pack, emotionally and telepathically; Pursuit-of-Midnight-Solitude quenched all fear of the darkness, suppressed her scent and made it easier for her to hide in the shadows; and now these purification elementals would help her to remain calm and in control of the Agrius in times of need.

As the steam around her cleared, Stalker was left standing, swaying slightly and with a serene smile playing on her lips. Her hearing seemed a little fuzzy, she thought she could hear applause all around her but it sounded very far away or as if she were under water. Slowly the fuzziness cleared and she looked around to see more than a dozen smiling people clapping and cheering.

Red Scythe took her hand again and led her to the centre of the circle.

'Now the time has come for your fighting heart to be judged by Odin. I call forth a volunteer Berserker to challenge Stalker-of-Night's-Shadow.'

'Right here,' a voice rang out loud and clear, barely allowing Red Scythe to finish his sentence. Stalker whipped around to see a young woman stepping into the circle. She was medium height and extremely lean, she had skin the colour of rich toffee that shone in the light and she wore her black hair in fine braids all the way down her back. Her eyes were cold and hard and a sneer played over her lips.

'Very well,' Red Scythe called out and the circle fell to order. 'Fury will be your challenger. The rules are simple. This is hand-to-hand combat only, no weapons. Innate abilities only, no assistance from allies. No killing blows. The winner will be the first to render their opponent prone.'

Stalker took a moment to appraise her challenger, she looked as tough as nails, and small enough to be quick too. But she looked young enough to not have a gross advantage experience-wise. The two of them began circling each other, just like wolves preparing to fight. Stalker moved slowly around the circle until she drew level with Shadow and glanced at him for what she hoped would be a sign of encouragement, but he was covering his eyes with his hand, his head bowed. Alarm bells started to ring and she reached out to him with her mind as best she could in her senseless human form. He felt her and looked up into her eyes.

Wrecking Crew was all she got from him, but it was enough. Now she knew that Fury's eagerness to volunteer was entirely personal and there was no way she would hold back from this opportunity to dominate the newest member of her rival pack.

With a deep breath of determination, Stalker took a step towards Fury and shifted into her Agrius form. Fury was only a split second behind her. Fury's fur was deep brown, tinged with red, her braids thickened, rather than disappearing and looked like whips running down her back from the top of her bestial head. She was snarling as she stared Stalker down, but Stalker remained calm.

Red Scythe was still stood between them, he raised his hands and the room grew instantly quict. Stalker's breath quickened, her eyes fixed on Fury. In her peripheral vision she was aware of Red Scythe dropping his hands and stepping quickly back to the edge of the circle. The crowd erupted in cheers and the two combatant shifters launched themselves at one another.

Fury landed the first blow, it was a bone splintering

blow to Stalker's left shoulder and she spun around with the impact of it. It was far stronger than it ought to have been and she knew instantly that Fury had tricks up her sleeve. But Stalker knew that she did too and used her incredible agility to dodge the next two blows. She was much quicker than Fury and long seconds passed with no blows landing for either party as Stalker ducked and weaved around her opponent and abandoned any attempts to land hits of her own.

She watched the way Fury moved and used her expertise in reading people to assess the increasingly angry beast opposite her. Fury had a very short temper and was frustrated already, she was throwing her all into every attempted attack, holding no reserves back. She would tire quickly. As she moved, she favoured her left leg and right arm and Stalker focused her keen eyes on that slow right leg. She was sure that Fury was right handed, so what was wrong with that leg? There was the tiniest trace of a limp there. An old injury perhaps. She could use that.

While she was so deeply focussed on Fury's leg, Stalker completely failed to see the next attack coming and Fury landed another excruciating hit, this time right to Stalker's jaw, she felt it crack and her huge teeth dug into her tongue. She roared in pain and backed away from Fury, but her opponent was relentless and pursued her across the circle. Hands of on-lookers made contact with Stalker's back and pushed her back into the fray, she used the momentum to run at her challenger, catching Fury around her middle and spinning her around. Stalker let go and left Fury catching her balance while she regained her own composure. Without waiting for Fury to right herself completely, Stalker launched herself forward and slashed with her talons at Fury's chest and just scraped the skin under her thick fur. It wasn't enough to do any real damage, only enrage Fury further.

The crowd around was chanting and clapping a pounding rhythm, feet were stomping too, it was so much noise. Stalker shook her head and tried to tune it out. She reached out and tried to catch Fury in a grapple, but the other shifter slipped out of her grasp and came at her with a vicious attempt to bite into Stalker's neck. Stalker twisted away and got behind Fury, grabbing her around the chest, pinning her arms by her sides. She used her own weight to flip Fury over her head and slam her onto the floor face first, right into one of the piles of hot coals from the purification ritual. Stalker heard something of Fury's crack and a nasty hope flashed into her mind that it was the bitch's nose.

Fury leaped to her feet, shaking her head and brushing burning embers from her body. Blood splattered from her mouth and left drops on the floor, a huge roar went up from the crowd. Stalker didn't hesitate, she locked her eyes on that weak right knee and launched herself at it. She bent forward and grabbed Fury's leg, she twisted with all her might and dislocated the knee as she pushed Fury to the ground, slamming her down on her back. Fury howled in anger and pain and Stalker roared as she felt Fury's talons pierce her left side and stay there.

The two of them were locked together, Stalker still holding Fury's leg and Fury's claws and fist buried in Stalker's side. Stalker snarled and felt pain racing through her body, it was excruciating, but she refused to let go. She had her, she had Fury pinned and undoubtedly unable to stand and continue the fight. She had won, if she could only hold on until Fury accepted it and relented.

But Fury hissed in her ear and refused to admit defeat. They stayed locked together like that for what seemed like an age. Finally Stalker felt hands on her shoulders and individual voices became clear to her in the sea of noise.

'That's enough. Break it up,' Ragged Edge called out above the din from somewhere nearby.

'Stalker,' Shadow's voice was barely above a whisper in her ear. 'You've won. Let go now.'

She was panting and moaning with the pain in her side, barely able to register what was happening.

'No!' Fury roared in her other ear and Stalker yelped as the talons were ripped from her flesh. Shadow pulled her away and two others had shifted into their Agrius forms for the required strength to drag Fury across the circle and restrain her.

Red Scythe approached Stalker with his hands up and Stalker realised that she was salivating and straining against Shadow's grip just as much as Fury was across the circle from them, she must have looked like a savage dog champing at the bit. She steadied her breathing and fought to regain control of the beast, she felt the purification fae calming her and the beast settled into a quiet rumble in her chest. She shifted back into her human form and slumped against Shadow. The pain in her side doubled and she clutched it with both of her hands as if trying to hold herself together. When she looked down and saw the blood pouring down her side and over her hands, she realised that she wasn't far wrong. She whimpered at the sight and tried to look away.

'Don't worry, it's not as bad as it looks,' Red Scythe said soothingly, bending to peer at her wound.

'I have a hole in me!' she cried desperately, but Red Scythe chuckled.

'You'll get used to that.' He straightened up and smiled warmly. 'May I take your hand?' He held his hand out toward her uninjured side and slowly she released her injury and took his hand with her own blood-soaked one, wincing as she stepped forward with him towards the centre of the circle. He gently lifted her arm and a massive cheer erupted all around them.

She was the victor and she had clearly been accepted as one of Odin's Warriors. Elation filled her and she felt a fire flare up in her heart. Odin touched her, she felt it. She felt her body fill with strength and speed and when she gingerly put her free hand to what had moments before been a gaping wound in her side, she felt mending flesh. A grin lit up her face.

Red Scythe released her and she walked slowly back towards Shadow. People moved in towards her, blocking her path and pushing past each other to congratulate and welcome her. She smiled and thanked everyone, but was desperate for the warm arms of her mentor. He pushed his way through the sea of people and grabbed hold of her, he pulled her into a protective embrace and steered her out of the crowd.

'Well done,' he whispered. 'I am so proud of you.'

'Th-thanks,' she stammered.

'Fury won't easily forget that fight, you know.'

'Neither will I,' she replied coldly.

'Now then,' he spoke a little louder. 'Where do you want your first tattoo?'

First Strike provided Stalker with plentiful quantities of the vodka she had so desperately craved earlier in the evening and once she was suitably numb from the alcohol she straddled a chair and leaned over the back of it, while he tattooed the rune for "Berserker" on the back of her neck.

A lively party had sprung up around them, though someone had had to take Fury home. Stalker tried to feel bad for the way the fight had gone, but she couldn't, she

275

felt very pleased with herself and at the same time extremely bitter towards Fury for making it so personal.

By the time her tattoo was finished her tongue and shoulder were completely healed and her side was well on the way.

'It's going to leave a scar,' Shadow told her after cleaning the blood off her.

'Cool,' she murmured into her glass of vodka, a drunken smile stuck to her face.

First Strike held out his right arm and showed her a silvery line all the way down the inside of his forearm.

'That's my initiation scar. Nearly lost the whole arm, but then Odin sent the healing fire and it healed right up in front of my very eyes,' he grinned. Stalker grinned stupidly back and realised that she was having trouble keeping her eyes open. She'd been through an extreme physical ordeal and was now drinking on an empty stomach. Not a good combination.

'Can you take me home now, please?' she asked Shadow and without a word of objection he scooped her up and made their apologies. Ragged Edge came outside with them and she vaguely heard him offer to drive them home before she passed out.

Chapter Twenty-Five

29th November

When Stalker woke up she was lying on the sofa in the attic of the betting shop. Daylight was spilling in through the skylight and it blinded her for a moment as her eyes adjusted. She groaned, her body ached all over and she felt sick to her stomach. She rolled onto her side and braced herself before trying to sit up. As her eyes came into focus she saw her whole pack sitting around staring at her with stupid grins on their faces.

'Morning sunshine,' Weaver singsonged in a voice that was much too loud.

'Oh god. Please, nobody speak,' Stalker croaked, holding her hands up in front of her. Several members of the pack stifled laughter but she ignored them. After a glass of water she was fit to stand and make her way to the kitchen for a family breakfast of sausages. She hadn't even had that much to drink, but the physical strain of the previous day and the lack of food were causing her to suffer now.

'I'd like to offer Stalker-of-Night's-Shadow huge congratulations for being initiated into Odin's Warriors.' Fortune raised his mug of coffee in a toast and the pack acknowledged him with a chorus of cheers and clinking of mugs. 'Whatever else anyone does today, I'd like everyone back here at seven for a celebratory meal. It's the first day of the full moon, which means that Eyes has survived his first month as one of us.' He thumped Eyes on the back and everyone cheered for him.

As the pack began to disperse Shadow took Stalker aside for a quiet debrief of the previous day.

'Red Scythe was very impressed with you and Ragged

Edge told me that he thinks you have a very bright future, he said that the stars were aligned and they would sing your song for centuries.'

Stalker looked at him with sceptical disbelief through bleary eyes.

'Hey, I'm just telling you what he said. He's like Weaver, he sees things. Don't let it go to your head though, you're still just a cub.' He gave her a gentle brotherly shove, she fought a wave of nausea and sat down.

Shadow sat next to her and pulled something out of his pocket, holding it out to her. It was a small, neatly folded square of dark blue paper, wrapped around something.

'What's this?' she asked, taking it carefully from his outstretched palm.

'An initiation gift from me. It's my way of congratulating you and welcoming you to my second family.'

She smiled and slowly opened the folded blue paper. Inside was a small disc of clay with a tiny feather pressed into it, a shining glaze coating the whole thing. It was attached to a fine leather strap, the perfect length to tie around her neck.

'Shadow, it's beautiful, thank you so much.' She smiled with gratitude and gave him a hug.

'You don't even know what it does yet, it's not just for decoration,' he said with a grin and helped her tie it around her neck. The clay came to rest on her chest just over her heart and she touched it lightly.

'What do you mean?' she asked, still playing with it gently.

'You know how Flames has those trinkets around his neck? And Weaver's gibbous moon necklace?' Shadow asked and Stalker nodded in reply. 'Well they grant them special abilities, this will do something special for you, as long as it touches your skin. Here, let me show you.' He took her hand and led her up the stairs. At the top he turned her around to face back down them and he flashed her a broad grin. 'Jump.'

'What?' She looked at him with alarm.

'Jump down the stairs. Trust me.' He pointed down the stairs, still smiling. Stalker had always trusted Shadow, ever since they first met. He had never given her any reason to doubt that trust and that bond, so she put her faith in him and leapt out over the steep flight of stairs.

She fell about three feet and then stopped. She hovered in mid air over the stairs for a few seconds and then ever so gently began to drift down to the bottom like a feather. She landed softly and silently, utter amazement filled her and she whipped around to gawk up at Shadow.

'Wow!' she cried. 'Seriously? Does it work from any height?'

He simply nodded, smiling at her elation.

She ran back up the stairs and hugged him again, thanking him repeatedly.

'I have errands to run today and have to take a turn in the shop, but I'll see you back here tonight. You take it easy today, get yourself back into fighting form. Fortune knows you need a little recovery time, I already cleared it with him.' Shadow accompanied her back down the stairs and they said a quick goodbye before he set off out on his errands.

Stalker found Weaver sat in the kitchen and sat down with her. Weaver was looking tired and worried.

'Are you okay?' Stalker asked.

'Not really.' Weaver was sketching furiously on a piece of paper. 'I thought it was a nightmare, at first it didn't feel like a vision, it was just like an anxiety dream. But I've been having it for days now and it's killing me. I can't sleep properly.'

She kept scribbling, not looking up. Stalker looked carefully at what Weaver was drawing. Fire. Lots of fire. Weaver threw down her pencil and pushed the pile of papers across the table, scattering them out. Stalker leafed through them, every page was covered in sketches, all featuring flames. There was one of an egg engulfed in flames, another of a figure clad in archaic armour kneeling and leaning on a sword with nothing but black inside the helmet. The last page was a drawing of a huge bird of fire, its wings spread wide.

'Is this a phoenix?' she asked, holding the page out to Weaver.

'I think it must be. I just don't understand. My visions are usually cryptic, but these are really frightening and it's like I'm in them, not just watching them.' She rubbed her face with her hands, transferring graphite powder from her fingers to her temples. Stalker decided not to point this out.

'I think you should talk to Flames-First-Guardian about this. I mean, he understands about fire. Right?' It was all she could think to suggest.

'Do you ever get the feeling that they're not telling us things? And why do they often refer to Artemis as Luna?' Weaver asked in a whisper. 'I know they're basically the same goddess, but all the other shifters I've met call her Artemis.'

Stalker blinked hard, caught completely off guard.

'What do you mean? What are you talking about?'

'Oh nothing, I'm probably just imagining things. You're right, I need to talk to Flames about this.' She gathered all of her sketches and got up from the table. 'I'll see you tonight.' She mustered a smile and left through the back door.

Stalker watched her go and sat frowning for a while, thinking about what she had said. She really didn't know much about what most of the pack did on a day-to-day basis, but she had been putting that down to her hectic training schedule and assumed that it would become clearer as she settled into normal pack life. Weaver had her doubting that.

Her phone buzzed in her pocket, distracting her from her thoughts. She had two messages from Rhys.

```
28/11. 16.04: Hi. Are you OK?
29/11. 10.37: Hi. Are you free today? I'd
really like to see you. R xx
```

'Shit,' she muttered. She was angry with herself for forgetting Rhys and the weird nature of their last meeting, though she knew she had a very good reason for Rhys slipping her mind. She was surprised to hear from him and doubly so at the invitation to meet up. When they had parted last time she had felt sure she wouldn't see him again.

```
Hi. I'm fine, thanks. Had a great night
with mates last night, bit worse for wear
today. How about you? I'd like to meet up.
We could go see a film or something.
```

She didn't want to expend too much energy and she really didn't think she could spend too much time talking with him, with so much that she couldn't tell him racing through her mind. Going to the cinema was just the thing. It allowed them to be together without having to work hard at conversation. She didn't care what they saw, she just wanted to chill out and be with him.

```
Sounds good. Meet me at the cinema at
1.30?
```

Came the reply. She sighed with relief and sent a message agreeing.

She decided to take some of her things back to her flat, as a first, tentative, step towards trying to return to her old life. She just had a few clothes and her dha, so she gathered them together and got ready to go out.

Wind Talker and Lily were working in the betting shop when it came time for her to leave. Stalker went into the back room of the shop and greeted them.

'Hey you,' Lily said warmly. 'Well done last night. I hear it was amazing.'

'Thanks. That might be you one day,' Stalker replied, grinning at her young friend.

'I hope so,' Lily said, returning her grin.

'I'm going out for the afternoon. Catch you both tonight for dinner, yeah?'

Wind Talker nodded, a small smile on his lips and Lily nodded enthusiastically.

Stalker left through the shop and walked briskly to her flat, where she showered and put her things away. With a quick once over in the mirror, she left to meet Rhys.

He was waiting for her outside the cinema in the city centre, wrapped up warm against the cold wind that had picked up but he pulled her into a tight hug and kissed the top of her head, catching her completely off guard.

'Hi,' her voice was muffled against his thick coat and it made her chuckle.

He released her and gave her a long look. Stalker tried to read him, he seemed sad and hopeful at the same time.

'I'm so glad you came,' he said at last.

'Me too, though I have to admit to being a bit confused.'

'Me too,' he said quietly, looking down at his feet. 'Let's just say that I don't think I can keep away from you and leave it at that.'

'Okay,' she said, feeling confused and relieved all at once.

They went inside, picked a film and bought popcorn. After a few minutes, Stalker felt warm and comfortable with him, she hoped that she would be able to get used to what she could and couldn't tell him about her life given a little time and for now was very grateful to have a normal day after what she had endured the day before.

During the film Rhys draped his arm around her shoulders and she rested a hand on his thigh. The close contact sent her heart racing and a deep yearning for more gnawed at her throughout the two hour film. When it finished they left, talking animatedly about the action in the film, but as they stepped out into the cold, grey late afternoon the conversation quickly dried up. Rhys took her hand and smiled like a nervous schoolboy.

'Do you want to come and hang out at my place for a bit?'

Stalker checked the time on her phone, it wasn't even 5pm yet, so she had some time before she needed to get back to the betting shop for the pack celebration. His thumb was stroking the back of her hand, sending sparks right through her. She was desperate to be with him and felt sure he was thinking the same thing, there were no mixed signals now. She grinned and nodded and they set off walking at a quick pace against the cold wind.

He led her through the city centre and out the south side, it had gotten dark already and the orange street lights lit their way. As they walked in easy silence she had a brief moment of hesitation, unsure where they were going and whether she might be encroaching on somebody's territory. Before they had really left the outer edges of what was considered the centre, he led her up a side street in a nice area of newly built apartment buildings and onto a narrow street of older terraced houses. She breathed a sigh of relief as they came to a halt outside one of the houses in the middle of the terrace, she knew they were still on unclaimed territory.

The door was black and reflected the orange light from a nearby street lamp. It was a narrow house, just one room wide, but was three storeys tall and was made from sandstone, every house on the street was identical and it looked very neat and clean.

When her eyes finished assessing the surroundings they settled back on Rhys, who was watching her with a small smile on his handsome face.

Rhys took her hand, drawing her back to the moment. He pulled her gently towards him, pressing her body against his and he looked down into her eyes with distinct longing. Their noses brushed together and Stalker closed her eyes as their lips met. The kiss was soft at first, but quickly deepened and became urgent and passionate.

She pushed him hard against the door and snaked her hands inside his coat, trying to find his hard body to grasp onto. His hands held her face tenderly, his fingers entwined in her hair.

Something tugged at her subconscious as they kissed, she ignored it, her mind lost in the moment. Strange images began to intrude, first smoke, then fire. She started to hear screams and she could ignore it no longer. She broke the kiss and stumbled backwards. A sudden pain shot through her entire body. She leaped backwards and stifled a scream. Rhys's face crumpled and he stepped forward, reaching out for her.

'What's wrong?' His voice was full of panic and she tried to focus on him, but the pain was so intense that she found herself doubled up in the street, clutching her stomach. Visions flashed through her mind of fire and bestial shifters locked in vicious combat, she felt fear and rage coursing through her but they weren't her emotions, they were coming from her pack.

'No!' she screamed and Rhys took a frightened step back from her.

She twisted around, afraid and confused, trying to focus on what was real in front of her and what was coming through the pack telepathy. It was a confusing jumble and she felt hot tears on her face.

Then there was nothing. Just as suddenly as it had started it was gone. She was crouched in the middle of the road, her face wet with fresh tears and she was trembling all over. She reached out with all of her senses, like grasping for straws. But there was nothing there, they were all gone. She tried desperately to touch the minds of her packmates, but it was like running in the pitch black. They were all gone. The telepathy was gone, not one soul to make contact with.

She stood upright slowly and tried to breathe, she was hyperventilating but she closed her eyes and called silently on the purification fae to calm her. Everything went still. When she opened her eyes Rhys was standing on the pavement nearby, watching her with a look of mingled worry and fear.

'I'm sorry,' she mumbled. 'I had a panic attack. I'm really sorry. But I'm fine now.'

He nodded and kept watching her, wordlessly.

'Do you want to come in and have a glass of water?' he asked hesitantly.

'No,' she answered, a little too quickly. 'No, I think I'd better go home.'

'Of course. Shall I drive you?' He took another hesitant step towards her and she reflexively stepped away, feeling tender all over from shock and deeply afraid. She didn't think it had anything to do with Rhys, but she couldn't stand to have him touch her.

'No. Thank you. But no.'

She turned and walked quickly up the road without another word. She turned the corner and looked around, the street was dark and empty, so she shifted silently into her fox form and set off at a sprint. Stalker had never covered ground more quickly, she raced up dark, secluded side streets and around the bustling city centre to avoid being seen. She tore north through the dark back streets of China Town, and within fifteen minutes of feeling the pack bond break, she was streaking across St. Mark's towards the betting shop.

She smelled the fire before she saw it. As she rounded the corner and rushed down her street the flames were flickering out of the hole in the terrace ahead and she skidded to a halt a few meters from where the betting shop should be. The street was filled with people, horrified onlookers pointed and cried. The fire had touched the neighbouring buildings, blackening the brickwork, but it didn't look like the fire had spread inside.

A scarlet fire engine sat in front of the shop, fire fighters were working furiously to contain the blaze, their hoses going flat out. Two police cars blocked the road either side of the blaze and officers were interviewing bystanders and setting up their blue and white tape. The blue lights on top of the vehicles cast eerie, moving shadows across the scene.

Carefully, Stalker edged around the crowd, hoping for a better look, but there was no way to get closer without being spotted.

She sniffed the air. Shifters had been here, their stink was all over the place and it had been recent. She didn't recognise the scents, but there were too many of them

286

jumbled up to make much sense out of it. She felt rage pounding in her ears, one-word questions punctuated each beat of her heart. Who? Why? How?

Through the legs of the assembled crowd, she was just able to see glimpses of the rubble. This had been a sudden and fast-burning fire leaving nothing in its wake. A great gaping hole in the middle of the terrace was all that was left, mirroring the hole inside her that her pack had filled.

She could contain it no longer, the feelings welled up and she turned her nose to the sky and howled, it was the haunting cry of anguish and despair, but also honour. She didn't care about the people all around her.

The terrifying sound ripped through the night and echoed off the buildings all around, covering the sound of her howl. An explosion shook the city and her head whipped towards the source. A great plume of fire and smoke billowed up into the night sky, followed by screams and sirens. The petrol station.

All around her people were screaming and running, some towards the explosion, but most away from it. Stalker felt panic rise in her chest and looked back at the remains as the crowd scattered. One police car pulled away, firing up its siren, which was deafening to her in this form and she ducked into the small front garden of the house she was standing closest to.

The fire fighters continued to work and the other police officers seemed unsure whether they should stay or go, but they stayed to direct the terrified public as they fled the scene.

Stalker watched from the shadows. Her home was in ruins, there was nothing left and strange shapes moved among the ashes and dying flames. Her first instinct was to run into the remains of the building and hunt for survivors, but the place was crawling with emergency service workers and it suddenly occurred to her that whoever did this might still be nearby.

She had to make a run for it, find shelter and figure out her next step. She was out of time so she ran, with no plan or direction, just the unbearable instinct to run for her life. She was afraid and confused. She didn't know what had happened but she did know that her pack was gone. She was alone.

Chapter Twenty-Six

Stalker's paws pounded on the pavement as she ran. The blind panic was subsiding, now she was mostly just feeling lost and shocked. The Blue Moon, her pack, was gone. Her home in the betting shop had been destroyed and her telepathic connection to her packmates was severed. She skidded to a halt and slipped up an alley at the southern edge of her pack's territory. She paced the alley, her red fur was damp from the drizzle that was falling from the black, November evening sky above.

She couldn't think clearly, her head was still ringing with the sound of the explosion and in her fox form it was always harder to think like a human, so she shifted silently. Her fingers went straight to the necklace resting on her chest, the small piece of clay, inlaid with a feather was safe and secure, but touching it sent her thoughts cascading into despair. Shadow's Step was gone. She fell to the floor of the alley and began to cry uncontrollably.

The bond with her pack had broken so suddenly and completely that she knew Grins-Too-Widely was gone forever. She knew that the Blue Moon's patron was dead, that was the only way for the pack bond to sever like that. If one or more members of her pack had been killed then they would have disappeared from her thoughts, but the others would have remained. But no, all of the voices went silent at once. Grins-Too-Widely held them together and now he was gone they were no longer connected the same way.

With a sudden spark of hope she wiped the tears from her face. The ancient shifter was gone, but the rest of the pack might not be. She had seen the rubble remains of the betting shop that was their headquarters and home. There were dead buried in there; the fire had been a flashpoint, an extremely hot and fast burning one, probably started by mystical means. There was no way that everyone got out of there alive. But she couldn't abandon all hope, it was rare for everyone to be in the building at 5pm. The petrol station had gone up too, the fight had obviously spilled to there and it was possible that there were other survivors there too.

Stalker leaped up from the ground and shifted swiftly into her fox form then set off at a sprint for the petrol station. She knew it would be crawling with emergency services, but she had to try to get as close as she could. She sprinted back the way she had come, then veered west towards the petrol station.

She soon reached a road block, a police van stood sentinel and tape had been strung across the road but she slipped silently and unseen into an alley and up a back street, slinking her way closer to the scene. The air hung heavy with smoke and it took some effort not to let it claw her throat. She could hear the shouts of command and the booming spray of the fire hoses and there was a red glow permeating the smoky air.

Stalker put her nose to the ground and inched her way through the smoke and the crowd of on-lookers, under the police tape and around the back of the fire engine. It was so hot, the blaze was like nothing she had ever seen before. She couldn't smell anything except the fire and smoke and frustration pounded through her temples. She managed to get close enough to see through the smoke and chaos to the hole that had been left in place of the petrol station, rubble was strewn everywhere and the tarmac was cracked and melted in places.

'Hey! Get out of it!' the shout caught Stalker off guard. A nearby fire fighter took an aggressive step towards her and shooed her away with his arms. She snarled briefly, this was her territory and it was a surprise to be ordered away from it. But she had her cover to maintain, so she turned tail and jogged back up the alley she had approached from.

She needed to find any survivors, she tried to think where to begin. Without the pack telepathy she had no idea where to start looking. A shadow twitched just ahead of her and her eyes went straight to it, searching the alley ahead, but the movement was gone. She knew what it was though, it must be Pursuit-of-Midnight-Solitude.

The darkness moved again, teasing her. It continued to flicker, giving her a much longer look at it than normal. The demon's normal behaviour was to tease and taunt her, appear and disappear to get her to pursue it. With a frown, Stalker padded forward. The demon didn't retreat, it stayed where it was, a shimmering shadow against the wall of the alley right in line of the glow from a street lamp, where there shouldn't really be any shadow.

Pursuit-of-Midnight-Solitude really wanted her attention, Stalker realised, this was no ordinary night of questing, the demon wanted to help. Pursuit-of-Midnight-Solitude twitched and then slunk out of the alley and out of view. With no hesitation, Stalker jogged from the alley and looked up the street. Her eyes locked onto the demon and she set off after it, chasing it up dark side streets and small alleyways, away from the prying eyes of Caerton's human inhabitants.

The demon led Stalker all the way to the north boundary of the Blue Moon's territory, towards Redfield park. As she approached the park, Stalker slowed down, something wasn't right. She smelled the ground, there had been a shifter here very recently and it wasn't one of her pack. She traced the scent carefully towards the park, where her nose was suddenly assaulted by four other scents. Boundary markings. The Wrecking Crew had clearly made a grab for Blue Moon turf. They must have heard about the attack and seized the opportunity to expand their own territory. Stalker growled. She wanted to beat them back and retake what she felt was hers. But she was alone and had no way to know how many of her packmates had survived. She knew she would have to let this go, for now at least.

Carefully she followed the new boundary marking, The Wrecking Crew hadn't taken much, they hadn't pushed their luck, but they had taken the park and a portion of the streets west of it. She picked out the scent of Fury, still fresh in her memory from their initiation combat only the night before, and now Stalker felt a violent surge of rage at discovering her scent on what should be Blue Moon territory.

Pursuit-of-Midnight-Solitude moved before Stalker's eyes and urged her to follow. They ran south, the demon weaving in and out of the natural shadows and taking the fox via the darkest, quietest route across St. Mark's and straight to the self-defence dojo where Stalker worked.

A familiar scent caught the air and she immediately focussed on it, tracking it for a few blocks, to the doorway she had collapsed in on the night of her first change. This was the first time she had been back here and a confusing mash of emotions flooded her fox senses. She tried to focus on the familiar scent, it was Fights-Eyes-Open, she was sure of it, he had been here. Was he looking for her?

She followed the trail and soon picked up another scent, Wind Talker! The two of them had been here together. The trail turned suddenly east, towards the human home that Eyes kept, where his human family lived. He must have gone there to check that they were safe. Stalker picked up her pace and ran into Crossway. The scents grew stronger and a third was added to their mix. Weaver, her dear pack-sister was with them too. Her heart pounded and elation filled her as she approached the right place. She rounded a corner and ran along the pavement, ahead she could see the place that she, Weaver and Eyes had hidden to guard his family and right there, in the same spot, she saw her fellow youngsters, stood talking in hurried and hushed voices.

She barked to signal her approach and the three of them turned to see her sprinting towards them, she shifted mid-stride into her human form, under the cover of a large tree, just in time to be caught in a tight group embrace.

'Thank Artemis!' Weaver was crying as she hugged her sister.

'You're all alive. Thank goodness,' Stalker whimpered, touching each of them and feeling completely overwhelmed with relief and excitement. 'The others? Are they...?'

Eyes shook his head.

'They're all gone,' he said sadly, his jaw tight.

'Lily? Was she there?' Stalker asked, urgently afraid for her young friend.

Eyes nodded slowly.

'She was closing the shop with Shadow. They were in the front and were the first to go down.' Eyes wiped a shaking hand across his forehead.

Stalker leaned heavily on Weaver and the two women had to hold each other upright. Silent tears streamed down Stalker's face.

'What happened? How did you all survive?' she asked, looking from one face to another, each showing a mixture of fear, shock and relief.

'We really should go somewhere private to discuss this,' Eyes said in a tired whisper, glancing around them.

'Where?' Weaver asked, despair in her voice. 'There is nowhere we can go, nowhere safe.'

'The Wrecking Crew have taken Redfield Park,' Stalker reported. 'I was just there. But I don't think it was them that attacked, I think it was just an opportunistic grab. They might make another push for more of Redfield and who knows who else might try to take advantage of this. This isn't our territory any more.'

A ripple of frustration and objection went around the group.

'We are still here. We may be young, but we can do this,' Eyes growled, trying to subdue the panic and desperation they all felt.

'Who did this?' Stalker asked, petrified of the unknown.

'The Phoenix Guard,' Weaver whispered, looking around cautiously.

Stalker looked at her carefully for a moment, remembering the sketches Weaver had shown her that morning of fire and a phoenix.

'Who are they?' she asked, deciding not to mention the premonition.

'Allies of the Witches,' Wind Talker hissed. 'Flames told me about them, they live out in the countryside beyond Fenwick.'

'So were the Witches involved in this?' Stalker snarled. She had doubted the sincerity of the message declaring the matter with Weaver to be settled and she wished now that she had made her doubts more vocally known.

'They must have let the Phoenix Guard cross Fenwick, at least,' Eyes spoke up. 'If they weren't actually involved in the attack they still facilitated it.'

'We really have to leave this until another time, we need to assess the damage in Hepethia at the betting shop and the petrol station.' Wind Talker said, his face set hard against the pain he must be feeling.

Stalker groaned, she had seen the state of both sites and

it hadn't even occurred to her that the damage would be reflected on the other side of the veil.

'It's not going to be pretty,' she sighed. 'I've been to both sites, the fallout from this is going to be huge.'

'Let's go,' Eyes said, but looked back at his house as Wind Talker took the lead. Stalker grasped Eyes' hand and gave it a squeeze. She knew how torn he must be feeling, wanting to go to his family, but knowing he had to help secure the pack and its territory. She hoped she could reassure him and that he would get to be home with his family soon.

Wind Talker led them across St. Mark's, the heart of what had been their territory. There was still a plume of smoke in the sky over by the petrol station a few blocks to the south, but they steered clear of it and headed for the betting shop. In the short time since Stalker had fled the scene, the street had almost emptied of bystanders and emergency services. Police tape was still strung up across the street, preventing anyone from getting close enough to see anything, but they could see the fire engine was still there and the flashing lights of a police car. The press had arrived, there were vans parked all along the street and cameras set up at the police tape with excited and serious correspondents stood in front of them, busily reporting on the bizarre flash fire.

Stalker and Weaver clutched hands and stood watching in silence. Eyes and Wind Talker looked like they wanted to charge the press and start hitting things, but Stalker trusted that they wouldn't do anything.

The house and shop were completely gone, it was just a gap in the terrace. The fire was out now, it was just a black, smoking hole.

'What happened?' Stalker asked, not really aiming her

question at anyone in particular, just a desperate plea for answers.

Eyes sighed and ran his hands through his hair.

'You were here, weren't you?' Weaver asked him, her voice soft and patient. He nodded.

'It happened just after I got back from work,' Eyes whispered, before leading them all away from the scene. He led them half a block away and sat down on the kerb. Stalker and Weaver sat either side of him, Wind Talker crouched in the street before them.

'They knew something was coming, but I don't think they expected it to be so fast. We never stood a chance. I think the only reason I survived is because Fortune kept them from chasing me. I think he sacrificed himself for me.'

Stalker gasped. She remembered the pain she had felt right before the bond was severed and she knew Eyes was right. She had felt at least one of them literally being ripped apart.

'Flames killed some of them. He blew up the petrol station on purpose.' Everyone looked at Wind Talker. 'He gave me his bag and told me to run. I protested,' he said stiffly. 'But he threw me clear and then blew the place up. He was stronger than he looked.' His eyes dropped to the floor, apparently ashamed, though Stalker knew he would never admit it. 'Flames sacrificed himself to take out the Phoenix Guard who chased us away from the betting shop,' he concluded with renewed stiffness.

'Where were you?' Stalker asked Weaver.

'The university,' Weaver replied, almost choking on the words, tears barely kept at bay. 'Flames told me to do something for myself, that I should have a break.'

'We were all kept safe,' Stalker whispered. 'They made sure of it. They all sacrificed themselves for us.' She

296

thought of Shadow's Step. Could he have known as early as that morning when he told her to be somewhere else? Weaver hadn't told Fortune, or the others about her nightmare visions of fire until later in the day, but Shadow and the others had always seemed to have other ways of knowing things. Weaver had kept quiet about that since the attack and Stalker wasn't going to bring it up. She probably felt terrible about not telling someone sooner and would have to carry that guilt with her for a long time. Stalker wasn't going to make it worse by pointing it out.

'Well then, let's make sure that sacrifice wasn't in vain,' Eyes said, standing up and shaking off his slump. 'Let's cross over and see what has happened on the other side of the veil as a result of the attack. We'll need to formalise our new border as a new pack and find somewhere to hunker down. There is bound to be a lot of spiritual and human fall out from this, police will be all over it and the press, for days if not weeks to come. We'll be busy.'

His energy was infectious and it spurred them all to action. They slipped down a back street, away from street lights and overlooking windows, then crossed the veil and set off back towards the betting shop.

They moved quickly and quietly through Hepethia, Stalker was aware of the attention that a group of them might attract, but the demons and fae seemed distracted. It seemed busier than usual too, there were frightening noises coming from inside buildings, shrieks and moans, then there was the relentless sound of televisions blaring out a news broadcast from inside almost every home. Stalker guessed that all of their neighbours that weren't gathered in the street were tuned in to the news to see what had happened, giving a surge of power to the electricity elementals and media demons.

Shadowy figures raced along the street, paying the

shifters no attention and from the cold air that followed in their wake, Stalker felt wave after wave of fear and chaos.

At the scene of the first fire it was quieter, there was police tape strung across the street as it was in the human world, but whatever crowds of demons and fae had been here had dispersed. A lone police van sat further down the street, it sat at the kerb purring like a cat, thriving on the energy at this place. They ducked under the tape and moved down the street towards the rubble. The police van demon snarled at them and lurched forward. The four shifters took defensive positions and the demon backed down, deciding not to take on four shifters at once.

Stalker's eyes went to the remains of their home. There was a gaping hole in the ground and the tarmac around it was scorched black. The buildings on either side were bent over double, warped from the heat and probably attempting to move away.

She reached out with her senses, trying to feel the veil and was shocked to find a gaping maw where their home had been. There was a hole in the very fabric of the universe, the veil was in tatters. She felt sadness and anger well up inside and threaten to spill. Weaver beside her was shaking and Stalker grasped her hand and squeezed it.

'I don't understand,' Stalker whispered. 'How did they do this?'

Just then, a rotten smell reached her on the wind, it was the smell of decay mixed with fresh tarmac and she whipped around to locate the source. A man stood nearby, watching them and the smoking rubble. It was part human, part demon, dressed in a black suit and hat, with a sallow face and he reeked of rot and darkness.

Eyes glared at him, the man smiled back.

'Who are you?' Eyes demanded, his voice echoing off the nearby buildings.

'I am Tar Peter. And you are?' His voice was thick and wet.

'We're the pack that claims this territory!' barked Wind Talker. 'What are you doing here?'

'Rubber necking,' Tar Peter said with a smile and small chuckle. 'One can't help slowing down to get a good look at an accident like this, one might see something terrible.' There was glee in his voice.

It was enough to tip the whole pack over the edge and they launched at him, shifting into their Agrius forms mid-leap. But Tar Peter was too quick for them, by the time the first of their claws was close enough to make contact the demon had sunk into the ground, disappearing into a pool of liquid tar.

Stalker wasn't the only one to snarl in frustration and pound the road hard enough to crack it. Amid the pack's snarls, terrible new noises rose up into the night. Stalker turned to look at the rubble and watched in horror as three great hulking demons clawed their way out of the hole.

Wait until you have to fight fire. The words of Flames-First-Guardian echoed in her mind as the flames rose up and took humanoid form. After the fire came fear, a horrifying demon with cracked black skin and a huge mouth alight with fire. Beside the demon was a construct of brick, metal and cables with smoke billowing from inside it. The three demons climbed onto the road and towered above the shifters, as tall as the buildings around them.

You have got to be kidding me, Stalker thought, unable to voice it with her bestial jaws. In an instant, Eyes was bounding towards the devastation construct with a warrior's howl. Weaver was hot on his tail and the two of them got stuck in to it, ripping it to pieces and throwing the discards back into the hole in the ground.

Stalker took a few seconds to assess the situation. Wind Talker had shifted back into his human form and was busy fishing through his bag, pulling out talismans and ritual tools. She had a hunch he was going to take on the fire elemental, the others had a good handle on the devastation demon, so she steeled herself to go after fear. She ran forward and slipped past the demon, dodging its massive claws and disorienting it. She kept ducking and weaving around it, slashing at it when she could without compromising her advantage of speed.

Pieces of the devastation construct kept flying past her, into the hole, the edge of which she danced around in her attempts to confuse the fear demon. Somewhere nearby she was aware of a crack of thunder and Wind Talker's voice chanting something into the increasing wind. The fine drizzle that had been falling started to increase and soon a downpour washed over them. The fire elemental twisted and writhed, steam issuing from it and filling the air around them. Stalker winced as the steam caught her side and scolded her arm and the side of her face. As she was shaking it off the fear demon managed to land a hefty blow and she felt her ribs crack as she was thrown back into the street and landed with a crunch on the tarmac. With a growl she leaped up and darted back behind the fear demon and tried even harder to get under its feet.

Wind Talker gave a satisfied bark of laughter before shifting into the Agrius form and leaping into the fray to get his claws dirty. Stalker kept distracting the fear demon while Wind Talker took advantage of its confusion and set about tearing chunks out of it. With an almighty howl Wind Talker managed to rip a whole arm off the demon, spilling its black ichor down its side and all over the road. Stalker needed no further encouragement and with a fierce roar of her own, she leaped onto its back and dug her huge bestial claws and ferocious teeth into its neck. Thick, hot liquid oozed out from under its charred skin and filled her mouth, it tasted foul.

The demon moaned and stumbled backwards. Stalker jumped down and dodged out of its way as it fell backwards into the hole in the ground, undoubtedly back to whatever hellish dimension it had spawned from. She looked carefully over the edge and watched it fall into black nothingness.

Panting, she looked around. The fire elemental was a steaming, black hulk, immobile and teetering on the edge of the hole. Wind Talker strode over to it and shoved it into the blackness. The devastation construct was nothing more than a scattered pile of debris, most of it had already been thrown back down the hole and Eyes was kicking the remaining pieces in. Weaver was nursing a broken arm and Eyes had blood all over his chest and a gash above his eye.

Stalker couldn't help but smile, they had taken on three very intimidating demons and had prevailed, despite a handful of injuries. She felt the fire of exhilaration from the fight and let out a loud howl of victory. Eyes stopped what he was doing and joined her, the others added to the chorus with their own voices and Stalker felt a little spark of a connection flicker through the pack. They had fought together and staked a claim to territory, which was enough to link them together as a pack.

The four of them came together, Stalker was the last to shift back into her human form and they all looked down into the pit between worlds and realities before turning to move away from it.

'We will need to mend the veil, but it will take preparation,' Wind Talker sighed, the last to move away.

Eyes put an arm around Stalker as they walked.

'We can do this. We can form a new pack. Retake what

was ours and avenge the Blue Moon,' he said with true conviction.

Stalker-of-Night's-Shadow believed him and knew in her heart that they would get through this together.

About the Author

H. B. Lyne was born and raised in Yorkshire and now lives there with her husband and children. She has always been fascinated by darkness and shadows, which is reflected in her writing. Lighter moments have included a fascination with unicorns and dragons, and a firm belief in faeries well into adulthood. Jotting down these observations in the form of fiction and poetry has always been a habit, but in recent years it has become a true vocation and calling.

When not chasing her two chaotic children around, Holly somehow engineers time to bring her fantasy creations to life on the page and also dabbles in politics.

http://www.hblyne.com

Also in the Echoes of the Past Series

Ghosts of Winter
Tides of Spring
Reaping of Summer

Coming soon:
In The Blood

The story continues in

Echoes of the Past
Ghosts of Winter

Prologue
Fights-Eyes-Open

Eyes strode into the shop. Shadow's Step sat drumming his fingers behind one of the little glass windows, Lily pottered about behind him tidying the back of the shop in advance of closing time. A couple of punters stood transfixed by the noisy televisions.

Eyes passed through the shop and into the house behind it. He heard raised voices in the kitchen. Fortune, it was always Fortune.

'Why didn't she tell one of us before now?' the Alpha was bellowing, as Eyes entered.

'What's wrong?' Eyes asked.

'Where is Weaver now?' Fortune went on, apparently not noticing Eyes' arrival.

'The university,' Flames-First-Guardian responded. 'I

told her to give us some space to handle this. I'm absolutely certain it is the Phoenix Guard and I don't know how long we have.'

Eyes looked from face to face, confusion and worry seeping into every pore of his body.

'Get back to the petrol station!' Fortune yelled at Flames. 'Do what you have to do.'

Flames nodded and left through the back door without a word. Wind Talker hesitated for a moment and then strode after his mentor. Speaks-With-Stone sat hunched at the table, her face and shoulders heavy with the gravity of the situation.

Fortune ran his hands through his thick hair and stared up at the ceiling. Eyes waited as patiently as he could bear it before he spoke again.

'Fortune?' he asked softly. Fortune's head whipped to him, his eyes wide with shock.

There was a moment of complete silence before the explosion. The sound of the shop window shattering splintered the air and Eyes leapt away from the door and slid across the kitchen table. Screams rang out and the room rapidly filled with fire and smoke. Fortune disappeared from view and Stone sprang from her chair, her body growing swiftly as she moved and sprouting thick fur all over. Her clothes disappeared, as if they had melted into her skin, and in place of her human face was the thick muzzle of a predator, the Agrius. She overturned the huge pine table with one clawed hand and bounded towards a shadowy figure moving into the kitchen through the thick smoke.

Howls and snarls ripped through the smoke and Eyes

cursed his blindness. He shifted into his Agrius form, as Stone had, and raced forwards, desperate to find someone to rip apart. He managed two strides before he was roughly tackled from the side and forced to the ground. He started to fight back, but realised in the scramble that it was Fortune who held him and was trying to shield him as someone stepped closer through the smoke, an unknown scent.

'Get out,' Fortune snarled in his ear. 'Run. Find the others. Stay safe. Look after them.'

There was a thud nearby and Eyes gasped in horror as he saw Stone's lifeless eyes staring at him, blood spattered over her face and hair.

Fortune leapt up, dragging Eyes with him, and heaved him out through the back door. Eyes went skidding across the gravel in the yard and crashed against the wooden fence. He jumped to his feet, suppressing a roar of fury. He looked back at the building; it was engulfed in flames. Fortune filled the doorway and two huge pairs of bestial hands grabbed him and dragged him back inside. It would take at least two of them to take the Alpha down.

Eyes' body shook with rage, he wanted to run back into the fray and fight but the words of his Alpha echoed in his mind, and with a snarl of frustration he sprung across the narrow back street and crouched in the shadow of the building opposite. He huddled in the darkness, watching half of his pack burn and feeling every blow of the fight. The thoughts and feelings of his pack mates swirled inside his mind; pain, fear and blind rage. He knew he had to leave to find the others, but he was riveted to the spot.

Then there was nothing. They were all gone, the connection severed.

'No!' he yelled, though it came out as a distorted growl. He clamped his clawed hand across his muzzle and shrank down into the shadows. Grins-Too-Widely was dead. That was all he knew for certain, and he tried to convince himself that Fortune and Shadow were still fighting, but the cold, sick feeling in his gut lingered and some other sense told him that Stone and Grins-Too-Widely were not the only ones to perish.

He kept still, his mind working furiously to formulate a plan. He had to get clear of the area, whoever did this meant to destroy the whole pack, he needed to get somewhere safe and he needed to find the others.

With his mind made up he shifted from Agrius into his wolf form and set off at a sprint for the petrol station, to find Flames and Wind Talker. They couldn't have got far before the betting shop was attacked, but perhaps they had continued to the fallback position. He would start there and gather the rest as soon as he could. He was nearly there when a huge explosion rent the air, the shock wave knocked him to the ground. *Hide,* a voice inside screamed. Eyes found himself truly afraid for the first time in his life and he leapt over a wall to find cover. He looked into the darkening sky and saw the vast plume of smoke billowing into the air where the petrol station stood. No one could have survived that explosion and he felt the truth settle on him; his fellow youngsters may have survived, he would have to find them, just as Fortune instructed, but their elders were all gone. They were alone now, and all the odds were stacked against them.

34843712R00181

Printed in Poland
by Amazon Fulfillment
Poland Sp. z o.o., Wrocław